Meet the Cutt

COLONEL R. A. "RAGS" C
Cutter left the GU Army when he ran afoul of Army politics. At large, Cutter realized that there was a need for his kind of expertise and created a fighting force for specialized, smaller-scale actions.

JO SIMS: A former PsyOps lieutenant in the GU Navy, Sims is drop-dead gorgeous and as adept with small arms as she is with her mind.

TOMAS "DOC" WINK: A former ER doctor, Wink is an adrenaline junkie who doesn't feel alive unless he is on the razor's edge defying death.

ROY "GRAMPS" DEMONDE: Previously the PR director for a major corporation, Gramps lost his family in the revolution and is always looking for a way to stick it to the GU.

FORMENTARA: A *mahu* and cybernetics whiz, Formentara is adept at installing and maintaining all kinds of bioengineered implants.

MEGAN "GUNNY" SAYEED: Gunny is a master weaponsmith and expert shooter. If it throws any kind of missile or a particle beam, Gunny can use it, upside down and over her shoulder.

*KLUTH*FEM "KAY": Kay is a Vastalimi who can kill using only her bare hands, feet, or fangs.

Praise for the novels of Steve Perry

"A crackling good story. I enjoyed it immensely!"
—Chris Claremont

"Heroic . . . Perry builds his protagonist into a mythical figure without losing his human dimension. It's refreshing."
—*Newsday*

"Perry provides plenty of action [and] expertise about weapons and combat."
—*Booklist*

"Noteworthy."
—*Fantasy and Science Fiction*

"Another sci-fi winner . . . Cleanly written . . . The story accelerates smoothly at an adventurous clip, bristling with martial arts feats and as many pop-out weapons as a Swiss Army knife."
—*The Oregonian*

"Plenty of blood, guts, and wild fight scenes."
—*VOYA*

"Excellent reading."
—*Science Fiction Review*

"Action and adventure flow cleanly from Perry's pen."
—*Pulp and Celluloid*

THE VASTALIMI GAMBIT

CUTTER'S WARS

STEVE PERRY

ACE BOOKS, NEW YORK

THE BERKLEY PUBLISHING GROUP
Published by the Penguin Group
Penguin Group (USA) LLC
375 Hudson Street, New York, New York 10014

USA • Canada • UK • Ireland • Australia • New Zealand • India • South Africa • China

penguin.com

A Penguin Random House Company

THE VASTALIMI GAMBIT

An Ace Book / published by arrangement with the author

Ace Books are published by The Berkley Publishing Group.
ACE and the "A" design are trademarks of Penguin Group (USA) LLC.

For information, address: The Berkley Publishing Group,
a division of Penguin Group (USA) LLC,
375 Hudson Street, New York, New York 10014.

ISBN: 978-0-425-25663-3

PUBLISHING HISTORY
Ace mass-market edition / January 2014

PRINTED IN THE UNITED STATES OF AMERICA

10 9 8 7 6 5 4 3 2 1

Cover art by Kris Keller.
Cover design by Lesley Worrell.
Interior text design by Laura K. Corless.

*This book is for Dianne, of course;
and for Josephine Herumin,
who lent me her name, if not her character.
Go, California swag, go!*

ACKNOWLEDGMENTS

This time, thanks go to:

Rory Miller, for matters thuggery and blind spots, though somebody'll have to tell him about this because he has his own blind spot—he doesn't read fiction.

Ginjer and the good folks at Ace, for once again putting up with me.

The women of Naggar NYC.

To the readers of my two weblogs: the general one, at www .themanwhonevermissed.blogspot.com, and the more martial one, www.silatseraplinck.blogspot.com. You're in the neighborhood? Drop by and chat.

If you look long enough into the Void, the Void begins to look back through you.

—FRIEDRICH NIETZSCHE

PROLOGUE

Amidst the machineries of the illroom, with their muted bioelectric drones and beeps, there were but three of them: the patient, the assistant, and *Droc*masc himself.

The air was cool, piped in and filtered coming and going, just in case, and sterile, lacking any real smell of its own.

"I am dying," the patient said. He had only just come out of the induced coma minutes ago. It was not a question. A Vastalimi in touch with his or her physical self would know.

"Yes," Droc said. One did not lie to patients.

"How long?"

"If the course goes as it has for most, another day. Two. With life-support systems, somewhat longer."

"Can anything be done to stop it?"

"Not that we have been able to determine. We had thought a hypothermetic coma might help. It does not seem to have improved your readings."

"I see. My claws are bound."

"There is a phase to the illness that becomes somewhat manic. During this, you would be a danger to others."

"Unbind them. I will not become a danger to others."

Droc understood. He nodded to the assistant, who quickly unlocked the bluntclaw gloves, freeing the patient's hands.

"Thank you, Healer."

"I wish that I could do more."

"One does the best one can, nothing else matters."

That was true.

"I will allow your family to visit you now."

"I am not contagious?"

"We don't know. We don't think so."

"Family, then. That would be good."

"Hunt well on the Other Side."

"I will endeavor to do so."

Droc nodded and turned away. The patient's family would visit, probably even if they knew the patient was contagious. They would leave, and the patient would ready himself, then commit *izvaditi utrobu*, using his own claws to disembowel himself. Even in *spokaj*, the trance that focused one's mind to the nth degree, it was not a painless death by any measure; but it was honorable and for most, much preferable to the thrashing, foaming, incontinent, mindless end to the disease, whatever it was.

The patient could have requested a soporific that would numb him, or a poison that would kill him quickly and without any pain, but he was a soldier, a highly ranked *pukovnik*, and he would not do so. That was the Way, and while Droc was a Healer, he understood it well enough. Vastalimi did not opt for the easy path simply because it was there. If one was leaving, the manner one elected when possible mattered to those left behind. And if you were a religious Vastalimi, it would matter to whichever god was waiting for you when you reached the Hunting Lands on the Other Side.

Droc was not particularly religious himself. If the gods responded to entreaties, they had never demonstrated it to him. Better his time was spent doing something that might work.

As he had said, the patient would not be a danger to others; he would be dead before the disease progressed that far, and honorably so.

Droc hoped that his sister would arrive soon and bring with her some answers. He was tired of watching his patients die. Death came for all, and some sooner than others, but even if He was the ultimate predator, when Droc fought, he hated to lose.

ONE

Vast. The homeworld.

It had been several years since Kay had left, self-exiled for reasons that were still valid. Nor would she be here now, save that her elder brother had reached out to her, and it was a call she could not refuse. Given her history, for him to ask her to return meant that the situation was dire enough to offset her past.

Dire enough, yes. It had killed her parents and several siblings. Coming home would not affect that, it was too late.

The grief swirled, but there was nothing to be done for them now. She had known when she left she might never see any of her family again, and there had been no help for that, either.

Lock it away in a room and shut the door.

It would be interesting to see how The People reacted to her return.

As the dropship fell from orbit, the planet looked more brown than blue; Vast had oceans, of course, but slightly more land than water, from large stretches of grassland along the equator, shading into woodlands as you looked north or south. Cities, of course, and visible now as the orbit crossed into nightside, albeit not so brightly lit as human cities. Vastalimi did not need as much light as humans did, and the darkness was muted anyway by the blaze of stars and the Twin Moons. When both satellites were full, you could read by their light though that was an infrequent occurrence; the balance of planet and moons and sun did tricks with shadow, though both moons were never completely dark at the same time. Made for interesting tides, the two moons, which orbited each other at an angle as they circled the planet. During Slosh, scientists came from all over to study and wonder.

Next to her, Wink Doctor said, "I've always wanted to visit this place."

He did not mention how difficult that was for anyone not Vastalimi; they did not encourage tourism on the homeworld, and the local laws were generally considered harsh by *ausvelters* come to call. Prey-species stayed away unless they were suicidal, and even armed and adept humans quickly learned that a visit to Vast could be fraught with deadly danger. As a Healer and a human, Wink would be much less imperiled than most, and Kay had made certain his clothing was embossed and holographically decaled so as to identify him as such.

Vastalimi Healers had a reserved status that allowed them to avoid most formal kinds of combat, and there was a grudging legal recognition for offworlders in general, and more specifically medical personnel. Perhaps it would be enough. Wink was adept with hands and weapons, but there were warriors on Vast who could claw him dead without raising a heartbeat.

Her, too.

With luck, she could keep Wink Doctor alive while they were here. She hoped the time on-planet would be short . . .

They had read all the available material on the illness

that had manifested, and its effects were known if the causes were not. Medical science here had hit a wall and been stopped. The answer lay past that wall, and she had come to see if she could help breach it. No doubt others had reached out for similar help, despite Vastalimi reluctance to ask for such.

The People did not like outsiders involving themselves in their business.

She looked at the projection floating holographically where a window might have been in the dropship. "You have read the material I gave you?"

"Yes."

"Forgive me for the repetition, but I wish to be clear. Remember that eye contact is permissible, if kept fleeting, and if you laugh or smile, try not to overtly show your teeth."

Wink nodded. "Yes. I recall."

Kay said, "*The Manual for Offworlders* is under constant revision, but there are bound to be omissions. I have been away for years, and during that time, no doubt new cults and fads have come and gone, so even my knowledge must be updated to avoid giving offense."

Wink said, "You worry about that?"

"I do not worry about it. I prefer to know, so as to have a choice."

His look indicated a certain amount of skepticism.

"There are warriors here who could defeat me without great effort," she continued. "Though my employment with CFI has given me a wider range of weapons and experiences than most who have never ventured away from Vast, duels here are usually constrained—traditional fights have traditional limits. My status as a Healer allows me to decline most Challenges, should I choose; however, there are some that cannot be refused if I have offered certain offenses. While I might elect to offend deliberately, I would rather not do so inadvertently.

"As a human and a doctor, you are exempt from most

Challenges. And no self-respecting Vastalimi would offer such—there is little honor in defeating an obviously inferior opponent."

"Thanks a lot."

"A statement of fact. We are faster, stronger, more martially inclined, and we begin to learn the ways of killing before we can walk. I can recall no instance of an unaugmented human defeating a Vastalimi in one-on-one to-the-death combat armed only with biological weapons.

"Augmentation will allow a skilled human to do so—Jo Captain has become a decent opponent in mock fighting, but even though she is an expert and augmented to approach our speed and strength, if the claws came out, her chances would be slim against a good Vastalimi fighter. Against a true master, she would have no chance.

"There are unprincipled Vastalimi, and some of them are willing to challenge offworlders simply because they want to see how it feels to kill one. I would prefer that you survive this visit.

"To this end, there is a phrase I wish you to learn: '*Ace ja stajanje.*' "

Wink repeated it. "What does it mean?"

" 'As I stand.' There are some rare circumstances under which you can be legally Challenged. You do not have the background to know when this could apply, but under some esoteric conditions, it could arise, and a determined assassin might figure out a way to manage it."

"So, what does 'As I stand' do me?"

"It means that if they acknowledge your response, you can, if you are fast enough, produce a weapon and use it. A gun is preferable, but you have some skill with a knife, and that might work though it is unlikely. If somebody challenges you, you respond with '*Ace ja stajanje.*' The instant they nod or say they accept, you draw and shoot them. Head shots are better than center of mass, but in either case, shoot and move away, quickly."

"This is legal?"

"It is. Vastalimi are intrinsically armed with teeth and claws and seldom anything else here, save for criminals and *Sena*. And the military, but they don't carry guns unless they are on duty. The response is thus a formality; however, it allows for the possibility of external weapons among those such as humans. It is my hope you will not need this but better to have it than not."

Ace ja stajanje. He got it—tigers didn't carry knives. "I understand. What are '*Sena*'?"

"Shadows. They are a kind of police though they have more responsibilities than those in human cultures. Their shoulder fur is dyed purple; no one else is allowed that. If any of the *Sena* speak to you, heed their commands immediately. To do otherwise risks instant death. They are empowered as—what is the phrase?—judge, jury, and executioner, should the need arise."

"Really?"

"Just so. It takes five years of training to become a probationary Shadow, another five for full certification. They are held in the highest regard. Their field decisions are seldom overturned." She did not mention that she had a sister and a male cousin who were Shadows.

"If you have a question, ask it. If we can avoid trouble, that would be best."

He nodded.

— — — — — —

The convoy was six vans, each the size of a ten-family dwelling, lumbering along on forty-four massive wheels, loaded to the brims with what looked like purple carrots. *Difrui*, the locals called the root vegetables. They were sweet, full of healthy vitamins and minerals and shit, and apparently tasty enough to have become one of the hottest-selling produce items TotalMart offered around the galaxy. Spendy little roots for foodies who like to go alien.

Jo had tasted one after they found out they were coming here. It was okay, but she didn't understand what the big deal was.

It was hot, dry, dusty, and aside from the engine noises, fairly quiet. The smell of the roots permeated the vehicles, and it was a not-unpleasant odor somewhat like stir-fried ginger.

"Here they come," Gunny said. "All twenty of them, cannon-foddering right on out of the fucking woods like they got the sense of tree stumps. Ah can't believe it." The mock amazement was heavy in her voice.

Jo nodded. The attack came from local east, through a stretch of thick trees that lined the road on both sides. It wasn't really a surprise—the sensors picked up the hidden troops a klick away, and, of course, that was way too easy. A feint. The question was, where would the *real* attack come from?

Jo was on the lead van, Gramps one back, and Gunny on the sixth one. They had drones in the air and a fair amount of hardware rigged on the vans, enough there even without the drones to obliterate twenty foot soldiers without raising a sweat.

"Gramps?"

"Got nothing in the skies. Nobody else in the woods I can see."

"They can't be that stupid," Gunny said. Her Terran SoAm accent made that come out like, "They cain't be that stoopid."

They had four armed drones in the air, and any one of them was enough to take out the ground attack. What were they missing? Had to be something else . . .

"Hey," Gramps said, "maybe they are. And wouldn't that make our jobs a lot—hello?"

"What?"

"Somebody just shot a bunch of missiles at our drones. Got, eight, ten, a dozen ground-to-air spikes heading at them."

Jo nodded. So much for easy.

She had her augs lit and running, listening, looking, searching the air for scents . . .

Gunny said, "And we got a tail and it's rolling up on us. GE APCs, two of them, Ah reckon it thirty-troop capacity each, more or less."

"We are going to need one of those drones," Jo said.

"I'm moving 'em," Gramps said. "Keep your shirt on."

Jo considered the situation. It wasn't a bad attack, especially if the convoy was using local guards without much military experience. Cutter Force Initiative had plenty of that, however.

The feint would occupy an inexperienced company's attention long enough to spike their drones if they'd had enough sense to bring any, and the armored ground-effect carriers could shrug off small-arms rounds long enough to catch the slow-moving convoy. Even if the APCs weren't mounting serious hardware, the troops would have rockets and grenades, and there was a good chance they could stop and destroy or maybe capture the agrovans. Not perfect, but probably enough for most cases, and also not cheap—your average bandit probably couldn't afford APCs and halfway-decent troops. The attackers must have thought this was going to be a snoozer.

Wonder who has the Masbülc military contract? Be a good idea to find out.

"I'm going to plink the ground guys," Jo said. "How are we doing on the drones?"

"Two of them are killed," Gramps said. "One more is at risk—fuck it, it's gone. The last one is treetop and looks to be clear."

"Send it back to spike the APCs."

"Already on the way."

"Save me one," Gunny said.

"You think you can hit something that small, Choco-latte?"

"Why not? We ain't talkin' about something as little as your weenie, are we?"

"That gets bigger."

"So you say."

Jo grinned. She turned her attention back to the incoming unit of ground troops. She had a laser-guided fifty mounted atop the ten-meter-tall van, caseless hardball, every twentieth round a tracer. She could almost hear Cutter's voice in her head as she lined the machine gun up on the nearest troops: *Short bursts. That ammo is expensive!*

They were three hundred meters out, not so far that she couldn't use her optical aug to see they weren't wearing anything other than standard, soft-ceramic armor. Which would not even slow a fifty's bullets down.

Gun fodder—and—likely somebody lied to them real good. *Don't worry, you are wearing armor.*

Jo triggered the weapon, her finger's pressure light enough to send a single round.

The fat bullet hit the first attacker square in the chest like a big hammer. He fell, DOA.

She targeted the second trooper. *Bam.* Another one down.

The van rolled over a rough spot on the road, and the bump was enough to cause Jo to trigger a triplet on the next shot. All three of them hit the next guy, but two of them were a waste. Fortunately, Rags wasn't here to see it. And she wasn't going to tell him although the recording cams would rat her out if he looked, and he would . . .

She swung the gun's muzzle a hair to the left. *Bam.* One more . . .

That did it. The remaining attackers scattered and retreated, heading for the woods.

She probably could have spiked them all, but there was no need. If you could nail a couple, and the rest ran off? Never knew but that someday one of them might be working for you. Well, maybe not this bunch, but still. Plus, it would save on the cost of ammo . . .

Gramps came on the opchan. "Special delivery from our drone—AP DU Lance, and . . . Adieu, Monsieur Personnel Carrier.

"Second one missed the wreck and is still coming. Stand by."

"Come on, Gramps," Gunny said. "Let it go. It's almost within mah range!"

With the fifty silent and her hearing-implant suppressors off, Jo heard the explosion as the second carrier ate the depleted-uranium-sheathed lance. Loud, even so.

"Dammit!"

"Sorry, Gunny. The DU is cheaper than the Magma, and you know how Rags is."

"Ah am gonna remember that, old man, next time you want something."

Jo grinned. Well, one attack, one win, within Rules of Engagement and legal. Could be worse. "Move along, folks. Call it in to the local cleanup crews."

Yep, not so bad. So far . . .

Jo remembered the briefing before they'd left the Solar System . . .

– – – – – –

Gramps had said, "Far Bundaloh? What's on Far Bundaloh? Aside from the iridium mines, there's jack there. It's an agroworld. Somebody looking to steal the crops out on the back forty? Rustle some meat critters?"

Jo looked at Gramps. "Even a blind pig finds an acorn now and then."

Gunny chuckled.

Gramps frowned.

Cutter, leaning against the wall by the door, nodded. Off his look, Jo said, "As you are all aware, TotalMart is our top customer and thus pays most of our bills. And since the current corporate philosophy is 'If anybody sells it anywhere, TotalMart does it cheaper and is more convenient,' then you realize that supply and demand depend on each other.

"Masbülc—for those of you living in a cave for the last twenty years, is TotalMart's biggest competitor. 'Biggest' is a relative term: They do seventeen percent as much business as TotalMart, so that's hardly threatening the corporate existence; however, that's still twice as much as Masbülc bottom-lined ten years ago. They are leaner, hungrier, and aggressive, and looking to cut a bigger slice of the pie. Decreased sales for TM means some executives will see it reflected in the size of their year-end bonuses.

"More importantly, we might see it reflected in *our* business.

"On FB, as everywhere else, Masbülc's ops have nipped at TotalMart's heels for years. Little stuff, mostly, misdirected delivery vans, cyberattacks on store systems, bribing employees to become sand in the machine's gears, like that. Probably the store there—only one of those onworld—loses more to pilferage and shoplifting than from what Masbülc's dirty-tricks harriers are doing.

"But it's not about the local store. FB supplies some exotic food exports that are sold galaxy-wide, and the biggest share of those flow into the TM system. *And* the Masbülc ops have gotten their claws hooked into that in a way that pisses off corporate uplevels."

Formentara said, "So we are spacing to the end of the galaxy to do what? Act as armed guards on agrovans full of roots and twigs?" Zhe raised an eyebrow.

Jo smiled. Formentara was an androgyne, *mahu*, and hir sex impossible to determine from a first look. Attractive, but . . . male, female, other? Jo didn't know; nor did it matter. Formentara was perhaps the greatest augmentation expert in the galaxy, and it was through hir grace that Jo functioned as well as she did. Jo was near the limit on augs, and without expert balancing of her physiology, that would kill her, and sooner rather than later. "Well, I wouldn't put it quite that way."

Gramps said, "What, are these vans pulled by teams of animals? Horses and stagecoaches?"

"You remember those from personal experience?" Gunny said, her voice faux-sweet.

He played the game: "Sure, my cousin invented them," Gramps said.

Jo said, "Far Bundaloh is at the end of the road, but it's not quite that distant in time. House-sized hovervans, mag-lev rail, and multiplex-sized wheeled bugcrushers move the crops around. It is true that some of these vans have been hijacked, and we need to stop that, but our basic role is to find the ops responsible and shut them down. That will entail convoy duty until we figure it out."

"I'll get a sleetgun," Gunny said. Her voice was as sere as a desert.

"Shotgun," Gramps corrected. He caught her smile and realized she had suckered him.

"Of course you would know that. Your cousin invent those, too?"

"Naw, Chocolatte, my brother did—right after he and I invented trees."

Gramps had only fifty-nine standard years, but he was older than anybody else here, beating Cutter by a few months, and the rest of them by at least a decade or two. Gunny never let him forget it.

Of course, Gunny and Gramps were in love with each other; everybody but the two of them knew that. Either of them saying so aloud would break their faces, and as far as Jo knew, they had not acted on it save to hassle each other; they seldom spoke without personal insults or a double entendre involved.

That made for some interesting interplay.

Hassles and insults and leers O my. But: When Gunny

had been shot on Ramal during the extraction of the Rajah's daughter, Gramps had slept on a chair in her recovery room until she came out of the healing coma. Just so, he said, he could rag her about getting hit.

Right . . .

Jo looked at Cutter.

He said, "That's pretty much it. Wink and Kay won't be here, we'll get a new medic."

"Gonna get a new Vastalimi, too?" Formentara asked.

"I wish. We'll just have to muddle through."

Vastalimi were worth their weight in platinum to any kind of military, especially small units like Cutter Force Initiative. The colonel made it clear he would hire as many of them as wanted the job, but that pool was fairly shallow. Vastalimi tended to stay home, and those who traveled and wanted jobs as soldiers of fortune didn't have any trouble getting work. They were faster, stronger, meaner, and deadlier than any human, and nobody with half a brain wanted to find themselves facing a Vastalimi with mayhem in mind. He was happy to have one and missing her already.

Cutter said, "So there it is, people. Pack, say good-bye to any new friends you've made, and let's get this mission in the vac . . ."

TWO

There had been, of course, more than a few Vastalimi on the dropship; however, it was the arrival on the planet and the debarkation into the terminal that really brought it home to Wink: Vastalimi in numbers far more than he had ever seen together before. Scores, hundreds, maybe a thousand of them, all about their business, and looking focused. Vastalimi didn't seem to loll about, they strode, marched, moved from one place to another in a determined fashion, all looking ready to pounce as necessary.

It was, quite literally, awesome.

They were shorter than human average, and while their aspects were hardly uniform—there were dozens of different shades and patterns to their short fur, their heights varied, and the males tended to be larger and heavier than the females—they all looked a lot like Kay. They had those preying-mantis-shaped heads, the apelike limb set, the feline grace to their movements, the tigerlike, short fur.

Put Kay in a clump of them and even as well as he knew

her, it might take a while to figure out which one she was. Different, but still they looked so much alike.

Wink at once felt very much the alien here.

He saw a male with shoulders dyed a deep purple, and that one was strapped—a handgun of some kind in a hip holster, along with other items on his belt. A Shadow, but only the one. Either they were really good, or they didn't expect trouble here. Probably both.

As far as he could see, there weren't any other humans in the terminal. No other alien species, either.

He got more than a few looks cast his way. He could almost feel the gazes measuring him. *Hmm. A human. What an odd mix of prey and predator it is. Should we examine it more closely? Poke it and see what it does?*

Voices were audible in the terminal, but the background murmur was in a language or languages of which he had only a few words. Not because it was difficult to learn but because it was difficult for a human to speak. The shapes of tongues and mouths and vocal apparatuses was markedly different between these people and Wink's own. He had a translation program in his com unit. He could use it to listen or to speak, after a fashion, at least for three of the most common local dialects. The computer could translate what the locals said into something Wink could comprehend, and vice versa. Plus it could read signs and approximate them. Although that was apt to be amusing, that reader. On the dropper, he had gone to the fresher, and the reader had rendered the Vastalimi words over the door as " 'Small Orifice of Excrement'; informally known as: 'Asshole.' "

There weren't any restrictions as to personal weaponry here. You could carry a knife or a gun if you could manage it on your person, and Wink had both concealed under his tunic. Not that they were particularly comforting. He was well aware of his survival chances in a dustup with a Vastalimi, and they were exceedingly slim. Not that he intended to see how that would go. Even with his risk-taking and dancing close to Dame Death, he was not suicidal.

Hey, bug-face, you don't seem so tough. Step off—or else—!

Yeah, or else *kill* me . . .

Kay stopped and looked around.

"You okay?"

"Yes. It has been years since I have seen so many of The People at once. It stirs emotions."

"I don't recall you ever said why you left Vast."

"Because I have never said why."

He waited, but that was the extent of her comments. She started walking. She did not appear to be looking for a reception committee.

"Is your brother coming to meet us?"

"No. He has much work to which he must attend. I am not a cub that I cannot find him."

Wink nodded. Different species, different social mores.

"Our baggage will be routed to our *domus*, which my brother will have provided for us."

"Customs?"

"Our passports were scanned before we left the dropship; had there been any problems, we would have been approached by the authorities by now. We need only to obtain a conveyance to the *bolnica*—our version of a hospital. There will be a cart waiting outside the port. *Droc*-Masc will know we have arrived and will be expecting us."

Wink became more aware of the stares he merited as they walked. Lot of looks.

Halfway across the terminal, a large Vastalimi moved to intercept them. He rattled off something in that tongue-twisting language of theirs.

The auto-engage feature on his translation program didn't seem to be working. Wink managed to flick his translator on manually as the speaker finished, routing the output to his earbud.

"—walk with this *jebiga* prey?"

Jebiga . . . Jebiga, ah, there it was: Fucking.

Kay responded in her language: "Companion is a Healer and human and exempt from *prigovor*. I am also a Healer."

"And exempt from *prigovor* also?"

"In this instance, yes. I can honorably decline; however, I will not. Do you offer Challenge?"

The larger Vastalimi stood silent for a moment. He must have heard something in her voice that convinced him Kay was not to be messed with.

Wink sure as shit heard it. He fought an urge to step back.

The male Vastalimi said, "Not at this time."

"Then move from my path or unsheathe your claws."

He moved aside.

As they reached the exit, Wink said, "Well, that was fun. Expect that to happen a lot?"

"It is possible. That one would not have been a problem had he persisted."

"Really?"

"One can tell by the way a being stands if he presents a real threat. He did not stand well. I am pleased to have made it this far without combat; I expected that I would have had at least one fight by now."

He raised an eyebrow at her.

"Welcome to Vast, Wink Doctor. It is not like anyplace else you have ever been."

- - - ⌐ - -

At the lab in the bowels of the *bolnica*, Droc nodded at Luque, the Chief of Research, a wizened old Vastalimi of 160 or so who had been in charge of the place since before Droc had been born.

There was no need to ask about progress. Had there been any, Luque would have informed him.

"I have new blood samples," he said.

Luque nodded. "We will examine them in their turn."

Every kind of tissue that made up a Vastalimi had been harvested and examined with the finest observational machineries available. The tiniest of retroviruses would appear to be planet-sized when projected onto the screens.

So far, nothing had been detected with them that offered a cause.

That did not seem possible.

The medical system on Vast was not as advanced as it was on some worlds; still, it was not primitive. If a Healer needed or wanted a device or medicines, and they were available commercially anywhere in the galaxy, they were free to buy and use them, including implants.

It was true that augmentation among Vastalimi was extremely rare—in twenty-five years of practice, Droc had never actually seen a case of it himself though he knew some Healers who had. Vastalimi did not hold with such things, at least the sane ones did not. Not all were sane, however.

Vastalimi were complex, but not particularly complicated creatures, and The People were, as a species, hardy. Many illnesses that affected other beings did not infect them. Cancer was rare, arterial diseases infrequent. Infections of the kidneys or liver or bowel happened, but the leading causes of death on Vast were old age, accidents, and combat, with everything else trailing.

Yes, there were agents that afflicted The People. Brain fevers, lung infections, blood dyscrasias and poisonings, mental issues, a host of things; however, most were nonfatal, most of the time.

Every test that Droc and the other Healers had run on the dying victims had come up negative for a causative organism. The agent did not chart as a known pathogen. Not a bacterium, fungus, or virus. Neither did it seem to be any kind of allergen, radioactive element, or detectable poison. Nothing to show it as a plasmid or episome. No evidence of genetic retroengineering had been detected.

Healers were at a loss.

People got sick, suffered a short and awful illness, and died. It did not seem to be militantly contagious, in that health workers exposed to the dying had not contracted it—as far as anybody could tell. Some family members and others in close proximity had been affected, including his own parents and some siblings. Of course, it might be like some retroviruses, with a very long and dormant incubation period. Perhaps the afflicted had been carrying the invisible seeds of it for decades.

Or perhaps it was black magic or a plague sent by some-body's malignant god, for all they had been able to determine.

It was frustrating. Vastalimi did not fear enemies, but to fight them, you had to identify them. If you did not know the cause of an illness, how could you combat it?

The body's reaction was more or less the same: It broke down, there was a cascade of signs and symptoms that mim-icked several known diseases or conditions. Systems failed; the direct causes of death varied, it was a matter of which organ or organs succumbed first. Droc had seen patients bleed from the eyes and ears and even the skin; fulminant fevers had cooked brains into seizures; hearts had raced into uncontrolled tachycardia or slowed to bradycardia and just stopped. Livers, kidneys, stomachs, bowels, lungs went sep-tic and died.

Many patients, once informed of the inevitable progress of the syndrome, opted for *izvaditi utrobu*. Suicide was quicker, less painful, and honorable. If he himself contracted the malady, Droc expected he would fight it to the end, to allow other Healers more time to study him. Yes, that would be a bad way to die, but it might serve some purpose.

His sister was here, on-planet, and she would be arriving shortly. She had been among the best Healers on their world when she had practiced the arts. She'd had skill, of course, but more importantly, she had sometimes been preternatu-rally able to intuit things that most Healers could not. It seemed empathic, even telepathic, how she simply *knew* what was wrong with a patient, sometimes simply by walking into the same room, no examination, nothing. A talent he did not have.

It had been a loss to Vastalimi medicine when she had left the planet. And a personal one.

He knew the truth, and Kluth's choices had been limited; he understood her decision. Exile had been, in some ways, harder than death. He did not think he could have done it that way. Whatever perceived dishonor there might have been, she had taken it with her and become a focus that drew attention away from her family. He understood why she'd done so.

Droc wondered where Jak was these days. Not so much that he would bother to look, but as an idle curiosity. Jak, who had walked away clean because of Kluth's sacrifice. Droc had despised him for that, then. Later, he had come to honor her decision, at least to the point where he could stomach being in the same hemisphere with Jak. Barely. He was not one to initiate duels, but he had considered doing so in Jak's case. Such a pleasure it would be to kill him. What a scathead he was.

Such a hard choice his sister had made. And one she should not have had to make.

Not that he blamed her. She had been at the wrong place at the wrong time, and there had been nothing to be done for it. It had been years, the parties involved had moved on. Some were dead, some no longer in positions of power, some shunted into places where they were no threat; still, there was a risk. Vial was still around, the scum-spawn.

Had he not asked it of her, Kluth would never have returned to Vast, and it could be the death of her, despite his current status.

But if she could help him figure out what was killing The People? Her death, his, they were nothing compared to that. She would be the first to agree.

Vastalimi did not fear death the same way that some other species did.

"My sister is coming. She has brought a human medic with her."

"A human? Interesting. I hope she can keep him alive long enough to be useful. How is Kluth?"

"Dutiful, else she would not be here."

"She is that. I'll call if I find anything. Don't hold your breath waiting."

"No. I won't."

- - - - - -

A row of vehicles was parked at the curb outside the port, small-wheeled, enclosed carts that could carry perhaps four, if two of them were small and flexible. "That one," Kay said, nodding at one of the carts.

"How do you know which it is?"

"One is as good as the next."

"What if it belongs to somebody?"

"Then they will have to find another. They won't mind. Such vessels are not prized among us. There are more than enough to go around. Were you not with me, I would simply lope. Why would I ride such a short distance if my legs are sound?"

"How short a distance are we talking about?"

"About nine kilometers."

"That all?" The air was dry, the temperature maybe twenty or so Celsius. Not hot, not cold. Still, it would probably make for a sweaty run, an activity for which he was not dressed.

"But at your pace, it would take much longer than using the cart."

"You are too kind."

She whickered, that soft, chortlelike noise that passed for a laugh among her people. "You probably haven't heard the expression 'Slow as a human.'"

"No, I have heard 'Nasty as a Vastalimi,'" he said.

She whickered again.

They climbed into the cart. She rattled off an address. The cart's motor came online, and the vehicle moved away from the curb. Apparently, the autopilot was sufficiently capable to operate the vehicle without Kay's help; she didn't offer it any.

The ride was bumpy, the seat hard and uncomfortable. The city was very clean, with wide streets, and there were more pedestrians than passenger carts though there were larger vehicles carrying what he assumed were necessities, cargo too large or being moved over too long a distance to be managed by a Vastalimi on foot. Most of the cargo vehicles appeared to be automatically operated, no drivers visible.

More than a few of those on foot were running, loping along at a good pace.

The air felt, smelled, even tasted exotic to him. Every world had its own feel that way.

It was all quite fascinating.

– – – – – –

Cutter looked up from his desk. "Any problems?"

"We lost three drones; other than that, nothing," Jo said.

"Three drones? Do you know how much those cost?"

"Actually, I do, since I signed the purchase order for them. Hardware gets used up in a battle, that's what it's for."

"No, it's there to be used if you *need* it."

"We needed it. We took out the attackers, including a couple of APCs that cost the other side way more than the drones cost us. They got some pawns, we got a bishop and a couple of knights. They'll think twice about trying something that stupid next time."

He nodded. He bitched about money all the time, but the truth was, if he kept his people safe, he was willing to spend whatever it took. "Maybe that's not to our advantage, helping our enemy evolve his smarts."

"More fun that way. Set 'em up, knock 'em down, that gets boring."

"*You* would get bored falling off a tall building."

"Depends on how long it took to get down."

"What's next on your agenda?"

"We have troops watching the trucks. We are thinking about taking a run to the farming community where they grow these purple rootnips, and seeing if we can figure out things from that end. What are you gonna do?"

"I'm going to visit the manager of the TotalMart store and see what other intel his ops have developed."

"I could do that, and you could go talk to the farmers."

"Nah. Nice cool monster-mart with good restaurants and a couple of hundred shops sounds like more my kind of thing than stepping around the ruminant-ungulate pies steaming in the pastures."

"I'll wear my old boots," she said.

"Wouldn't it be easier just to avoid stepping in it?"

"Never seems to work out that way. And funny, coming from you."

He laughed.

- - - - - -

Kay nodded at her elder brother. They exchanged greetings, ritual face licks. She noted that he seemed happy to see her, and probably not just because he needed her help.

Well. It had been years. And some major things had happened.

"Our parents and siblings?"

"They died well," he said.

She nodded. She had already grieved, but it was still a shock. Death came for all, and it was never a matter of "if," only "when."

The way of it. Nothing to be done.

She and Droc had been close when she had lived here.

He had urged her to stay, offering his full support. Brave of him, and she had appreciated it.

Kay introduced Wink Doctor.

The two males gave each other nods of acknowledgment. Humans did not lick, they gripped and shook hands on such occasions; Vastalimi did not. The clasping of hands was supposed to show, according to what she had learned, that the humans were giving up a measure of lethality. It stemmed, so the story went, from the days when humans carried knives or swords, and demonstrated that the dominant hand—usually the right one—was empty. And with the dominant hands thus occupied, the ability to draw a weapon was also hindered.

Vastalimi had killing claws on hands and feet, were generally ambidextrous, and there was no ritualistic greeting that would convince anybody they were unarmed or incapable of a killing response—because both assumptions were demonstrably false. If you knew somebody well enough for face-licks, you trusted them, and usually that meant family.

Family was different. There was seldom danger from family.

"My sibling speaks well of your abilities, Doctor Wink." He spoke Basic.

"Good of her to do so."

"Would you like to see some of our afflicted? We have several in various stages of the malady."

"Of course," Kay said.

"This way."

He turned and walked away. They followed.

When they walked into the room, Kay had a visceral reaction to the feel of death in the air. It had been a while since she had been around dying Vastalimi, and the three strapped to the beds here were certainly close to expiration. There was the smell, of course, but something else, something . . . wrong about them she couldn't quite pin down.

She had been a skilled Healer, but it was *intuicija* that had set her apart from most other Healers; that sudden, unexplained, in-the-blink-of-an-eye knowledge, a certainty of what was wrong with a patient. Some Healers had it when they entered the profession; some achieved it along the way; some never had nor got it.

It was, she had learned, both blessing and curse . . .

She had never been able to control it, to summon it. It happened, and there seemed no reason in particular why it did or did not. Of a moment, when it occurred, she simply looked at a patient and knew what their problem was. Over the years, it had come to her hundreds of times.

And when it happened, it had never been wrong.

Her brother knew that, and he looked at her, waiting. Hoping.

She shook her head. "Not for sure. But there is *some-thing* . . . It seems . . . unnatural."

"How so?"

"I cannot say for certain. Whatever the cause, it feels wrong. Not like any disease I know."

"Ah."

Wink said, "May I examine one of the patients?"

"You are not worried about contracting the condition?"

"Have you determined that it is contagious?"

"No. We have no idea what it is. We haven't seen a vector pattern."

"Well, even if it is contagious among Vastalimi, chances of interspecies jumping to humans are small."

"Small might still be fatal," Droc said.

"Everybody dies, Healer. A comet might fall on us tomorrow."

Droc glanced at Kay, and gave her the barest hint of a smile. *I like this human,* the expression said.

Kay nodded and ghosted the smile back. *They have their moments.*

Droc held one hand up to indicate the nearest patient.

Kay followed Wink to where the ill male lay.

Even if you knew little about Vastalimi physiology, it would have been easy to see that the male was distressed. Wink Doctor had experience with a number of aliens, including Kay herself. He would bring a fresh and objective viewpoint. Maybe that would help.

Kay would examine the ill, too, but she suspected that the cause would not be found that way. Maybe something she had learned in her time among humans would help. And maybe Wink Doctor would have some ideas, for he was one of the best medics among them in her experience.

THREE

Jo and Gunny and Gramps went to see the head of the farm co-op that focused on the *difrui* crop. It wasn't too far from where CFI had set up camp, a few minutes by hopper.

They had PPS direction and sat imagery, so Jo wasn't expecting to find an adobe hut at the end of a dirt road, but even so, it looked more impressive than the images had suggested.

The place was probably four or five thousand square meters under a dura-tile roof, ferrofoam construction, with twenty-five-meter-tall evergreen trees, flowering shrubs with red and blue and purple blossoms, a reflecting pond, and neatly trimmed short-grass lawns.

Hardly an animal pasture full of old turds, this.

TotalMart had paved the way for CFI, too, so the people were all smiles and nice-to-see-you when they arrived.

They were ushered into a conference room with a waxed, flame-grained hardwood table, deep reds and oranges, one wall of clear plastic looking out at the reflecting pool. Painting on the opposite wall, a meter-tall metal sculpture of a

harvesting machine in one corner. Everything about the
place said quality, and nothing looked cheap.

"Must be good money in purple roots," Gunny said.

"Else we wouldn't be here," Gramps said.

Before Jo could say anything, a tall man with short gray
hair and teeth that practically glowed they were so white,
arrived. He looked fit, wore a gray silk unitard that hung
perfectly on his frame, with matching leather slippers that
looked sprayed on. Maybe forty-five, and he seemed comfortable in his skin.

"I'm Director Kreega," he said, and flashed his perfect
teeth at them. "Everybody calls me 'Chet.'"

Jo returned the smile. With a twitch that was almost
reflexive, she lit her Stress Analyzer aug. "Chet. I'm Jo Sims,
this is Megan Sayeed and Roy Demonde."

"Please, sit. How can I best help you, fem?"

"I expect you have been briefed on the recent encounter
with the, ah, bandits and the convoy?"

"I have. Excellent work. TM Corporate assured us that
Cutter Force Initiative was a first-rate organization, and I
am happy to see that so quickly demonstrated."

Jo shrugged that off. Protecting some big trucks from
some half-assed hijackers? No big deal.

"The attack was only a symptom, sir, and while we can
treat those, we are more interested in curing the cause of
the disease."

"Of course. That would be Masbülc," he said, his smile
fading.

"Probably true, if our intel is correct. However, the more
we know about the situation here, the quicker we can remedy
it. We have, of course, seen your reports, but if you wouldn't
mind telling it to us again?"

"Of course." He leaned forward slightly. "Some months
ago, we were approached by a buyer who represented Masbülc. He made an offer for our next crop, which was in the
beginning states of first harvest. As I am sure you know, *difrui*

grows year-round in this climate, and in a good year, we will get three harvests."

Jo nodded. So far, nothing to tweak her Stress Analyzer, nor did she expect any such.

"The man—I believe his name was Proderic"—he pronounced it "prod-er-ick"—"offered a premium, twenty percent higher than the going market price. Of course, we turned him down."

"Why didn't you take it?"

He leaned back slightly, gifted her with the smile. "We have a long-term relationship with TotalMart. Our contract with them had yet to be renewed, but we expected them to make an offer. Masbülc is a fine company, but . . ."

"You didn't want to piss off the big dog?" Gunny said.

He chuckled. "Just so, Gunny. We might be a short-rocket planet out here, but we aren't brushing alfalfa seeds from our hair. The couple million extra we'd have made taking Masbülc's offer isn't much compared to what TotalMart could send our way in the next decade."

Still no lies, but a blip, nonetheless. She filed it away and continued.

"So tell me about this Proderic. What was your sense of him?"

"Well. He was slick, sharp, smooth. Had that professional salesperson aspect about him, a good listener, smiled a lot, quick to answer any questions, and all the responses on tap. Hinted that Masbülc would be interested in a long-term relationship and willing to pay premium rates for a five-year contract.

"He was short, had a tan or faux that darkened his skin, indicating that he either spent a lot of time outdoors unprotected or wanted to convey that impression. His clothes were nice enough to impress but not so expensive so as to raise eyebrows in wonder. He arrived in a rented flitter with an assistant, a young woman who appeared to be chosen for her physical beauty, which was considerable. When he saw me look her over, he hinted that she might be willing to, ah, stay behind and work out details of the contract with me personally, no matter how long it might take."

Jo nodded. No surprise there. Sex had sold stuff ever since stuff had been around.

"When I was adamant that we weren't ready to accept his offer, he asked me if there was anything he could do to change my mind." There came a short pause. "You have viewed the conversation?"

Jo nodded again. She had watched and listened to the recording as a matter of course. But how Chet felt about it? The vid couldn't convey that.

"He asked me to reconsider before making a final decision, that he would get back in touch later. I didn't hear any direct threat in his words, nothing that could be taken as such, but . . ."

"Go on."

". . . there was about the man in that moment a sudden sense of . . . menace. Nothing upon which I could put my finger, and say, 'There! That!' but a feeling. Rather like standing just outside the cage of a greatcat. Were it not for the fields between you and the beast, it would think nothing of swatting you dead with one clawed paw just because it felt like it."

"Thank you," Jo said. "I won't take up any more of your time. We will keep you posted as to our investigation."

Chet nodded. "Thank you, Captain."

Outside, in the warm afternoon sunshine, the three entered the hopper and switched on the garble field as the engine cycled up.

Gramps said, "Interesting. He telling the truth?"

"Far as my aug could tell," Jo said. "But there was something."

Gunny and Gramps exchanged looks. "Go ahead, Chocolatte, you know you want to."

"Age before beauty," she said.

Gramps grinned and shook his head. "Well, as I recall—and for a man of my advanced age, memory is such a porous and transient thing—and please correct me if I am wrong, but when you introduced us, you didn't mention any ranks, did you?"

Gunny nodded. "Amazing. You caught that."

Jo headed off the exchange: "Nope, and yet Chet knew to call you 'Gunny' and me 'Captain,' and none of us are wearing anything that denotes rank."

"Gramps here is sometimes pretty rank when he takes off his boots, but, yeah."

"So he does his research," Jo said. "Nothing wrong with that though it does make you wonder. Was he just showing off by letting us know he'd checked us out? Or did he screw up and let that slip by accident? And does it matter either way?"

"Another of the many questions we will undoubtedly address," Gramps said. "Wheels within wheels . . ."

As the hopper spiraled up through a thousand meters toward cruising altitude, the Doppler on the tactical control panel pinged.

"Incoming attack," the computer's vox said.

"My, would you look at that," Gramps said. "Somebody is shooting at us."

The computer could do it and would in another half second, but Jo preferred manual. She hit the e-chaff spew and tapped the power control to full. The thrust shoved them back into the cushions as the hopper, one of theirs and unobtrusively rigged for combat, shot almost straight up, zipping through three gees in a couple of seconds.

"Take it easy! I had a big lunch!" Gramps said.

The missile, ground-to-air, had been fired from a couple of klicks out and was most of the way there, but the e-chaff spew caused it to slow and think about things. Jo's finger hovered over the gat-control, in case the rocket was smarter than an IR or pulse-guide weapon.

Apparently, it was. Instead of following the chaff, the rocket changed course and headed for the hopper. Interesting.

Jo lit the gat.

The hopper slowed, gravity eased up, and the vessel veered a hair to port as the gat-port snapped open. The electric gun opened up, six barrels atwirl, eight thousand rounds a minute of 10mm EU caseless, laser-locked onto the incoming rocket. A two-second burst was more than enough. Way more.

Rags would probably give her shit about how the computer could have done it in one second, thus saving 133 rounds, but fuck it, better safe than sorry. If they got spiked? The computer wouldn't care.

The heavy metal sleet tore the rocket to pieces five hundred meters out, shredding it into metal-and-plastic confetti. No boom, as the bits fluttered and fell in the warm afternoon.

"Smart rockets don't come cheap," Jo said. "Looks like the opposition is ramping things up."

"We need to go find it and have a look?" Gramps asked.

"No point. We'd find out it was a rocket and maybe back-walk where it came from, but the shooter will be long gone, if he was even there when it lit. Could have been a din running it."

"Well, at least we won't be bored on this op," Gunny said.

"How could anybody be bored when you are around, Chocolatte?"

Jo shook her head. Sooner or later, somebody would tell them to get a fucking room and get to fucking. Be interesting to see what their reactions would be when it finally happened.

She waved at the com.

"Cutter here."

"You check the feed from the hopper's squirt?"

"Why would I do that? Don't *you* know? Aren't you there?"

"So far. But somebody doesn't want us to be."

There was a pause. He'd be calling up the telemetrics on the hopper. Before he could speak, she said, "And don't even go there about overfiring the fucking Gatling gun, Rags."

"I was only going to say, 'Nice shooting.'"

"Bullshit you were."

He laughed. "Come home. We need to sit down and think out loud about this."

— — — — — —

Kay didn't expect her visit quite so soon, though it wasn't a complete surprise. Wink was at the lab, talking to Luque, and it wasn't as if Kay had all that much to do. She walked through the decontamination field, waved her hands back and forth to make sure they were completely bathed, and through the two positive-pressure chambers. Into the waiting area. Other than her own fur, she had nothing on that could carry germs. Not that they had found any such.

Leeth stood there, as if she were a statue, staring into infinity. It was well-known that the *Sena* could stand in a meditative trance for hours without moving, their minds hard at work on whatever they wanted to consider in detail. They seemed unaware of their surroundings at first look, but it would be a mistake to assume that. *Sena* slept aware.

Two seconds through the door, Leeth spoke to her: "Kluth."

"Leeth."

Her sister appeared much the same as Kay remembered. Trim, taut, with the bril-*hide* weapon belt of her trade slung low on her hips, pistol on one side, swand on the other, the com, recorder, and PPS snugged midway between. The official stain on her shoulders was an electric purple, freshly applied.

She was every centimeter the walking Rule of Law, and a subvocalized word into her com would bring a dozen more like her running if she needed them. Unlikely that she would *need* such help. To assault a Shadow was to die; if not in the moment, then soon afterward. Everybody knew that. It happened rarely. As far as she knew, there were no unsolved attacks on Shadows unless some had happened since she'd left.

Shadows were immune to Challenge while on duty. Any Challenge from anybody. Offer one, they could shoot you down without a second thought if they felt like it.

Even the military stepped wide of the *Sena*.

"I grieve for our parents and siblings," Kay said.

"As do I. We have never been a particularly fortunate family."

That was the extent of their expressed grief. People died. Some sooner, some later, that was the way of it. The dead moved to another country.

"You look sleek. Apparently soft, alien ways have not made you entirely fat and slow."

"As being *Sena* has apparently done to you. Gained a kilo or two, Sister?"

Leeth whickered. The Shadows were among the most dedicated of Vastalimi. They trained to keep their minds and bodies as close to peak condition as could be maintained. There were no fat, dull *Sena*. A fitter group of The People was not to be found, everybody knew that, too.

Kay had always been able to make her sibling laugh; good to know she still could.

"I didn't expect to see you in this life again."

"Nor I you. I could hardly refuse our elder brother's call in this case."

"Agreed. Can you help?"

"It remains to be seen."

"And what of your human *pas*?"

"He is not my pet, but a colleague. He has great skills as a medic, and he brings an unbiased perspective. As I am sure you already know in great detail."

"Unbiased? As opposed to . . . ?"

Sleek, and her wit undimmed. Right to the pertinent comment.

Kay smiled. "Tell me, have politics ceased to function since I left? No more power-hungry, self-serving, ambitious Vastalimi to be found here?"

Leeth whickered again. "Would that it were so, Sister. But surely you don't think somebody would use this illness to their advantage?"

They both whickered at that one.

"I take it you have not found such links."

"Not as yet. How is life among the humans?"

"Better than many would expect. They have their own kind of honor, they can be brave and loyal. Slow and weak, generally, but they are matchless with small arms. You have heard, 'Never shoot with a human'?"

Leeth said, "A teat-tale to frighten cubs, I always thought."

"Not entirely. Two of my human team members can out-shoot any Vastalimi I have ever known."

"Is that so? You are likely unaware that I am the current *Sena* pistol champion and ranked third with the issue carbine," she said.

"Only third?"

Leeth looked away, a brief flash of embarrassment flitting across her face. "I had a bad match. I shall do better next time. I—" She caught the hint of Kay's grin.

"Ah. You pull my fur."

"Who better than your own sister to do so? I expect the third place was but a fluke. You always were the most driven and talented among us. But even so, there is one called Gunny who would defeat you eight of ten with any common sidearm or shoulder weapon, and *she* loses to Cutter by the same ratio when they vie."

"Interesting. I should like to see them shoot." She paused. "Have you had Challenges?"

"None so far. Perhaps those who might have offered such have either died or moved on, or perhaps, forgotten."

"Unlikely those directly concerned have forgotten."

"Well, I have been here but a few hours. Word is yet to get around."

"It will."

"I expect so. I have learned some new skills from my adopted pack that may be of use."

Kay caught the hint of another question in Leeth's demeanor. She said, "I thought so at the time."

Leeth blinked, surprised. "To what do you refer?"

"The question you did not ask: Was Jak worth it?"

Leeth shook her head. "You could have been a great *Sena*, sibling. You have an uncanny knack for clawing to the heart of the matter, a clarity of vision. And *now* what do you think?"

"Probably not. I have yet to see him."

"But you will."

"Of course."

"His alignment has changed."

"To be expected."

"I have never heard him speak of you."

"Also not a surprise. The questions I will need to ask him are not personal but about our problem."

"You think Jak is involved?"

"I cannot say. But his uncle was the third to die from the malady."

"Yes. I recall." Leeth nodded. "You seem . . . calm about things."

"The years away have given me a perspective I would likely not have achieved here. Humans do not see the world as we do. There are things to be gained from them."

Leeth whickered again. "You always were more liberal in your views about such things."

"But was it not you who used to tell me that the more you knew, the better? That knowledge was the sharpest fang?"

"I have missed our discussions, Sister. I would not have

chosen the path you did, and I have wished more than once that you had taken a different one, but *zevot krut*."

"Yes, often life *is* hard. I cannot complain; many have it worse than I."

There came a short pause. "I have duties. We will speak again, assuming we survive our days."

"I shall endeavor to do so," Kay said. "And offer hopes you will do the same."

"Sister."

"Sister."

After Leeth was gone, Kay was somewhat surprised at the emotions that had roiled up within her during their short meeting. Leeth had been the brightest light of their litter, always faster, sharper, more ambitious than the rest of them. That she became a Shadow had been no surprise. She always had a rigor in all her activities and a keen sense of justice. The *Sena* could not expect more from one of its own than Leeth brought to the job, for even in that august body, she was above reproach.

That she came to see her tainted sibling? Nobody would lift a lip in her direction. Certainly not if they knew what was good for them. *Sena* were restricted from offering Challenges, save for most special circumstances. They were exempt from *any*.

It was the talk of Jak that had stirred her, even more than the loss of her siblings and parents. Death claimed all, there was no point denying that. But Jak was still alive. She had, she'd thought, put all that behind her, let it go. So she had thought.

Having Leeth as a resource would likely prove beneficial. The gnawing little pest in the back of her mind had increased its activity. If this disease was not a natural phenomenon, then somebody had unleashed it upon The People for reasons that would need be discovered in order to determine who had done it, and from them, how it could be stopped.

When you hunted, there were several ways you might

proceed to take unseen prey. You could follow a trail; you could circle around and try to get ahead of it, to intercept it; you could guess where it might go and get there first and wait. You could use bait or a lure. Any might work, but determining which was the fastest and surest was the quest. Dull hunters went hungry. Really dull ones got themselves killed.

Sometimes, prey would outwit even the fastest and sharpest hunter and escape. It happened.

But she was not going to let that happen this time.

FOUR

Cutter leaned back in his chair and considered the problem. It wasn't really that much of one, relatively speaking. They had a pretty good idea of who the opposition was, and it was a matter of tracking them down and having a spirited discussion with them.

Sometimes, it would take guns. Sometimes lawyers, sometimes money. TotalMart had them out here to kick ass, but if he determined that buying off the opposition was cheaper? The runners would write a transfer and pay the toll, and Cutter and his troops could move along to another job.

Corporate liked that about CFI, that they would make the report even if it meant they put themselves out of work. So far, that had always resulted in more jobs being offered in short order, and he was good with that. Sometimes a win was decisive, and sometimes it came from packing up and walking away. Nature of the biz.

Jo and Gunny and Gramps would poke around and figure out what was what, and when they did, then there would come a battle plan. Meanwhile, they had enough seasoned troops to guard the root shipments. Industrial espionage was doubtless on the table, and processing sites being sabotaged, local growers being kidnapped, and the like might still happen. CFI had already started offering classes to local bodyguards and their expertise to any police agencies who might want it.

CFI had been down this road a few times.

The GU Army hadn't sent over a rep yet. Buried somewhere in all the briefing material was the report on them, but Cutter hadn't bothered to find and read it yet. It didn't really matter, at least at this point. They were HQed near the big mines and not close, but it was only a matter of time. The local commander would know what was going on in his or her backyard, and either somebody would come to call or he'd get a com telling him to report to the base ASAP for a chat. Regular Army didn't have much use for private military, but fuck 'em—he had enough of that organization when they had set his unit up for a snafu not their fault. The uplevel dicks had pissed on a bunch of good officers to make sure nobody came after their guilty asses. Only reason he had been allowed to retire instead of being court-martialed and sent away was because he had friends among the generals who owed him. They knew he was getting screwed, but their influence only extended so far.

We can keep you out of the stockade, Rags, but we can't keep you in the Army.

No point in dragging that up, done was done, and in the end, he was doing okay . . .

Maybe it was time to break out the bourbon and have his daily drink a little early, hey?

No. It could wait. Not the least reason being that he didn't want to wait. One drink, expensive booze over ice, to be enjoyed, not used as a crutch . . .

The incoming com chimed. The sig said the caller was Colonel Sett, Galactic Union Army HQ . . .

Speak of the devil . . .

Sett? That name sounded familiar. Sett . . . ?

Cutter waved his hand at the com. The threedee image of a man looking at the camera appeared over the com, quarter scale. "Cutter here."

Even as he said the words, he recognized the face. It was still lean and angular, dark-skinned and the hair shaved or depilated, a few more wrinkles here and there. And it had been First Lieutenant Sett the last time he had seen him.

"Mica Sett," Cutter said. "How the hell are you?"

The man grinned. "Other than being posted to the asshole of the galaxy, I'm doin' jest fahn, Rags."

"How long has it been? Fifteen years?"

Sett nodded. "About that. The Aleutians, that little revolution that took down General Papirósa."

"Yep, what a clusterfuck that was. So, asshole of the galaxy, but a full bird colonel?"

Cutter didn't ask the next question: Was Sett sent here as punishment that would wind down his career, or because it was a necessary posting on his track to keep going? Sometimes with the Army, you couldn't see what they had in mind: A rathole in the middle of nowhere could be a curse or a blessing, depending.

Sett must have known what he was thinking. He said, "And if I don't screw it up, a good shot at general within two years if my sources can be believed. The politicians have been convinced by the GU Army lobbyists that we need more boots on the ground. More boots, more freshly minted generals to direct them how to step. Better me than some others."

"Congratulations."

"Thanks. Been a long time coming. Uh, Rags, you aren't going to be part of the problem, are you?"

"Not if I can help it. I'm here to protect the root-growers from bandits."

"Yeah, we know about that. I sent patrols out, but we are

stretched pretty thin here, I can't afford to keep troops with every van on the road."

"What they hired us for. We keep the trucks from being jacked until we can figure out who is doing it."

"At which time, you will give me all the particulars so that I can stop them."

"Well, of course, Mica. Absolutely."

They both grinned at that. He could chop the bad guys into fine soyburger as long as he wasn't too loud and obvious about it, Cutter knew. Within the ROE, there was a lot of leeway, and as long as he didn't make the local commander look bad, nobody gave a toad's ass. And if he could make him look *good*? So much the better.

Never hurt to have TotalMart call up your commander and allow that you were a fine fellow well met.

Sett didn't speak to Cutter's history, nor did Cutter expect that he would. Sett would know what had happened, the Army underground com being what it was. No point in bringing up bad memories.

"Seriously, Rags, I need to keep a low profile here. I come away from this posting without any fuss, my name shows up on the lists. I get the star holograms, I wind up a Systems Commander somewhere comfortable, nice bump in pay, the usual perks, a good place to park until we get another shooting war."

"Not my job to screw that up," Cutter said. "This should be a by-the-numbers operation. The opposition hasn't thrown anything at us we can't handle, and unless they up their game, we'll run them down and be done here, a few weeks, maybe less."

Sett nodded. "You will keep me in the circuit?"

"Sure. Nothing to report yet, but soon as we get something, I'll pass it along."

"Thanks. You were always a stand-up soldier. I have to run; base command is like being nibbled to death by ladybugs. Maybe we can get together and clink glasses."

"I'd like that."

"Good talking to you," Sett said.

After they disconnected, Cutter smiled to himself. He and Mica Sett had met as lieutenants together a lifetime ago, bumped into each other a few times since. They hadn't been best buddies, only had a nodding acquaintance, different platoons, working soldiers in the same action; still, Sett would cut him a little slack based on that. The good old days always seemed better in distant memory than they had actually been at the time.

Not that he thought he would need much slack. This didn't look to be complicated as an op; at least not so far. And better that the local army commander was inclined to give you a break than not. Take what you could get.

— — — — — —

Formentara said, "If you would." Zhe gestured toward the table.

Jo nodded and reclined on the padded support. The field hummed as she entered it, and Formentara began waving hir hands over the control panel, initiating the system's reader. The room smelled faintly like patchouli, but even with her augmented senses, Jo couldn't nail down the source of the pleasant odor.

Formentara went into hir work trance.

Jo never forgot how lucky she was to have somebody with such outlandishly good skill adjusting her augs. Formentara was a genius, second to nobody when it came to this. Not only did zhe create new augs that went from luxury to necessity in short order, zhe was the best there was at maintaining installations. The level of complexity in somebody with more than a few augs was mind-numbingly complicated because of the imperfection of cybernetic interfaces. Your biology suffered, hormone systems, major organs, the balance of this and that, they were all prey to damage. Most if it was minor, but it added up over time. Some if it could be repaired, but some of it could not be.

Somebody with one major aug up and running lopped around five years off his or her life span. Five augs, could be twenty-five years. Aug hogs who ran twenty systems? They were pretty much fated to live fast, die young, and leave hideous corpses. You could be superwoman, but you paid the price, and the run wasn't long.

Jo currently had fourteen augs. Which meant that she could expect to live to be seventy, maybe eighty, out of a normal span of 150 years. That was the cost, and because of who she was and how she had come to be that way, she had elected to pay it. That's how it went. Nobody lives forever.

But when she'd come under Formentara's care, that had gotten her a snort. "Camel cark!" No reason she couldn't live out a normal span if a technomedic kept things balanced properly.

And how many technomedics could properly balance that many systems? Jo had asked.

Counting Formentara hirself? Two. Maybe three . . .

"Okay, that's it," Formentara said, breaking into Jo's memory. "All done."

"Everything okay?"

Zhe laughed. "You are kidding, right? Of course everything is okay. You forget who you are talking to here?"

Jo sat up.

Formentara's smile seemed a little forced, and Jo's ability to read such things was also augmented. She had inbuilt stress analyzers. Lies were pretty easy. Fugue was a little harder.

"What?"

"What 'what'?" Formentara said.

"Listen, you know how good my microexpression reader is, you installed it. What?"

Formentara nodded. "Hoist on my own petard."

"What does that mean?"

"Means I should have known you'd pick it up." Zhe paused. "You are running out of room, Jo. You are balanced now, but . . ."

Jo nodded. "So if you come up with some neat new toy, I can't have it?"

"I didn't say that. But there are limits to what even I can manage. Two, maybe three more, that's it. What that means is, you will have to be more careful in your choices. Once you hit the limit, I'm not going to give you any more."

"I understand."

"I'm not sure you do, but that's the deal, remember."

"Yes."

And it made sense; everything had a limit, even the edge of the universe was out there somewhere. She couldn't be immune to that.

As a soldier, Jo's combatware was useful, and she had more of that than anybody she knew still walking around. Some of the others—com, proprioceptives, high-end sensories—were icing on the cake. Being tended by Formentara was priceless, and if she decided to sneak off and get another aug elsewhere, that would be elective suicide—it might take a couple of decades, but she'd be going down, no question.

If Formentara couldn't keep her stable, nobody could.

Of course, she could be KIA on any op—that was part of the risk.

She had good reasons why she had started along this road. And the pull to keep going farther was an addiction, as much as a chemhead's lust for drugs or a wirehead's hunger for juice.

To be stronger, faster, smarter, more impervious to pain or injury, able to do what no ordinary human could do? It was a powerful draw. How many humans could play hand-to-hand with a Vastalimi and hold their own? How many could see into the red or violet, hear radio waves, stand on one foot with their eyes closed for as long as they wanted?

Not many.

Mostly, she didn't think about it. Now and then, it shone through her mind. The candle that burns brighter burns out faster. She'd accepted that. But once Formentara had told her she could have both? It was a miracle. She'd be foolish to give that up.

Still . . .

"Well. I'll just get more picky," she said.

"Maybe I won't come up with anything else you'll want." They both grinned at that one.

"That might be. What are you working on?"

"Ultimate orgasmware," zhe said.

"Shit you are!"

Formentara laughed. "Well. I could if I wanted."

"Every male in the galaxy would want to buy that one. And more than a few fems, too. You could retire a multi-billionaire in a couple of weeks."

"I could. But where would the fun be in that? I already have more money than I know what to do with. Why would I need more?

"Okay, you're done. Come back for a recheck next month."

"Yeshir."

FIVE

Wink was a good medic, better than many, but his expertise was in meatball surgery and battlefield vectors. He could take care of the problems that arose in a small military unit most of the time. Injuries, diseases, allergies, what usually afflicted troops on an active operation. Cuts, breaks, burns, bullet wounds, STDs, flu, neuroses and psychoses, malfunctioning augs, a boxcar of things. What the machines couldn't DX, he could usually manage on his own. He had enough training to know how to isolate and treat unknown bugs on an alien world that rarely affected humans, a decent knowledge of field epidemiology; but he was not a number cruncher who could program a shitload of esoteric information into a computer and have it spit out a miracle cure for something that a million other scientists had tried to do and failed.

Still, there was the chance that his eyes might spot something the Vastalimi Healers had missed, if only because they didn't look at things the way humans did.

But as he looked at the Holographic Impious Particle

microscope's scan, he didn't see anything that pointed him in a direction. He had already viewed dozens of tissue samples, and if there was an unknown bug in them, he hadn't spotted it.

The old Vastalimi, Luque, had given him the run of the lab, and while he got more than a few curious looks as he poked around, nobody had bothered him. Luque ran a tight ship, and any of the employees who wanted to cause trouble apparently didn't last long. Just as well. He didn't want to use that as-I-stand phrase if he didn't have to.

Not as if Wink was averse to risks; he had danced with Death more than a few times, and while he didn't tell people, some of them knew: He enjoyed it. But there was the dance and there was suicide, and he wasn't suicidal. Fighting with Vastalimi might as well be that for most humans. Maybe Jo could keep up with one, all her augs. He couldn't, and he knew it.

He looked at the scan again. A view into the depths of a brain cell, and each organelle was accounted for, there weren't any anomalies not in the catalogue. Nothing missing, nothing that shouldn't be there.

You could compare every bit of this or that against what it was supposed to look like in an ideal state and see how it stacked up. Some parts were perfect, others less so, but there weren't any foreign invaders who didn't belong—no tiny sharks swimming in the Cytoplasm Seas, no dragons dug into the periplasmic caves.

Surely, if something was too small for the HIP scope to detect, it would be too small to do what the illness was doing to the Vastalimi?

If it was an infective agent at all . . .

Wink rubbed at his eyes. If the Vastalimi researchers hadn't seen it, he wasn't apt to, either; they saw farther into the red and violet than humans by a considerable margin, and the problem wasn't fresh eyes, human or otherwise.

No, they were missing something, there was a blind spot,

and the nature of such things was that if you knew what it was, it wouldn't be a blind spot . . .

He'd have to talk to Kay about it, but his feeling was that she was probably onto something when she said it felt artificial. The Vastalimi had lived on this planet for millions of years, and pretty much any pathogen that could have arisen naturally had, as far as Wink could tell. Sometimes you figured out what something *wasn't* rather than what it *was*, and what was left was your answer.

And sometimes you didn't find an answer at all.

— — — — — —

"Got a visitor," Gramps said. "Probably you want to see him."

Cutter, bored with background reports he had put off reading and not unhappy to find another reason to put them off a while longer, said, "Send him in."

"Best of the afternoon, Colonel, sah."

"Singh? I didn't expect to see you here."

The young man, all of twenty or so, approached, back straight, to stand in front of Cutter's desk.

"At ease, Singh, have a seat."

He did so.

"So you've come to take me up on my offer."

"Yes, sah. You do not seem surprised to see me."

"Yes and no. I know you were loyal to the Rajah despite his, um . . . behavior. But I heard he died. So on the one hand, you could have stayed on Ananda and not had that complication any longer. Then again, with him gone, you would be free to work where you wish if your hitch was up.

"Long way from there to here."

"And it took most of my savings to afford the trip."

Cutter smiled. How great it must be to be young and enthusiastic enough to pack everything into a shipping trunk and space halfway across the galaxy, hoping there'd be a job when you got there. Surely the gods did sometimes watch out for fools and children . . .

"Well, as it happens, we are always on the lookout for loyal and experienced troops. I know about the loyalty, and while you haven't had as much time in the field as we normally prefer, I also know the quality of your training was first-rate, given as how it came from us. And that you can pull a trigger when it needs to be pulled.

"Go see Gunny. She'll find you a bunk and get you squared away."

The boy's face lit up in pure joy.

"Thank you, sah! My debt is boundless!"

Cutter shook his head. "You'll earn your pay, Singh, and Gunny will work your ass ragged." But from the boy's smile, Cutter knew that hard work wasn't any kind of impediment, not even on his pradar . . .

SIX

As they finished their midday meal, still-warm *foof*-rats with a pungent blood sauce, Droc said, "So, how are things? As you recall them?"

She picked a bit of meat from between two teeth with her forefinger's claw, flicked it onto the plate. "Mostly. Many of the faces are different, but the flow seems to be the same."

"Your meal was acceptable?"

"Quite tasty. So much for the canard about *bolnica* food being uniformly awful."

"Well-fed patients behave better. Can't have them getting up to go seek prey because the food stinks."

She nodded. "I do find it somewhat odd that I haven't gotten any Challenges," she said. "It has been several days, and I expected at least a few."

"Disappointed?" Droc gave her the briefest of smiles.

"No, just remarking; however, I remember that facial expression, Brother. You know something of which you are not speaking."

"I do not *know*, but I have a suspicion."

"Which is . . . ?"

"Our sister the Shadow."

"What of her?"

"She applies the law."

"And what does . . . ? Ah. Yes. I see."

"Good to know that your wits haven't completely evaporated during your association with the humans."

There was really no need to say it, but Kay said it anyway: "You think our sister has let it be known that she will be especially rigorous in her application of the law regarding *prigovor* in my case."

"If I had to gamble on the premise? Indeed. Even though you and I know that Leeth would not knowingly break the law, she might . . . ah . . . bend it a bit. And if she would not do that much? There are more than a few among The People who believe that *Sena* abuse their power and adjudicate matters to their own ends when it serves them.

"Someone who might consider challenging you, just to see if they could win, might think that a Shadow peering over their shoulder for the slightest error is a matter of some concern. I would; even a careful person can misstep in matters of protocol. Were Leeth to hint at taking special care in investigating such, it would not be illegal, merely suggestive. Word would get around quickly."

Yes. A Shadow looking at you with interest was to be avoided.

Kay nodded. "Family first."

"Of course. 'My sister and I against my cousin; my cousin and I against the pack; my pack and I against the world.' Are your humans so different that you have forgotten this?"

"Not at all. If anything, they are much like us in that regard."

"For their own kind, you mean."

"It depends on how you define that. They have become in many ways my pack."

"Made you an honorary human, have they?"

She whickered. "No, but Cutter's tribe behaves as family, regardless of blood. There are more than a few of my cousins and a couple of sibs I would trust less than I do my humans."

"Sister! I am shocked to hear this!" He smiled to give that the lie.

She shook her head. She had put all this behind her when the orbital ship took her aloft those long years ago. Now and again, memories of how it had been surfaced, but sitting here, talking to her brother, knowing her sister had her back? It was a powerful draw. Family *did* matter. Was it possible that enough time had passed so that the idea of being here at home was not totally unrealistic?

Probably best not to consider that option now.

"How goes the investigation?"

"Slowly. There are many people to whom I must speak, to gather information before I find a scent I can follow."

He glanced away, and his thoughts were, of a moment, so easy to read as Leeth's had been that he could have spoken aloud.

She said, "Yes, and Jak is among them."

"Did I mention his name?"

"Might as well have; I had no trouble hearing your thoughts."

"Hear these, then. He is offal," Droc allowed. "Dried white dung is worth ten times more, and probably tastes better."

"You never cared for him."

"With demonstrably good reason."

"Nonetheless, he has a direct familial connection. If I am to investigate, I must go where I must to find answers."

"The only answer Jak will provide is how worthless a Vastalimi can be and still retain the ability to breathe."

She shook her head. She had come to realize that herself . . .

Wink sat in the rear of the cafeteria, eating what was the least-bloody-looking thing they had to offer. A lot of what was on the menu was still alive when you selected it. It would be killed and butchered to order as you watch. *Is it fresh? Observe . . .*

There were a score of Vastalimi in the place, and most of them had seen him here often enough over the last few days so that they didn't just sit and stare at him anymore. Nobody had initiated a conversation, which was fine by him.

There were a lot of fascinating things here, and their medicine was more advanced than humans' in some areas and less so in others. Much more trauma than pathogens, which went along with his own skill set.

He looked at his food, some kind of rootlike thing, it had a consistency of a half-baked yam and the color of meconium. It didn't taste too bad, more *umami* than anything. He had eaten worse. He hadn't asked what it was; better to not know . . .

So far, he had read tons of material and was probably getting an education on Vastalimi healing superior to that of all but a handful of nonlocal doctors in the galaxy. Not why he had come, but hey, take what you could get. Never know when it might come in handy.

There were a pair of Vastalimi seated at a table nearby, and with his earbud hidden and the translator's gain turned up a bit, he was able to overhear their conversation easily. He felt no guilt about listening since a lot of the time, he was the subject.

He had gotten pretty good filling in the blank spots the translator left in the conversations though it still wasn't perfect. What he overheard the two Vastalimi talking about was fascinating, as much for their attitude as the content.

The taller one said, "Did you hear about the Rel?"

Rel were pear-shaped bipedal herbivores, about the

height of an average human but half again as heavy. They were hairless, had a spongelike grayish flesh, and they liked to decorate their skin with bright paint or dye.

"Only thing I know about Rel is that they taste like hide glue."

"This one sneaked into a bog freighter and managed to get into Northport undetected."

"Came to Vast *deliberately*? Scat you say!"

"Raeel's Own Truth."

"Why would it do that? That's crazy."

"So it was determined to be later. Mad as a stoned sackfly."

"Continue."

"It had been altered. Augmented."

"A Rel." The translator didn't catch the disbelief in the shorter one's voice, but Wink heard it clearly enough. He was getting better at that, too.

"Sped up, increased strength, and drugged to make it brave."

The shorter one didn't speak to that, only waited.

"Steel claws had been grafted onto its paws."

The shorter one finally got the direction of the story. "You pull my fur."

"Not even a single hair. It came here to fight. Prey."

"Fuck your father!"

"Exactly what I said when Karsh told it to me."

"What happened to this Rel?"

"It tried to challenge the first person it saw. You recall Svark, the freight handler?"

"The fem who likes fems?"

"That's her. The Rel stepped up, blathered something about claw-to-claw combat. Waved its arms about.

"Svark killed it before it finished its speech."

The shorter one nodded. "Of course. Probably had to shower the rest of the morning to wash the stink from her fur."

"Armed, belligerent, altered *prey*. Here. On Vast."

"Perhaps the End of Days approaches."

"You jest, but it may be you speak more truth than you know. There is the Scourge that kills and no cause for it. Kluth is returned, with that furless Terran over there in tow. And now, prey with fake claws and an obvious death wish? Strange times indeed. Best you make your peace with Raeel."

"Too late for that."

They both whickered loudly.

Wink wondered what they would think if they knew *that furless Terran* was listening. He was not, however, tempted to tell them and find out . . .

Jak's place of residence had changed. It was upscale, in the richer side of the district, and while many of The People did not care for things, Jak had always had a fondness for toys. Anything that made him feel better or look better or create a deeper impression on those around him? He would have it, could he get it.

Back when they had been a pair, that had seemed somehow amusing. Part of his charm.

The corridor was wide, with windows that gave a view of cultivated grounds, and the room in which she found him had tall ceilings, an entire wall open to the outside save for an air-curtain, and art objects carefully placed around the room. Jak sat on a couch—well, more like he *posed* upon the couch—of what looked to be a mottled, white-and-black alien animal hide she didn't recognize, and he came to his feet immediately when she stepped into the room. His in-command stance, as she recalled it.

*Jak*Masc looked much as Kay remembered him—tall, lean, fit, insouciantly at ease in his own fur. As handsome a male as any, more so than most, and very much aware of it. He'd had his claws enameled in what looked like matte-finished platinum. His fur had been brushed until it gleamed.

Obvious his fortunes had risen. Plating and hand-brushing like that weren't cheap, and he hadn't done those himself. And this place?

She had wondered what it would be like to see Jak again; what he might say if somehow such a meeting, however slim the chance, ever took place.

How are you? How have you been? I'm happy to see you. I've missed you . . .

His words, now that the moment had come, were not among those she had imagined:

"How stupid are you, fem, to be here?" The edge of anger was a cold razor in his voice.

She had, over the years she had been away from Vast, reconsidered the actions that caused her to leave more than a few times. Jak had been a major part of her motivation.

In this moment, her actions seemed far less compelling than they had been at the time.

Far less compelling.

She said, "Droc asked me to come back to help him deal with a medical problem. It was my duty to do so." She paused a moment. Before she had spent time among the aliens, it never would have occurred to her to finish her thought the way she did: "What would you have done in my place?"

The question surprised him, she could tell. The Kluth he had known would not have gone down that path. "I would have found a compelling reason to stay away. It's too dangerous."

Her sister had tried to warn her, she realized in that moment: His alignment has changed. I have never heard him speak of you . . .

The brief, tiny spark of hope that he might be concerned for her safety was quickly extinguished. "Your presence will likely roil mud long settled. It would have been best for all that you never returned."

Best for all?

No. Best for Jak . . .

There had been a time when that thought would never have blossomed in her mind, either.

Well. Things change. Worlds move.

How low do the young and foolish fall . . .

That self-centered arrogance that once she had taken for decisive confidence was painfully evident. Hard to believe she had failed to identify it. It had taken being away for years before the truth finally visited her, creeping in like a caterpillar on hair-fine feet as she lay waiting for sleep . . .

How on Vast could she have *ever* considered becoming life-mates with Jak? How could a fem ever have been so densely *oblivious*?

Desire, she realized, was a thick fog that could completely obscure reality. Thinking with one's *ruta* was not thinking at all . . .

It had taken a long time to percolate through her, the realization of her mistake. Even moments ago, some part of her had held out a minuscule hope that she had been wrong. That Jak would rush to her, embrace her, lick her face in joy at seeing her.

Desire breeds hope. But hope was, finally, snuffed out with his words.

She had left her home, given up her life, in no small part to protect a male, who, in the end, wasn't worth her sacrifice. He hadn't been the only reason, but she had counted him high on the list.

Stupid. She had been stone-headed stupid. No getting around that. He was what he was, evident for all to see, and she had missed it. Her family had tried to tell her, and she had ignored them.

No fem so blind as one who will not see.

Well. Live and learn and survive. Sometimes a hard lesson.

"I was sorry to hear about your family, but—why have you come to see me? You put me at risk by doing so."

Self-centered, arrogant, *and* a coward. She had realized that, too, else he never would have let her leave. He would have stepped in front of her, to shield her. He had not.

It was embarrassing, how thick she had been.

It made her want to spit. Instead, she said, "Your uncle was among the first who died of the malady. I need to know about his activities before the illness manifested."

"Why?"

"That is not your concern."

"If you want my help, it is."

"No, it is not. My brother's status is much higher than it was when I left Vast. He is in charge of the investigation into the cause of this malady, which has now affected hundreds of The People, including *our* family. He has been given great leeway and full authority to conduct his inquiries, and I am his agent. You can help willingly, or I can call the *Sena*, who will compel you to it."

"You would do that to me?"

Once, the look he now gave her, the throaty *jebati*-me trill in his voice, those would have melted her into mindless lust. Not now. "The choice is yours. And save the growl for a fem who just left the den, Jak. It won't work on me anymore."

He sat quietly for a moment, no doubt considering his options, deciding which would serve him best. He did not look comfortable.

Kay enjoyed watching him squirm. Revenge was as much a part of her makeup as any other Vastalimi's. He deserved to suffer, and even a small amount was better than none.

"Very well. What do you want to know?"

"I need your uncle's movements before his death."

"I have already given that report."

"And you and I both know it was less than complete. Unless Uncle Teb had a major change of philosophy since I left Vast, he was not a person to spend his time walking the path of Right Action. He was rich and he was crooked and he would not pour water to douse a newborn cub on fire unless he was paid for both water *and* his effort. That he had enemies is a given, and your sanitized report is fiction by omission."

Jak said nothing.

"I will know what illegal and immoral activities he was involved in. You can tell me, or—"

"—Yes, yes, you will call the Shadows. How is your dear sister these days?"

"Probably salivating at the chance to prod you with her swand and listen to you scream. She never liked you to begin with and likes you less now. Tell it to me or sob it to her."

She heard his teeth clash. It was quite satisfying.

"I will tell you," he said.

She smiled.

SEVEN

In the dojo behind the mess hall, Gunny shook her head at Singh. "But what if you lose your knife? Or break it?"

"I find it hard to believe either might happen. My great-uncle made the *chhuri* well, and in the field, I wear it always."

"But you remember your bare-handed match against Gramps?"

"I could hardly forget it. 'Old and treacherous beats young and strong every time.' I learned."

"Absolutely. You take showers?"

He looked at her as if she had sprouted a second head.

Before he could speak, she said, "It was rhetorical. You carry your knife in there with you?"

He gave her a look. "No."

"So if you are attacked in a shower, what do you do? Wave your willie at them?"

"That would probably terrify them."

Gunny grinned. Give the kid credit, he kept trying.

"Or maybe they from Long Dong village, and they'd die laughin'."

She hefted the zap. This was a training weapon that looked like a regular knife, save that the dull, but electrified blade delivered a shock if it touched you. Gunny had once had a combat teacher who used live steel and had the cuts statbonded as you went along—she still hated the burned-pecan smell of that nasty spray glue, and it had been messy; but, sometimes a sharp enough edge? You got ratcheted up and didn't even feel it, you just looked down and noticed your blood welling. Not to mention when somebody got overenthusiastic and sliced a tendon or poked out an eye, and you had to spend some quality time in rehab.

In training, you wanted the student to know instantly he or she had been tagged, and the electric blade made the point, left no doubt. It called forth "Motherfucker!" in a hurry.

Gunny was more of a shooter than a cutter—Wink was their precision guy when it came to knife work—but her philosophy was simple: When the tool you had was a knife, then you'd cut or stick somebody enough so they'd bleed out, and the party would be over. Insert point or edge, repeat until hostility ceases, wipe off, go home.

If you were close, within six or seven meters, and if you started first, you could tag most humans with your blade before they could draw a sidearm to stop you. You needed to know that on both sides of the equation, and you needed to know how to use or defend against a knife.

She flipped the zap around so that the handle jutted from her hand toward Singh.

"Squeeze the handle three times, that lights it," she said. "Come at me."

"How should I attack? High, low, left, right?"

"Up to you. Since Ah won't know what is comin' in a real attack, knowin' what is comin' in advance isn't a fair test."

Not strictly true, she knew. He might not tell her what he had in mind, but his stance, the way he held himself and the weapon, his balance, all of those she could get if she were paying attention. She should know what he was going to do anyway.

Singh held the knife in a saber grip, point forward, edge down, in his right hand. He put his body behind the knife, right foot leading, and began to centimeter toward her.

He was going to fake high and stab low, she could tell. He was used to using a longer blade. She had his reach figured.

His nostrils dilated as he inhaled—

She jumped in, threw a hard left punch at his face, and when he instinctively raised the knife to block, continued the punch into a left parry and smashed him underhanded on the solar plexus with her right fist—

—Breath gone, stunned, Singh slashed at her highline as he fell back from the impact, and she turned her left arm so the back of it covered her. She felt the jolt from the electric charge across her forearm midway between the elbow and wrist. She pivoted left and swung her right hand across her face in a hammerblow that ended on Singh's wrist. The follow-through turned him to his left, and the impact knocked the knife loose from his grip. She slid her left foot behind him, caught his shoulders with both hands, and dropped into a squat. The move jerked him off-balance backward to land on his butt, then his back. She scooped up the fallen knife and laid the edge onto his throat—

"Ow, *fuck*—!"

Game over.

She stood, extended a hand to Singh, helped him to his feet.

He shook his head. "That won't work a second time," he said.

"Ah should hope not. But it doesn't have to; it only needs to work *once*. Real knife, Ah'd have a six-centimeter-long slice on my arm, no major bleeders, wiped clean and glued shut in a couple of minutes. You, on the other hand, would have a cut throat and would be pretty dead in another couple of minutes."

He nodded. "I'd like to learn that move."

"No, not really, you wouldn't. What you need to learn are

simple motions, general patterns that will happen automatically when you track what is incoming. A specific defense set up in advance almost never works. If you think, 'Well, Ah'll block this way, then counter like so,' you'll find yourself skewered more often than not. Bare-handed defense against a knife is a last-ditch and desperate action, Oh, shit! moves. Conscious thought is too slow. Good chance you'll get cut or stabbed as part of it, and if you know that going in and are willing to take it to win, you can win. If you fall apart at the sight of your own blood, you will lose and maybe die.

"What Ah'll show you are some patterns. Covers and responses. You drill them until they become part of you, and if you have them when the turd hits the turbine, maybe you'll use one that works."

"'Maybe'?"

Gunny nodded. "Yep. Old sayin' is 'You're not an ape, use a tool!' Your bare hands are for when your knife breaks; your knife is for when your pistol runs out of ammo; your pistol is for when your carbine is dead. Carbine is for when you can't be somewhere else.

"More tool than you need is better than less. Bare-handed stuff is a low-percentage game, for when you can't run and can't get a better weapon. But it only needs to work once to pay for itself. In our biz, sooner or later, you might find yourself up to your ass in enemies with nothing to wave at them but your own biological tools. We started into this back on Ananda, but it's a never-ending game. Better to know what you can do and do it than to roll over and die."

"Yes. I see."

"Good. Here, take the knife and try again . . ."

- - - - - -

It was late when Kay and Wink left the medical facility, headed for their quarters. Another long day without anything much useful to show for it.

It was only a couple klicks to the cube, and as long as

she didn't want to run, he didn't mind the walk. Loosen some of the tension he'd built up.

They weren't any closer to a solution. It was frustrating. You'd think with all that civilization had to offer in such situations, you could find answers.

It was a little warmer today, still not hot. Never really got tropical, Kay had told him, but it did get a lot colder. The season was summer; come winter, it would drop below freezing and stay there for weeks. Not surprising, given the double-coat thickness of Vastalimi fur—they did better in the cold than in the tropics.

As they crossed the road, the streetlights offered only a faint, yellowish gleam. They were dim because Vastalimi didn't need as much illumination as humans did. Made Wink realize that a nightsight aug might not be a bad idea though the chances of getting one here were way below slim. Vastalimi *really* didn't like such things. When Kay had found out that Formentara had sneaked a tracker into her, back on Ananda? She'd nearly blown an artery, according to what he'd heard. Vastalimi didn't do augs.

Well. He wouldn't be here that long. He could get used to it. Or carry a lamp. Not like he didn't already stand out everywhere he went . . .

The street wasn't crowded, only a few vehicles moving back and forth, and no other pedestrians near them . . .

Wait. On the other side, leaning against a building, there was one, a big male, and he was definitely focused on Kay.

Wink could almost taste blood in the wind. He slid his right hand back to his hip pocket and grabbed the butt of his pistol, eased it free, let it hang behind him. He edged his left hand around to the handle of his knife . . .

Kay noticed. "Don't do anything inciting," she said.

"You know this guy?"

"I do."

"He looks like trouble."

"He is. Let me handle it."

Wink nodded. "If you say so."

— — — — — —

Kay resisted the urge to extrude her claws as they walked across the road.

When they were ten meters away from him, *Vial*masc said, "Well, if it isn't the hairless *ruta* who ran. You won't escape me this time."

He spoke barely passable Basic, and she knew that was for Wink's benefit.

Kay smiled at him. "Is *that* the best you can do? One would think that a fighter who used to have skill could rise above such a pedestrian insult."

Vial shrugged. "It's not the talking, Kluth, it's the doing that matters. And you will find that my skill is unchanged from the time you observed it last."

"Good."

"Good?"

"One hates to kill a worthless opponent, there is no honor in that."

"After I finish you, I'm am going to shred your tame human."

"He is legally immune to Challenge."

"Challenge? Hardly worthy of that, is he? I'm going to exterminate him, as I would any other pest."

"You think?" Wink said.

Vial glanced up. Saw that Wink held his knife in his left hand.

The big Vastalimi whickered. "How amusing! What do you think you are going to do with that stubby toy, ape? Wave it and hope I die from fright?"

"No, actually, I planned to use it to cut your balls off and stuff them into your mouth after I shoot you with this." Wink held up his pistol in the other hand.

Vial looked at Kay. "You were speaking of honor? None among humans, is there?"

"As I recall, you said you were going to slay him as you would a pest, no Challenge involved. It thus would be your own arrogance that caused your death. Not that it will get that far."

He whickered again. "Really? I am larger, stronger, extremely more experienced, and far more adept. Do you really think you have any chance whatsoever?"

"Absolutely. Unlike you, my skills have improved since last we saw each other. I have spent some years on alien battlefields. They fight differently than we do. I know things you do not."

"Really? I doubt it."

"Offer *prigovor* and find out." She radiated confidence.

"I hear that your sister the Shadow watches over you."

"Not your concern. Challenge or don't, my sister won't trouble you as long as you do not cheat. Offer it."

He stood silently for a moment, considering.

She was not going to scare him off even if he believed her. He was a professional killer, an assassin, and he had certainly been hired to take her out; he couldn't walk away and expect anybody to employ him again. Plus, his own sense of honor could not allow it. But even a tiny crack in his confidence was to her advantage. A small doubt might make him pause when he should move or hurry a move he would better let ripen.

Sometimes, the smallest advantage could lead to victory. It was valid to take it if it was offered.

Kay was not at all sure she could beat him, but there was truth in her statement. He would hear it.

Vastalimi chased and caught their prey, usually attacking from the sides or from behind, now and then face on, by bounding and launching themselves with claws extended. That shaped how they moved, how they thought.

Most of their formal fighting techniques were based on the principle that one's deadliest opponent would be another

Vastalimi. And that was sound since no other intelligent species near their size could defeat them claw-to-claw. You trained for the opponent who could beat you, and that was another of your own kind.

Humans did much the same, but despite their inferior strength and speed and senses, if you balanced those, sometimes their close-combat systems would offer something a Vastalimi simply did not expect to see. If a fight went long, that likely wouldn't matter, but against an augmented human who quickly did something completely unexpected? The fight might not go long. A single mistake could be fatal.

Jo Captain could, in mock fights sans claws, defeat Kay four times of ten. That was fairly amazing—few Vastalimi would believe her if she told them that. *A human? Even an augmented one? You pull our fur!*

But it was possible, because a million years of evolution was hard to put aside. Jo had learned this and devised ways to counter ingrained Vastalimi techniques. And Kay had then learned ways to recounter Jo, so she did have skills few other Vastalimi would have had a chance to develop. It might not be enough; still, it was what she had.

Finally, he spoke: *"Career nama borba do pojedinac inače oba nad nama umreti."*

Let us fight until one or both of us die.

"Neka bude tako," she said, giving the ritual response.

Let it be so.

"I don't suppose you want to tell me who hired you?" she said.

"Hired me? You don't believe I offer this on my own?"

She didn't smile: "I don't think you would put incense on your sire's funeral altar unless somebody paid you to do so."

"Who cares what a dead fem thinks?"

Kay didn't take her gaze from Vial as she said, "Wink, if I lose, and Vial leaves without offering you any threat, you must allow him to live."

"Fuck I will. You die, I'm going to shoot him and desecrate his corpse. In fact, I think I'll do that right now to avoid the wait."

"No. It's not our way. If he attacks you, you may defend yourself. But even Vial is not so stupid, as long as you have a gun trained on him."

Vial faked a yawn, showing his fangs. "The human does not really matter," he said. "He lives, he dies, nobody cares enough to pay for it. I can forgo the small pleasure."

"Wink, if you kill him, it will bring dishonor to my memory and to my family. You must not do so without direct provocation."

"He kills my friend? That's provocation enough."

"No. Please."

"You beg a *jebangje* human?"

"I ask a favor of an honored comrade. Wink?"

"All right. If he twitches in my direction, he dies. If he walks away, he lives."

"Thank you."

Kay untabbed her belt and let it fall.

Vial's claws snapped out with a loud *snick!* "As I stand!"

"And as *I* stand—"

He charged—

He was bigger and stronger, but not faster, and his attack was direct, intended to take advantage of his superior reach and power. His claws would reach her before hers could reach him, they both knew that.

Three meters out, he leaped, an angled dive, upper body leading, his arms extended fully, fingers outstretched. If she offered a block, he would shred that arm and strike with his other hand, cutting the line of her second block if she tried it, and bowling her over with his weight—

Kay waited until he was in the air. Then she fell onto her back, a move no Vastalimi would ever do in a death match, offering a vulnerable throat and belly to an enemy. As he flew over her, she thrust her foot up, claws extended, and caught him just above the groin. Instead of ripping, she shoved upward, turning his flat dive into a flip—

It was a move she had learned from Jo and one she had used on the augmented human who had attacked her and Formentara on Ananda. She knew it would work on a human, and a Vastalimi would have no reason to expect it at all.

It took Vial by complete surprise.

He snarled as he rotated—

She continued the motion, came up in a backward roll, did a half twist, and was already moving before he landed on his back, hard—

He hit, and scrabbled to come up but it was too late—she dropped to her knees and stabbed downward with both hands, burying her right claw in his throat and her left in his face and eyes—

He screamed, a primal, wordless roar, and swiped at her, scoring her chest and slicing the muscle under her left arm, but she was already moving, diving away, and rolling—

Vial came up, blood pouring from his throat, his eyes gone, screaming—

"Ja volja ubiti te!"

"No, you won't," she said. "You aren't going to kill me or anybody else, *paid* assassin. You are done."

He tried to circle for another attack, tracking her by scent, but she matched his steps, staying outside his range.

He lunged—

She moved out of the way.

It didn't take long for the shock and blood loss to drop him to his knees. And when he fell face forward, she knew he would not be getting up again.

– – – – – –

Wink sprayed the skinstat from his aid kit on the last claw cut. The liquid quickly hardened to a flexible film, sealing the injury shut. "I think that does it," he said. "You'll have scars if you don't get them resected. That pec is going to be sore for a few days, too."

"Thank you. The fur will hide the scars. The muscle will heal."

"That was amazing. So . . . quick."

"He was very good, a first-rate duelist if not a true master. I didn't expect to win, much less as undamaged as I am. He made a mistake. I gave him warning."

"Yeah, I noticed." Wink chuckled.

"Some funny thing I missed?"

"Not really. Just that if he had won? I lied. I was gonna say *Ace ja stajanje!* and shoot his furry ass dead anyway. He wasn't going to gloat for long."

She whickered. "I expected that you might. I confess that the thought gave me some comfort."

"Now what?"

"We call the Shadows, report the incident, and with luck, will be at our quarters in another half hour and able to get some rest."

"That's all?"

"It was a formal Challenge; he is dead, and I am not. That's how it goes."

"Yeah, and I'm a witness."

"Not necessary for you to speak to it," she said. "The *Sena* who comes will accept my statement."

"Really?"

"Why would they not? And it will probably make subsequent challenges less frequent."

"Why?"

"Vial was one of the best-paid duelists among us. Hundreds of kills. In the light of his death, those who knew his skills? Likely they will think carefully before offering *prigovor.*"

"You said you thought somebody hired him."

"Somebody certainly did. Vial didn't kill people for free."

"Why?"

She shrugged. "An old matter, from before. He missed his chance when I left Vast. Back then, I would have died. My experiences offworld gave me an edge. I—" She stopped, hearing the faint sound of footsteps. She recognized the tread.

"What?"

Kay looked down the street, saw the approaching figure.

Wink caught her look and turned. His hand drifted toward his weapon. The light was too dim for him to recognize the approaching fem for what she was. "No need for that," she said. "The *Sena* have arrived."

"Did we call them, and I missed it?"

"No."

When she drew near enough, Kay nodded at her. "Wink Doctor, this is Leeth. My sister."

"Doctor," Leeth said. "My sibling thinks most highly of you."

"She does?"

"Else you would not be on Vast." She looked at the corpse on the sidepath. "I see that Vial finally found you." She looked at the bonded cuts on Kay's chest. "And that is all he managed to do?"

"He was not as good as he thought," Kay said.

"I have seen him fight, and he *was* that good. It would appear that you were better than he thought."

Kay shrugged.

"I am required to ask: Was this a valid *prigovor*?"

"Yes."

"His or your Challenge?"

"His."

She nodded. "So noted." She looked at Wink. "My joy to make your acquaintance, Wink Doctor."

"Sister."

"Sister."

Leeth turned and walked away.

"That's it?"

"That's it," Kay said. "Are you hungry? I could eat."

EIGHT

"They got cute on us," Gramps said.

Jo looked at the projection over her desktop. "They got smart on us."

The image floating in the warm air—the cooler was on the fritz—was of one of the giant-wheeled transports the growers used.

What was left of it. Still had wisps of smoke rising from the shattered vehicle, which looked as if somebody had fired a high-velocity bullet into a pressurized plastic container and it had peeled apart in the ensuing explosion.

"Casualties?"

"Six killed outright, another dozen or so seriously wounded, a few more with minor injuries. All civilians. The carrier was full, so the cargo was a total loss."

Jo nodded. The laws regarding civilian deaths in corporate conflicts were tricky, varied from world to world, but interstellar corporate policies had evolved over decades to cover such things. Local authorities might not like it, but they had to live with it. Sometimes.

He continued: "Looks like they got attractant nanos into the reactant for the fuel cells. These big suckers burn that up pretty good. Somebody topped off the tank, the catalyst was small enough to squeeze through the filters, *kaboom*."

Jo nodded. Attractant nanos were great for sabotage. There were usually two or three varieties, none of which would do anything alone but which would seek each other once introduced into a fluid medium. When they combined, they made something else altogether, and the timing of that combination could be calculated in advance. "The growers assured us they had enough security on the fuel depots."

He gave her a tiny shrug. "They were mistaken."

Jo sighed. "Get our engineers out there and show them the error of their ways. And backwalk the employees on-site and in the fuel chain. I'd bet on social engineering over secret ops skulking through the yards unless they were really good."

"Yep. I'm on it."

Rags came out of his office, shaking his head.

"Can't win 'em all," Jo said.

"Maybe not, but they don't pay us to lose them."

"We have ears out. We should get some intel we can follow up on pretty quick."

"Before they blow up any more of our client's trucks, I hope."

— — — — — —

Gunny had spent too much of her life in pubs and bars around the galaxy, but at least these days she got paid to go. There was a shitload of information to be had when people gathered together and got drunk or stoned; asking the right one the right question could be of great value.

To be honest, it could also be dried-up rat shit, but you never knew until you got there which it would be. If you were part of any military group, good intel was worth its weight in platinum, and if you were in a unit as small as the Cutters,

everybody was liable to be pressed into duties other than
pointing and shooting. Kay usually got to hunt down and
find out things from aliens; Formentara did tech; Gramps
followed the money; Wink was the medical guy; and Gunny
wound up in the local watering holes trolling for street scat.
Each according to his or her ability, and what did that say
about her?

Knowing who your enemy was, where they were staying,
how adept and how many of them there were? That could
be the difference between kicking ass or getting yours
kicked. Knowledge was truly power in any kind of war, from
a planetwide shoot-out to a local set-to.

There were some perks to the bar scene. On Ananda,
there had been this handsome young bouncer who had filled
her ear—and other things, too—and that was a win-win
encounter. Good intel, good times, a nice memory to have
in the vault.

This pub? It didn't look so promising. The place was
called The Mole Hole, in the mining city of Adit, and it
was fairly full of hard-ass miners, off shift and looking to
get plastered, laid, and in a fight, not necessarily in that order.

It was a ramshackle, rough place, heavy plastic walls
overlaid with spongy soundproofing, a tile floor with a drain
in the center, furniture bolted down and built to withstand
a hundred-kilo miner being slammed into it. Stools, tables,
that was it.

There was a small stage at one end, but no band in atten-
dance. The music was recorded, Rototope Retro, which she
could take or leave, not so loud you couldn't hear yourself
think or talk but not much quieter than that.

The pubtenders—there were three of them—looked like
weight lifters, heads shaved, wearing sleeveless tunics. Their
skin showed lots of pulse-ink tattoos, more than a few unre-
vised scars on them, heads, faces, shoulders, arms, and some
of them obviously knife wounds or zap burns. Hard men,
willing to mix it up, and obvious they had done so.

They were drawing a lot of beer from taps and shoving foamy steins at waiters and waitresses.

The mirror behind the bar was scratched and stained and had a bullet hole spidering one end; unbreakable, but never meant to be pretty and only going to get uglier with age.

The bottles and combustibles were behind sliding, heavy, kleerplast panels under the mirror. Closed, you could throw rocks at 'em and not do any damage to the hootch or toke supply.

Exhaust fans on the ceiling sucked the thick smoke up and out, but they were working hard to keep ahead of the fragrant cloud that hung a meter or so over the tabletops.

Gunny figured they came in with a hose after everybody left and blasted the whole place, letting the water drain into the big grate in the center of the slightly depressed floor. Utilitarian. A place to get stupid, pass out, thrown out, and no frills.

She'd been in worse, though not lately.

Apparently, the miners didn't mind the decor or lack of it.

She was glad she had dressed down from her previous trip for pub work: She wore a loose tunic that fell halfway down her butt, baggy pants, both of standard gray-on-black synthetics, definitely not cut to show off her figure. Her precharged air pistol was SOB-carry, 4mm shocktox darts. She wore dotic boots to midcalf, but the plain pair, not her good faux ostrich leathers. She had a short dagger in the right boot and a swand in the left. The four-finger ring of fake emeralds on her right hand was actually a pretty good knuckle-duster. Sometimes there wasn't time to reach for a weapon, and a hundred grams of hard stone and metal thumping into somebody's temple could do wonders as an attitude adjuster.

There was a bouncer on the door big enough to make the three tugs behind the bar look small, but he didn't do a weapons check when she arrived, just took five New Dollars and waved her in. No e-tags spray or ink stamps for her hand. Either the bouncer would remember you if you went out, or you had to pay again.

She worked her way to the crowded bar, found an empty spot, and nodded at the tender. "Beer, whatever dark is on tap."

He nodded, sloshed a chocolate-colored ale into a big stein, and set it in front of her.

"Two noodle."

She put a five coin on the counter. "Keep it," she said.

That got her a lopsided grin. "Thankee, fem. Enjoy the brew, enjoy the view."

He moved off to serve another customer.

Gunny felt the man to her left start to move as she sipped the ale. Pretty good, the beer, but she put it down quickly because she could tell by his shoulder motion what he was going to do. She bent slightly, caught the handle of the dagger, and pulled it from its sheath in her boot just as he put his hand on her left ass cheek.

"Nice 'n' tight—urk!"

The point of the dagger under his chin drew a spot of blood as he tried to pull back.

"Don't even twitch. Yes, it is nice and tight and it is *mine*. You touch it again, and Ah will open you up from ear to ear just to watch you bleed out."

He was about her height, maybe half again as wide, and built like a brick. Not bad-looking, actually, and he smiled. "Got to like a fem with a knife that fast," he said. "*Mea culpa*, sorry." He held his hands wide.

She gave him credit for the smile, given the knife digging into his throat. She pulled the blade back.

"I'm Stuude," he said. "First-Shift Drill Pusher, Adit-One."

Like they were being formally introduced. She had to smile at that.

"You can call me Gunny," she said. She lifted her right foot and resheathed the dagger without looking.

The tender who'd served her nodded. "Nice," he said, appreciating the knife work.

"You aren't from around here, are you?" Stuude said.

"Nope."

"Didn't expect so. Fems come in here, a hand on the ass doesn't usually merit even a fuck-off look. Mostly they know that, or they'd go somewhere else. But you aren't your run-of-the-shift barflit, are you? Military, right?"

"Yep."

"Let me buy you another of whatever you are drinking, apologize for my presumptuousness."

"You talk more like a professor than a tool pusher."

He regarded her for a moment. "That's pretty good, Gunny."

She waited.

"As it happens, I used to *be* a professor. Comparative Alien Literature, University of San Basho."

"Long way from there to here. How did you wind up working the mines?"

"Well, the classic answer is, 'Just lucky, I guess.'"

"What's the real answer?"

"Truth is, I was *un*lucky. I had a gambling addiction, it blew through me like a force-six hurricane, took everything wasn't nailed down. I woke up one day in debt to my hairline, spouse gone, job down the toilet despite my tenure. I looked around; working here was the most money I could make honestly. Another year, debts are paid, I can maybe find another teaching position.

"Assuming, of course, a touchy fem doesn't skewer me for playing grab-ass."

She laughed. Men. Never knew what you'd run into.

"And what, might I ask, brings you to this armpit of a pub in the bad section of a town that has no particularly good sections?"

Sometimes, you played your cards close, didn't tell anybody anything. Sometimes, depending on the feel of a situation, you could be a little more forthright. If Stuude here was a tool pusher who could fake being a college professor, he was smart enough to have been one anyway. She said, "Ah'm working for a private military unit. We were sent here to protect some local farmers from hijackers."

He smiled. "Reminds me of an old joke: 'My father drives a freight roller without any wheels.'

"And you say, 'Really? What holds it up?'

"And I say, 'Bandits . . .'"

She smiled. "You take off points on your students' grades if they didn't laugh at your jokes?"

"Only a few. So you are protecting the farmers. How does that get you into the Mole Hole? You think the bandits hang out here?"

"Maybe. There is a lot of information flow goes along with the drinks or smoke. Sometimes somebody knows somebody who knows somebody if you get my drift."

He nodded. Sipped at his beer. "Intel run."

"Yep."

"And right now, you are trying to decide if I'm worth your time?"

"Got to love a professor-turned-drill-pusher that quick."

"I haven't heard about this, but I know a lot of people who know a lot of people. I can maybe find out. Tell you what, meet me here tomorrow off shift, same time, you can buy the beer, and we can talk."

"Why would you bother?"

He smiled. "Not every day I meet a woman like you. Lot more fun than powdering rock all day. Although probably more dangerous."

"Done," she said. "Ah'll see you tomorrow, Professor."

"You can stay long enough to finish your beer, right?"

Behind them, somebody cursed in Basic, and there came the sound of impacts, fists on flesh. A few people at the bar glanced that way, then back at their drinks or smoke.

"Stop," came a deep voice.

She turned in time to see the giant bouncer plowing through patrons like an icebreaker through a couple centimeters of surface slush. Didn't even slow him down.

The two men fighting didn't notice him until he arrived and grabbed each one of them by the neck and peeled them apart.

"What part of 'Stop' didn't you understand?"

He slammed the two men into each other; their heads colliding made enough noise to be heard over the background walla of the patrons.

He let go of the two stunned fighters. "Leave. Two days before I see you here again."

He turned and walked away.

"Maybe you know another pub a little less rowdy?" Gunny said.

"As it happens, I do. Follow me and I'll show you; we can meet there instead of here."

"Good deal."

Follow the money.

It was amazing how often those three words would show you what you needed to know. Of course, it wasn't always easy, but there were ways to get there, and early on, Gramps had shown a talent for things related to money. This was why he handled it for CFI, and having the ability to wave some of it around did wonders to loosen tongues—if he waved it at the right time and person.

In the branch office of the Bank del Galaxico, the somewhat unctuous manager seated across from him seemed to be exactly the fellow for whom he was looking. The man's name was Wentferth, and his hair was a fine, pale brown cloud, electrostatically held in place.

Gramps immediately thought of him as "Fluffy."

"So, how may we assist you, M. Demonde?"

There were only a few humans in the place, most of it

being given over to din-stations, and it had a cold feel to it. Not much cash in the building, Gramps would guess, just another electronic transfer point. Long way since people traded grain for eggs . . .

"Well, I represent Cutter Force Initiative, an A-Class Small Military Corporation. We have an engagement here on Far Bundaloh, and we would like a bank for our operation. Salaries, procurement, the usual."

"Yes, of course."

"We could simply use our main bank, GFY, but we have found that it is better to have a local contact who can provide services the bigger banks sometimes can't be bothered to deal with."

"We at the FB branch consider service one of the bulwarks of our business."

Bulwark? Who used words like that? He said, "Good to hear. We aren't talking about major money, only a few million."

Fluffy almost drooled at that. *Only* a few million?

"Let me call up a deposit contract—"

"Well, here's the thing. I must confess I have spoken to representatives of the Bundaloh Miners Association, and they have offered a generous interest rate if we use their credit union."

"BMA is a fine organization, to be sure, but they don't have our resources, M. Demonde. You would be better served by BG across the board."

Gramps allowed himself to look indecisive. "BMA is smaller, but they are eager for our business. They've offered some sweeteners."

"Which BG will match and exceed. They can't beat our interest rate on short-term-yield CoDs."

"There is one thing they seemed somewhat reluctant to do."

"Name it."

"There is another SMC operating on-planet. As it

happens, they are the opposition to CFI on our current assignment. I would very much like all available information on them. Nothing illegal, of course, no confidences broken, nothing untoward. A man in your position would surely have access to such information."

"I confess I have not heard about this competing military corporation," Fluffy said. "Certainly, they are not depositors here."

"But you could find out where they are keeping their money? And perhaps some, ah . . . background information?"

"For a client who is willing to put a few million New Dollars into my bank? I am certain I can."

"I was hoping that you would say that. Why don't we transfer, say, a million or so into a new account to get things rolling, and the rest when you have something for me?"

"I'll punch up the deposit agreement, M. Demonde."

"Call me 'Gramps.'"

Fluffy smiled.

Gramps returned the smile. "Always a pleasure to do business with a man of the galaxy," he said. He almost added "Fluffy," but fortunately managed to hold off on that.

NINE

Wink sat at in a chair outside Droc's office, waiting for Kay and Droc, playing with his knife. He spun and twirled the stubby-bladed weapon this way and that, rolling it from hand to hand.

The knife was a spearpoint design, dropped just a hair, with a short, thick blade. It was single-edged, Damascus, four kinds of tool steel blended and hammered until there were 416 layers. The metal had been acid-etched to show-case the folded pattern; the steel was darkened to shades of gray and black and thus would not reflect light to draw attention in the night.

That helped it function, and it also made it pretty.

Hammer-forging made for a strong, pliable steel, and the temper gave it a hardness that held a razored edge. The handle was also fat, a cylinder longer than the blade, stabilized maple burl, pressure-stained a deep red. The guard was a sculpted oval, the same steel as the blade. It was a functional, useful knife, and Wink was most comfortable using it. He was, after all, a surgeon, at ease with sharps, be they steel, vibratos, or obsidian. When your main tool is a knife, best you learn how to use it well.

This was something he tended to do when there wasn't anything else to occupy him, and he'd had this particular knife long enough so that it had become a well-practiced and smooth activity.

In a fight where he had to use it, he'd never risk dropping the weapon by dicking around with such moves. Wink knew guys like that. Somebody threatened them, a knife would appear magically, they'd give it a few showy spins to let whoever it was see they were good, and not to be fucked with, and apparently such would draw the "Oh, shit!" reaction often enough to short-circuit trouble.

There was something to be said for this. A big cat flashing its teeth might scare off lesser predators.

For his money, if he had to pull a knife, it was going to be because he had to use it pretty soon, and that meant whoever was in his face or coming up on his back was probably already past the point of being shooed off. When the adrenaline flowed, those small movements you could do in your sleep almost reflexively tended to go away—it was the nature of the system. Big muscles, the ones that worked for running and jumping and getting the fuck away from a predator, those took over, and fine motor control went into the toilet. Wink had seen guys who could plug the bull's-eye on a target all day long at fifty meters miss an incoming trooper at spitting distance with an entire magazine's worth of ammo.

Primal fear could be a killer.

Shoving a knife was a big motion, not like squeezing a trigger.

Twirling it was not a big motion. And if your weapon was a knife, you most certainly didn't want to *drop* it when you needed it most.

As an adrenaline junkie, Wink tended to slide past that—he lived for the rush and had learned how to function when it took him for the ride. Chances were, he was going to hit his target, or stick it, just fine.

Of course, handling the knife like this made it into an extension of his hand. He did that with his handguns, too. If you were completely familiar with a weapon's balance, the heft, the way it would move if you did this instead of that? That was a plus, come the real need . . .

The door slid open, and Kay came in, followed closely by Droc.

Wink slipped the knife back into the sheath behind his right hip. It was old-style, cloned-leather rather than pressure-formed plastic. A bit bulkier, but more organic. Plus, he liked the feel and the smell of leather.

"Anything?"

Kay shook her head. "Completely nonreactive for zoodozoa."

"Damn."

It had seemed like a promising lead. Zoodozoa were a pseudolife-form discovered eighty years ago in a methane sea on some godforsaken moon somewhere. Not exactly flora or fauna, they had viral-like qualities, were as small as medium-sized varieties of viruses, and they had been implicated in some esoteric illnesses among humans. The zoodozoa tended to hide inside cell nuclei, where they were hard to spot even if you knew to look for them, and while they caused problems, they didn't replicate with any kind of predictable regularity, nor in numbers enough to jump out at somebody trying to find anomalies. Sneaky little bastards.

"Some of my colleagues are beginning to invoke notions of religion or magic," Droc said. "We are cursed by the gods for our hubris and the like."

"Yeah, well, if that's the case, we are shit-out-of-luck," Wink said. "But excuse me if I don't buy that one."

"Not religious?"

"Actually, I don't have a problem with the idea of

something beyond the physical. Lot of strange stuff out there in the galaxy. But I don't believe in a deity who manifests as a giant white-haired old man in the sky setting up roadblocks, hurling lightning bolts, or striking us down with assorted plagues. That seems awful petty for any kind of being capable of building or destroying universes with the wave of its appendage. Why bother?"

"Who can know the mind of a god?" Droc said. "And it would be a white-furred old Vastalimi and not a human around here. Our deities are territorial."

Wink looked at him. Funny guy, Kay's brother.

"However, I agree with your assessment of God," Droc continued. "I see Him as a twirler. He sets the galaxies in spin, then moves off to other serious business. Whether He or She will be on the Other Side when our spirits arrive there, if indeed they do? Who can say? I also doubt that an omnipotent being needs to poke a finger into the doings of Vastalimi or humans or any other species on an individual level."

"On the other hand," Kay said, "if that were the case, we could importune God to lift this particular affliction and perhaps Zhe would see fit to do so, if we asked properly."

"You believe that?"

Kay smiled. "Not for a human second."

"Which leaves us where we were before."

"Well, it eliminates another possible cause," Droc said.

There was a pause. Then: "Epidemiological inquiries have come up empty, other than the illness has occurred in families or in close associates. I am positing some kind of intentional introduction of an unnatural causative agent by unknown parties," Kay said.

"Based on?"

"Based on the theory that somebody wanted to kill Vastalimi deliberately using a method that wouldn't likely be traced back to them. Either a particular target, without regard to sequelae regarding others; or with mass murder in mind, for whatever reasons."

Wink nodded. That made as much sense as a natural, completely undetectable disease, more so, actually. More diabolical creations had come from labs proportionately than from nature. Why somebody would go to this much effort, were that the case, might be beyond easy measure, but that it was possible? People had been coming up with ways to kill each other since people became such, and they had gotten better and better at it . . .

"We have studied the patients with this affliction from various standpoints," Kay said. "Primarily medical, then geographical, genetically, environmentally, looking for links that would isolate a natural cause. If the illness is artificial, then we won't find those particular links. So we need to examine other factors, based on that notion."

Wink nodded. "What might they have in common regarding their sociology rather than biology. Who are their friends and enemies? Who might they have pissed off?"

"Exactly," Kay said. "If there is something that links them together worth murdering them for, and we can find it, we can backtrack that and figure out who is responsible."

"It is a thin theory," Droc said.

"If you have a thicker one, Brother, I'm ready to hear it."

Droc shook his head. "A small chance is better than none."

Wink said, "So, how do we start?"

"The Shadows can parse much of it. They have the ability—if it can be found, they can find it—if they have sufficient reason to look. They might need more than a theory, though my sister will at least listen. We can continue our own investigation. We know the names of those afflicted, and in which order they became such. The dead will have family, friends, coworkers, and they are potential sources of information.

"If we ask the right person the right question, it might open a door."

"Works for me," Wink said. "Let's go places and talk to people."

— — — — —

Gunny was dozing off in her chair when Cutter said, "Okay, what do we have?"

They were in the conference room, the walls still smelling faintly of ferrofoam-setting solution, a not-particularly-pleasant chemical stink.

Gramps said, "I have the bank they use, and where they buy their local supplies, courtesy of our new banker, Fluffy."

The others looked at him. "A nickname, based on his hairstyle. I didn't get a location. Probably they have a bivouac somewhere away from their main camp, too, but we can poke into the deliveries."

Cutter nodded. "Formentara?"

"Like so many of the stone-age planets you drag us to, this one is lacking much in the way of technology." Zhe kept hir face deadpan. "They do have augmentation parlors here—mostly muscle and endurance augs for the miners, a few that offer more than basics. I was able to determine that there have been a few soldiers newly arrived, in for tune-ups, and a backwalk of their payments for such services link to the corporate account Gramps found."

"Which is a shell," Gramps added. "'John S. Mosby & Associates.'" He smiled.

Cutter grinned, too.

"What's funny?" Jo asked.

"Our competition has a sense of history," Cutter said. "John Mosby was the leader of a military unit on prespace-flight Earth during a large and nasty early-industrial regional war. Led a group of rangers, guerrilla forces, hit-and-run against much larger armies. Quite successful, albeit they were on the losing side.

"Mosby was, I believe, a colonel by the end. He was known as the Gray Ghost, based on uniform color and his ability to vanish when pursued. You should brush up on your history, Jo."

"Friend of yours?" Gunny said, smiling at Gramps.

"Johnny? Sure, knew him well. One of J. E. B. Stuart's boys. Great soldier. Became a diplomat after the war. He was a lawyer, but I never held that against him. I thought you were from that region—why don't you know this?"

Gunny shook her head. Point to Gramps, for the research.

"Gunny?" Cutter said.

"Scuttlebutt from the pubs, but my source seems fairly reliable. Seems there's a group of 'religious tourists' who have rented a parcel of land a couple hundred klicks southeast of Adit. Some kind of retreat, so the story goes. They've built a camp and seem to be importing a lot of supplies in heavy-duty vans and hoppers. Maybe they are erecting big idols or something."

Cutter said, "So that gives us something to look into, doesn't it? Can we get a spysat overfly?"

"Not unless we launch it ourselves," Jo said. "The locals are touchy about such things. Might could hack into one long enough to get a view, but if they are running camo, we won't see anything."

"Do we have a bird in stock?"

"Not as such. I could buy us one."

Cutter shook his head. "Seems like a lot of expense, given as how we have all you highly trained and well-paid soldiers who can figure out cheaper ways to put eyes on the site."

"Might could sneak a couple of firefly drones over, drop a few birdshit cams in," Jo allowed. "Though if they are any good, they'll find and disable those pretty quick. Even the on-demand-only transmitters would trigger halfway-decent scanners, and they'd zap the cams."

"Which would tell us something, wouldn't it?"

"Yeah, either they are undercover mercs or really paranoid religious nuts. Unfortunately, it would tell them something, too.

"Too bad Kay isn't here. She could sneak in and out, nobody the wiser."

"Well, I leave it to you, Jo. It's why you get paid the big money."

"Thanks. I've been meaning to talk to you about a raise."

"Next assignment."

"That's what you always say, Rags."

"And don't you want a consistent commander? Besides, what would you do with more money? I have to force you to take leave now as it is. You probably have more noodle in the bank than the rest of us put together."

"No," Gramps said, "that would be Formentara. Zhe's richer than some planets. And zhe doesn't spend it, either. I had that much, I'd retire."

Jo shook her head at Cutter. "Amazing how good you are at changing the subject."

"Mark of a good commander. You gonna stand around all day or get us some useful intel?"

TEN

Jak was no less truculent than he had been before, but he tried to keep it hidden better. Perhaps because Wink was with Kay this time, and Jak did not want to reveal anything that might put him at any kind of disadvantage in front of a human. Given that she already knew what a *kurac*-head he was, he wouldn't put much effort into trying to sway her.

He couldn't help himself, though. When he saw Wink next to Kay, he said, "So this is your tame human I've heard about." He spoke in *NorVaz* instead of Basic.

Jak didn't know that Wink Doctor had an unseen translator feeding his earbud, and the sound was low enough so that Jak couldn't hear it.

Before she could speak, Wink said in Basic, "Yes, that would be me. I have heard much about you, too." He smiled, not showing his teeth. "All manner of things."

It was a good insult. Veiled, not enough to trigger a Challenge for slander between two Vastalimi, and Wink would be immune to such in this case anyway. Nicely played.

Still running on surprise, Jak said, "You understand me?"

"Oh, I understand you perfectly well."

That shut him up.

Kay said, "I have more questions about your uncle."

"Ask them, then." He had to clench his jaw shut to keep from saying something else that would make him look bad.

Kay already knew the answers to the questions she meant to ask. Jak's responses were less important than his knowing she had a purpose in asking and what that purpose was. She was on the hunt, she had quarry, she was seeking a trail, she wanted Jak to know what it was and, generally, where she was heading.

They went through her list, Jak growing more impatient and wary with each question, and finally they were done. They left.

On the walk back, Wink Doctor said, "Okay, what was that all about? You already knew all that stuff, didn't you?"

"Yes."

"You think Jak is involved? Trying to rattle him?"

"No reason to think he is directly involved. But Jak is weak. He will speak of this to somebody, and word will get around that we suspect the illness was a deliberate attack upon The People."

"Ah."

"If we are wrong, it won't matter. But if we are right, it might provoke someone into *doing* something. People suddenly made nervous by the notion that we are looking for them. Skittish prey will make mistakes."

"Won't it also make you a target?"

"A risk I am willing to take."

"Hmm. I had a thought: Could Vial have been a part of this?"

She considered it. "Possible. Although we had history that he might have thought necessary to play out. I suspect he was contracted to challenge me before I left Vast and never got the chance to act on it. But maybe somebody took out a new contract."

"Somebody worried about you could hire somebody else."

"Yes. And there are those swaggerers who would dismiss Vial's abilities as inferior to their own willing to try. However, they will now know that their actions will fall under careful scrutiny."

"And this means what?"

"It is technically illegal to Challenge for hire, though the crime is hard to prove, and thus the law seldom enforced; however, with the Shadows paying close attention, potential challengers will thus have to step with care, and anybody who would hire them would know there would be a chance they could be found. They might not wish to risk such."

"That's something, at least."

"I would rather they try, and give me a direction in which to go. Meanwhile, I am going to talk to my sister. I should be back soon. I'll meet you back at the hospital."

– – – – –

They were in Leeth's office, a spartan cubicle mostly devoid of decoration. There was a window, screened and open to the outside, so the air wasn't so stale.

There was a computer terminal on a desk, two chairs, and a row of silvery medallions, a dozen or so, mounted on small, stripewood plaques on a shelf. Awards for winning various competitions: shooting; martial arts; *Za*, the Vastalimi version of three-dimensional chess.

Only Firsts were on display.

"Don't keep the second- and third-place medals?"

"What joy in showcasing a loss?" There was a pause, and she shook her head. "I am unconvinced."

"You can't see the possibility?" Kay asked.

"Of course I can see that it is *possible*. But I find the idea hard to believe."

"That somebody would do it? Or that they could?"

"Both."

"Yet the problem persists. The top Healers on Vast have been unable to find a cause, using the best available equipment and tests."

"Which does not mean your theory has any more weight. One does not automatically follow the other."

"No. Save that we have eliminated all kinds of possibilities, to the point where we have no idea how to find a solution. We must look at other things. To ignore this might be a critical error."

Leeth was obviously skeptical.

"I have a feeling," Kay said. "Not as strong as some of the times when I have *known*, but there is something there."

Leeth looked at her. She knew of Kay's ability in unsubstantiated diagnoses. She raised an eye ridge. "Really?"

"Yes." Kay wasn't above using that to add impetus to her request. "Consider the gravity of the situation. So far, the deaths have been relatively few, but without a cause, there can be no treatment, so any new cases that arise will continue to have a one hundred percent mortality rate. If the rate of infection increases, it could become pandemic, epidemic, and the death rate catastrophic."

"Or it might disappear as quickly as it appeared."

"True. But that's a completely passive approach, and we are not prey to sit frozen and waiting for the end. If it does not stop, or if it increases, what then? What is the cost then?"

"High," Leeth allowed.

"*Sena* investigate. So let them investigate this."

"Easy to say. We are stretched thin, you know that. The pool of qualified applicants has never been deep, and those who will make it through the training? Not many. We are always working simply to replace those who die or retire; we never seem to gain. Fewer of our young ones now elect to travel the Path. When I began, two or three thousand hopefuls would apply each year. Now? We are lucky to get a third as many.

"Each of the *Sena* has much more territory to cover than we did, even five years ago. There has been talk of . . . relaxing standards."

It was Kay's turn to raise an eye ridge. Relaxing standards? Oh, Leeth could not abide such a foolish concept. Her loyalty was to the Shadows, first, last, and always. To put somebody *unqualified* by her measure onto the streets? An abomination.

"It is true. The People as a whole simply do not realize how critical the *Sena* are. Something must be done. But in the meanwhile, to spend effort on this will take resources from our other areas we can ill afford."

"Surely crime is not so rampant that such a potentially disastrous situation should be ignored? How many murders have there been, compared to those who have died from this mystery plague in the last few months? It's a matter of priority, and *Sena* make such choices every day.

"Besides, Droc has been given a clear and wide path to pursue this. If you need resources, he can make certain that you get them. I see no reason why the Hierarchy wouldn't allow such an investigation under your leadership."

"Under *my* leadership? You play to my ambition?"

"Well. *Some*body has to be in charge—and who is better qualified? Aside from which, given your relations with the lead medical investigators? Would not that be a selling point?"

Leeth nodded, if grudgingly so. "You make a valid argument. I will approach my superiors regarding the matter. We will see what can be done."

"I appreciate it."

Leeth grinned. "You could always talk the shrells right out of their burrows, Sister."

"If my theory is right, we are dealing with much worse than a pod of vermin chewing on maize stalks. If they exist, perhaps you can find them."

"Yes," Leeth said. "Perhaps I can."

— — — — — —

"How'd it go?" Wink asked.

They were on their way to the garage to collect a vehicle. The Vastalimi to whom Kay wanted to speak personally was more than two hours away on foot, and she would forgo the pleasure of a nice run in the interests of time. A ten-minute ride in a hot and smelly cart was better than spending four hours for what might turn out to be a wasted trip anyway.

"As I expected. My sister is too good a Shadow not to consider that a crime might have been committed, and mass murder is high up the list of things to be looking into. I allowed as how the Hierarchy would certainly allow her to run such an investigation, and that Droc could channel enough money their way to make sure she got the resources she would need.

"She is unrivaled among the *Sena* in her dedication, to the public good and to the Shadows themselves; however, she is also ambitious. Heading such an investigation and solving the crime, if one is found, would add greatly to her prestige. She is fated to become a high-ranking officer. A successful mission here would make that happen sooner rather than later."

Wink grinned and shook his head.

"Something funny?"

"No, just interesting how much humans and Vastalimi are alike in some ways. Organizations seem to run for reasons that don't always seem apparent."

"Here, family is important," she said. "What reflects well or badly on one can reflect the same way on one's parents, siblings, offspring, or even more distant kin. The primary goal here is to find a cause for the illness and stop it. If that means Droc and Leeth will wind up elevated in status or popular esteem? I see no harm in that."

"Me, neither," he said. "More power to 'em."

The garage where the vehicles were kept was noisy and stank of lube and hot fuel cells. Kay headed for the nearest one.

"Do we need a card or some kind of key?"

"No. They are not kept locked. They are just carts."

Wink shook his head. Take a human's cart without permission, and many of them would kill you without a second's hesitation. "What about this guy we are going to see?"

"*Shan*masc," she said. "Jak's cousin, another nephew of Teb, who was the third to die of the malady."

"And we are talking to him because . . . ?"

"Because Teb was a world-class criminal who had claws in many illegal activities. He was a thief, gambler, sold illegal chem, ran unlicensed prostitutes, and likely had people killed. He would have enemies who might throw something like this at him and not care about bystanders who died."

"Wow. I mean, I guess since you have cops, you have criminals, but somehow I didn't think much about that until I met your sister."

"We have our share of baddoers and sociopaths. Not as many as human worlds, of course."

"Oh, of course."

"Uncle Teb was among the worst, but he was passing clever, and the threads never led directly to him, else the *Sena* would have taken him out long ago. I don't know if Shan is involved in Teb's business, but if he is, the *Sena* don't show evidence of it. He doesn't need to be—Teb put away enough money so his family can live like royalty all their lives through the great-grandchildren."

They climbed into the cart. She waved a hand at the control panel, then rattled off an address. The cart's engine powered up, and they began to roll toward the garage's door.

She shook her head.

"What?"

"I mentioned prostitutes. Such activity is not illegal if licensed. Uncle Teb had scores, maybe hundreds of them, illegal, and he was the first Vastalimi to import aliens for the purpose. Males and females, mostly humans."

Wink considered that. It was no revelation that interspecies sex went on around the galaxy. When he'd been in college, he'd had a human roommate who had a thing going with a Rel female. Human males were randy enough to stick a willie into a damp spot on a carpet, so that wasn't a surprise. He hadn't gone down that road, having limited himself to humans, and fems only, but he could see the attraction. Everybody needed somebody.

"You ever been tempted?" he asked.

"By a prostitute?"

"No, by somebody other than a Vastalimi?"

She thought about that for a moment. "Tempted? Yes. Acted upon it? No. Until recent times, it was illegal here and considered enough of a perversion to cause consternation if it was made public. The laws have relaxed, but there are still many of The People who think anybody other than Vastalimi are prey, and you don't fornicate with prey, you eat them."

Wink let that one rattle around for a while without speaking to it.

"No," she said.

"'No,' what?"

"I don't consider you prey. In case that's what you were wondering."

"There's a missile dodged," he said.

She whickered.

ELEVEN

Jo went to make the recon of the site. She was alone.

She took a ground cart to a wooded spot ten klicks away, after dark, the lights off once she got close, using her augs to navigate. Having built-in nightsight was a useful toy when you wanted to keep a dark profile.

And she had a shiftsuit, for all she didn't like wearing it; it was a big plus. The suit was proof against a bunch of small-arms fire and eyes using the human spectrum, plus it could rascal basic pradar, to a degree. Yeah, it slowed her down and was awkward, but she wasn't going to fight, only to spy, so it was to the good.

Besides, even in the suit, she was faster, stronger, and could see and hear and all like that better than anybody not running top-of-the-line augware. It balanced out.

To see and not be seen; the best spy was one you never knew had been there, and that was her goal. Go in, find what you needed, get out.

She had picked out a path, and while it wasn't the most direct, it was unlikely anybody would be out taking the night

air until she got right to the encampment. If they had half a
brain among them, there would be pickets, and the local
sensors might catch a quick bounce if she wasn't careful,
but she knew where to put her feet, and she'd been doing
this a while . . .

"Jo? You on-station?" Gramps.

The com was tightbeam, shielded, and encrypted, the
suit's rather than her own radiopathic aug, so even if somebody detected it, they wouldn't know who it was or what
they said. And her hidey-hole was in the radio shadow of
an agrotruck-dispatcher station, with coded chat spewing
all over half a dozen channels, and one more sig wouldn't
raise any eyebrows on somebody bored and channel-
surfing.

Proper-planning-prevents-piss-poor-performance.

"I'm here."

"Copy. Get a nice nap, it's a long walk."

"Ten klicks? An evening stroll. I'm leaving on
schedule."

"Got that. Take care. Call us if you'll be late; you know
how your mother worries."

"Why don't you go bother Gunny? I'm a working fem
here."

"Yeah, sure, sell that one to somebody else, I know better.
You'd pay us to do this."

She discommed but grinned. He was right about that.

- - - - - -

Military camps ran in shifts, day and night, so there wasn't
any time that would be completely dead; however, most
planets had diurnal/nocturnal cycles and were more slack
once the local sun went down. Big civilization ran like the
military, but on less-populated worlds, the clock sometimes
slackened in the middle of the night. Humans could adjust
themselves to all kinds of cycles, but left alone, most of them
would be up days and sleeping nights. An army base would

have fewer interactions with civilians as a result and be less busy.

Besides, in a human camp, only sentries and a few scope-watchers would be apt to see in the dark, and you took every advantage you could.

Jo was outside the perimeter, which in this case was a quik-stretch wire fence three meters high and topped with needle-barbs. The trick was in getting past the wire where there was a blind spot, where a cam wasn't apt to be looking, and guards were somewhere else.

From the drone-flyover recordings, Jo had a good idea of the camp's general layout. They had elected not to drop disposable cams, so as to not alert anybody to possible visitors.

She looked at the layout. There, the HQ prefab; here, the barracks; over that way, storage units. Ferrofoam domes, most of them, wearing simple electronic camo and set among trees so they'd be hard to spot from orbit if you didn't already know where they were.

Her suit's scanners told her the fence was inert, no zappers, and not even motion sensors in the wire, which was sloppy but cheaper. On a site where you weren't expecting visitors, this was often SOP: Put up wire to keep the curious and local livestock out, call it good.

If visitors with any skill came round? Not such a good idea.

What was it about being in command that made spending a noodle when a tenth *might* suffice seem like a good idea? Corporate mentality? People who didn't understand that a gram of prevention was worth a kilo of cure . . . ?

It was never a good idea to underestimate one's opponent when he was armed and might shoot you.

Of course, if they did? So much the better for your team.

She could find a dead zone, run a cutter down the wire, and slip through. She didn't need to spend a whole lot of time snooping around, just enough to verify what they already suspected, maybe get some numbers, see what kind of gear these Masbülc mercs had, then glue the wire back together and toodle off, with them none the wiser.

Whoever had put up the fence hadn't done so close enough to the trees so somebody could climb up one and drop over the top, so they weren't totally inept.

There was a place, just there, where the fence was mostly blocked from view inside the camp by a shed close to the wire. Again, sloppy—always best, when you had the room, to leave open space between the fence and the nearest cover. Were this camp hers, she'd at least have a cam on the back of that maintenance shack, eyeballing the wire, and maybe a guard patrolling that stretch every so often.

Well, if it were hers, she'd never have put the fence that close to the building in the first place, the wire would be lit and sensored, too . . .

Then again, if it looked too easy, it could be a trap. Probably wasn't, but you didn't lose anything if you assumed the worst; assuming the best could get you spiked.

Don't see a guard? Must not be any.

No guards, and no obvious cameras, but, of course, a lens could be so small as to be invisible, or built into the wall's camo. And since it seemed like an invitation to *Come on in!* she decided to decline.

It took half an hour of edging along, playing scan-ghost, until she found a place she liked better.

Generally, the perimeter was fairly well lighted, biolumes mounted on posts next to the fence every thirty meters, casting a bluish green glow bright enough to see movement. But the terrain had a dip in it, and the line of sight not as clear for distance, the light posts lower. As long as she moved slowly and carefully, the shiftsuit would take care of anybody looking in the human spectrum. Somebody might be running a scope, but the suit's confusers would make it look like a scan-ghost on any but top-of-the-line sensors, and she knew how to move so she could enhance that impression if anybody was paying enough attention to notice.

What's that?

Scan-ghost. See how it drifts back and forth? Floats away like that? Fucking cheap gear!

Jo approached the wire, creeping. She mentally marked the location, then used a vibroblade cutter on the wire, drawing a line that followed the mesh pattern. She watched, waited, then eased through the opening, made sure it didn't gape behind her, and began to slowly work her way across the ground, drifting back and forth. The ground was mostly covered in grass that came to midshin, mowed, but not for a couple weeks, she guessed.

She moved, stopped, moved, tried to make her motions float aimlessly, as a sensor-ghost would. Gradually, she made her way closer to the nearest building, which was a big storage unit with large doors. Probably a garage of some kind, maybe a hangar for aircraft, hoppers, or flitters.

She opened a small entry door—wasn't even locked— and sure enough, the place was full of rollers and ground-effect vehicles, ranging from two-seaters to troop carriers that would hold a platoon.

She had an on-demand squeal, and she attached it behind a dust plate on a midsize roller. The little semiorganic caster was inert, not putting out any kind of signal, but if you beamed a certain series of radio frequencies at it, it would emit a very short PPS sig. A scanner might catch it, but it would ordinarily be too fast to triangulate and find even if somebody did hear the squeal, and the sig would tell its operator where the roller was.

So even if they picked up and moved the camp, the Cutters could find it. Or at least this vehicle . . .

She slipped out of the garage, carefully closed the door behind herself.

Let's see what else they had here . . .

She was feeling pretty good about her sortie, having

avoided any guards patrolling and keeping to the shadows when she became aware she was being watched.

Nothing she could see, but she knew.

She froze. Did a slow scan, her augmented sight ramped up to the maximum. Nothing. Nothing . . .

Wait. There. Thirty meters away, in the shadow of the big dome. A figure.

She had her pistol out, covering the target when it moved from the shadows and headed toward her. The light here wasn't bright, but her aug was more than enough to see it, and it was—

A Vastalimi!

The alien drew closer. She wasn't holding a weapon, and she was dressed much like Kay usually was, which was to say, wearing nothing but a belt with a holster and a couple of items clipped to it.

Jo came up from her crouch. She held her pistol low, pointed at the ground.

Five meters away, the Vastalimi stopped. In clear Basic, she said, "Ho, intruder. Have you anything to say before I rouse my comrades?"

Jo realized she was in trouble. At a dead run, she could make it to the fence well before the yard filled with soldiers, and she'd have a head start outside the base, albeit they'd have vehicles. Of course, there was this Vastalimi, who could give her a head start and still beat her to the wire.

She could shoot the Vastalimi, but even as fast as Jo was, that might be iffy, and nothing less than a fatal hit would stop the call for help.

Not a lot of choices. She hadn't expected to come across a Vastalimi here.

Jo said, *"Career nama borba do pojedinac inače oba nad nama umreti."*

The Vastalimi blinked at that. "*You* offer *prigovor*? How can you even *know* about such?"

"I have a furry friend," Jo said.

"Ah. That explains it. Why is he not here instead of you?"

"She's busy."

"A human who offers a Challenge. I have heard such things, but I didn't truly believe them. You are serious?" She sniffed, inhaling deeply. "You are multiply augmented."

"Of course. I'm nearly as fast and strong as you are."

"Even better. You qualify the Challenge?"

"As I stand," Jo said. "Of course, I'll put the pistol down and get out of the suit, and I'll use a knife, to offset your claws."

She whickered. "What a story this will make around the hunt fires! A human who gave *prigovor*!"

"You accept?"

"Oh, yes, I could not miss such an opportunity. But keep your knife sheathed, fem, and I will do the same with my claws. I would not take such an advantage, four to your one, there would be no honor in such a victory. Blunts will do well enough. I might not even have to kill you."

Jo grinned as she put the pistol onto the ground. At least she had a chance. She stood and began to peel off the shift-suit. Underneath, she wore a thin polypropyl bodysuit and slippers, nothing else.

"Will we be having company?"

"Unlikely if we are not too noisy. I am the camp's primary guard after dark. Nobody bothers to patrol or man sensors."

Jo nodded. She understood that. There was no need. One Vastalimi was more than enough for such light duty. Obviously.

"I'm Captain Jo Sims, of the Cutters."

"Ah. Your group has bested mine in several encounters."

"We're just getting started on that."

"As are we. Recall a recent vehicle explosion?"

Jo nodded. Of course, that was how they got past the farmers' guard to the fuel supply—they had a Vastalimi. Knowing that alone justified the sortie.

They obviously hadn't been using her much yet.

She whickered. "I am *Mish*fem, Em to my friends, and now to an honorable, if mad, human. Shall we dance?"

"Whenever you are ready." Jo smiled and showed her teeth.

Em crouched and Jo knew she was going to leap. They did such extremely well, the Vastalimi.

And it was to Jo's advantage that she knew it . . .

- - - - - -

Shan was young, at least he seemed so to Wink, and his fur was dyed or stained in bright splotches, with sections of it cut short or even shaved to the skin, as if he were wearing a jester's motley. He wore some kind of skeletonized helmet, thin strips of what looked to be platinum or iridium, glowing with a kind of rainbow sheen. He was outside the doorway to a large home, watching as Kay and Wink arrived, fifty meters away as they pulled the cart into a parking area.

"*Bukvan*," Kay said, under her breath.

His translator rendered that as "fop." Which didn't do him much good—he knew it was derogatory, but not exactly what it meant. So he asked her.

"He is a preener," she said. "He affects dye, jewelry, even clothes, to impress with his appearance. He spends considerable time on it each day, I would guess."

"Doesn't seem to be working on you."

"I do not begrudge the young their exuberance and folly. If it kills them, too bad, but their choice. That headlet he wears? An entertainment receiver. Probably cost what an average, honest citizen makes in a year. And he will have a *brijač*—a fur cutter attending to his chosen look, trimming, shaving, dyeing. Shan is a person who has wealth and glories in flaunting it. I find such ostentation lacking subtlety."

Wink chuckled. "When I was young, there was a fad among humans in my set for migratory tattoos. Skin nanos that would creep over one's body, interacting with other images, pulsing and flashing pictures that ranged from gross to obscene. I had a red-demon installation on my right shoulder that would crawl up a sub-Q net to my neck to meet the blue demon from the other shoulder, where they would fornicate in glorious, glowing purple for an hour before ebbing to their stations."

"And you thought this amusing?"

"At the time, yes. We did it more to irritate our elders than anything else. Fortunately, they were temporary tattoos, a year or so half-life and fading completely after that. Good thing, else many humans my age would look pretty silly. What seemed so funny and cutting-edge and radical at fifteen more often than not seems passing lame at thirty."

"Shan was born to wealth, he takes it for granted, and the source of his fortune was come by illegally. We have a saying, 'If you are looking for justice, look for it on the Other Side.'"

Wink nodded. "We have a similar sentiment."

She opened the cart's door and alighted; Wink exited the other door.

"So it is true!" Shan called out. "You have a human who accompanies you! Is he expensive? My human whores cost a fortune!"

"If I'm supposed to be your dog, maybe I'll bite him," Wink said.

"I would let you, save he would kill you if you tried. He has been training under master fighters since he came back from *Seoba*, in late cubhood. Only a few years, but even so, he is, according to my sources, passing adept."

"Good as Vial?"

"Certainly not, but no doubt he believes that he is. You can smell it on him."

"Maybe I'll shoot him from here."

"Kill him before we get our answers?"

Wink laughed.

They moved closer.

"Come in, come in, I have been looking forward to this," Shan said. "Is it true that you bested Vial using some sneaky Terran technique? Somebody supposedly has a recording of it, but I haven't been able to find it." He spoke excellent Basic.

Since it was obvious he knew who they were, Wink didn't wait for an introduction, he said, "All Terran techniques are sneaky, didn't you know? Best you never take your eyes off us."

Shan flicked a glance his way. "Really?" He hesitated a moment, then said, "Ah, you pull my fur! I didn't know Terrans had senses of humor! Excellent, excellent, come in, come in, I'll have a flagon of tirgwine decanted, and we can talk!"

He was like a kid with a new toy; Wink thought he might start bouncing up and down he seemed so full of himself.

Well. You were allowed to be young and stupid, when you were young and stupid, and if it didn't do you in, you might get older and wiser. Wink found himself kind of liking this Vastalimi.

- - - - - -

Em attacked just as Kay had done when first they had started sparring, straight ahead, powering in with speed and agility. That had worked the first couple of times Jo had danced with Kay because even as augmented as she was, Vastalimi were still faster. But the biggest part of fighting was not speed, nor power, but position. Being in the right spot and the right moment, with the right stance, those were worth more. A tiny step took less time than a big step. Faster to get set than to attack.

Em's leap was the product of millions of years of evolution, her personal experience, and Jo meant to short-circuit both by advancing her timing and taking the right spot before Em could get there. A strong stance in position was an advantage.

Jo wasn't your run-of-the-norm human, plus she had experience in hand-to-hand combat with a trained Vastalimi.

Em was in for a big surprise—

—but even as she thought this, and Em flew toward her, Jo's brain calculated the trajectory and speed and she realized she had made a mistake—if Jo took the ground she wanted, she would get there too late. Em had advanced her own timing with a quicker, lower leap—

Jo dived away, the fastest way to clear herself. Hit the ground, rolled, came up, and spun as Em landed and skidded to a stop.

Eight meters apart, they faced each other.

"Good," Em said. "I didn't expect that."

Abruptly, Jo realized what she had thought was her biggest advantage wasn't so. It had been a mistake to assume so.

"You have danced with trained humans before," she said.

"Yes, and I realize that Kluth has done the same with you. Which makes it yet more interesting. Was Kluth a better teacher to you than my human was to me?"

"That's how I'd bet," Jo said.

Em whickered. "Am I an ovum?"

Jo felt herself grinning. "Can't blame a fem for trying."

They circled carefully to the left, edging closer.

When she was at the limit of her step-and-a-half range, Jo charged. This time, she retarded her timing, offering a move that made it appear she was moving faster than she was, but actually slowing down her approach—

—Em reacted, stepping in to intercept but arriving too fast. Before she could correct, Jo dropped and snapped out a kick, adding range by the lowering of her stance—

Her right heel smacked into Em's leg, a little higher than her aim. Instead of the knee, it hit her thigh. It was not a crippling strike, but hard enough to knock Em into a half-assed turn. That gave Jo enough time to come up and spin for a back kick with her other foot, aimed at Em's low ribs.

Something else Vastalimi didn't like to do, show their backs, so the move was again unexpected—

Em dropped, turned slightly, took the heel on her shoulder, and again, it was enough to knock her off-balance, but not a telling blow—

Em dived away and came up, covering before Jo could follow through.

"Excellent! My human has not shown me this! I'll remember it and—*jebati!*"

Jo heard the sound of voices at the same moment and thought the same thing in Basic: *Fuck!*

"Go," Em said. "Hurry!"

Jo stared at her.

"We need to finish this without interference," she said. "If they see and catch you, they might damage you or kill you, and that would be wrong. I will divert them. We'll meet another time." She grinned.

Jo nodded and smiled back. "Yes. Another time."

She grabbed the suit—Rags would kick her ass if she left that expensive piece of hardware behind—and ran for the fence.

— — — — — —

The wine Shan provided was excellent, the best Kay had ever had, and he was a convivial host.

"So, you are keeping the Vial-killer move to yourself?"

"Wouldn't you?"

"Yeah, sure. From what I hear, you'll probably need it again. Sooner or later, though, somebody will figure it out."

"Sooner or later, we are all plant fertilizer."

He whickered loudly. "So I hear, but I intend to live forever."

She noticed Wink smiling, and she could tell he found this youngling amusing. Well, he was not without a certain charm.

"So back to business. Your uncle's death came as a surprise?"

"Yes and no. On the one talon, Uncle Teb had a *tzit*load of enemies, so somebody's spiking him was always a possibility. But he was careful. He never went to the shitter without a couple of armed guards who'd check the hole for hidden bombs before he squatted. Food was checked, visitors screened, he never went anywhere without a tactical team scouting and securing. I think there were five or six assassination attempts in the last couple of years. He didn't get a scratch in any of them.

"Old Teb was clawproof; even the Shadows couldn't get anything illegal to stick to his fur, not after thirty years of trying.

"So in theory, somebody could have killed him if they spent enough money and tried hard enough, but they'd have to be rich and really good.

"On the other claw, catching some disease and rotting away in a few days? Never saw that one hiding in the short grass. Teb was a health fiend, he ate *prey*-food, didn't drink enough to stone a flea, no drugs, and even the *ruta* he stuck his *stidnik* into was certified disease-free. He was never sick a day in his life I knew about."

"Who stood to gain by his death?"

"Other than me, you mean?"

"Yes."

"Some of the people in business with him."

"And that's not you?"

"Oh, no, no way! I never stepped a *ruta* hair into Teb's world. He didn't want that, neither did I. He had clean money—at least as far as anybody who looked at it can tell, including the *Sena*—and that's all I have ever touched. I party, but it's all legal, my whores are registered, and if I don't starting buying towns and moons and *tzit*, I'll have enough legal money to stay rich for, like, forever."

"And the names of those who were in business with your uncle who might benefit from his passage?"

"Ffuf! Ask the Shadows. I'm not saying *any*thing about

*any*body when it comes to that. I don't talk about them, they leave me alone."

"What if they think you did talk about them?"

"They won't. This conversation is being recorded, time-stamped, and sealed in a particular vault. It's available to Uncle Teb's business associates anytime they want to have a look and listen." He smiled. "Transparency is my best defense. I have no reason to cause my dear departed uncle's friends any grief, nor will I. I mind my business, keep my claws out of theirs. Live and let live."

When they got back into the vehicle, Wink said, "Kid is smarter than he looks."

She nodded. "Yes. But he did tell us something of value."

Wink said, "That his uncle was a health fiend and very careful."

"Yes. Alone it might not mean anything, but it seems unlikely that Teb was out tramping in the high grass where he caught some esoteric and hitherto unknown disease."

"What next?"

"Teb was third to die. We need to speak to the families of those who were first and second, then fourth and fifth. We need to find the connection among them."

TWELVE

"So, they have a Vastalimi?" Cutter said. "That's too bad."

"Doesn't sound like a very loyal one," Gramps said. "Otherwise, she wouldn't have let you go."

Jo shrugged. "If I had to guess, if somebody like me showed up and had the same conversation with Kay, she'd probably do it that way, too."

"You reckon?" Gunny said.

"They look at the galaxy a little different than humans," Jo said. "Hadn't you noticed?"

"Well, that's neither here nor there," Cutter said. "We have a location on the enemy force, and we need to do something about them. I will channel a com to corporate and see if they want to spend or shoot, and we can go from there."

"Seems like a good plan," Jo said.

"All right. Go polish stuff and drill the troops, we'll wait to hear from our employer."

Cutter headed to his office. So far, so good. The exchanges they'd had with the opposition forces had mostly gone their way, and now that they knew about the Vastalimi, that would make them pay better attention. Moving along well.

In his office, he was running some scenarios, playing war games against his computer, when Jo stuck her head through the door.

"Rags."

"Yeah?"

"We got a message from our spy at the port."

"Yeah?"

"Seems a passenger got off one of the dropships a few minutes ago might concern us."

"And . . . ?"

"Look at the image. She's using the name 'Melinne Cutter.' You know her?"

He stared at her. "What?"

The projection in front of him swirled and coalesced.

No fucking way . . .

Cutter stared at the image. It was either her or somebody who looked enough like her to be a twin or a cloned sister, and he didn't buy that one, either.

Yes, it was a small galaxy; now and then, you'd run into somebody you knew from another world and another time, but those were usually people in the same business, and if you were a soldier, you went where the wars were, so that wasn't completely unexpected. He'd been in the Army for a long time, and not all those troopers had been killed off or retired yet. SoFs, the good ones, got around. You bumped into each other.

Sure, you walk into any gathering, there would be folks with matching birthdays: That would usually get a show of at least a couple–three hands. But if you asked about a particular day matching, the numbers went down. How many here born on this date?

What were the odds of meeting your ex-wife halfway across the galaxy on a backrocket planet that had nothing on it she would have come here looking for?

He didn't believe it was a coincidence. And if it wasn't, then what was it?

"Rags? What's going on?"

Jo hadn't known him when he and Melinne had been together. He'd never told her the story; hadn't told anybody else all of it, either, though Gramps knew some of it.

It hadn't come up, but Jo was family now. And it would be hard to shut this door and pretend she hadn't seen it.

He had been carrying it for a long damn time. She was his CO, and his friend.

"I used to be married." He paused. "That's her."

"Wow."

"Come in, sit."

She did.

"It's a long story."

"I don't have any appointments. And you know I want to hear it."

He paused, gathered his thoughts, considered where he should start. Or even if he should. It was such a shock.

Melinne . . .

"We met when I was posted in Johannesburg; she was eighteen and drop-dead gorgeous. Melinne was young, beautiful, smart, a blast in the sack. Came from poor stock in SoAf, got herself into trouble. She was engaged to a local, he gave her some expensive token of his affection, a bracelet, she ditched him and sold it, he was pissed off about it.

"I had a word with her suitor, he backed off. She and I fell in lust, connected, and had good times. After a time, getting linked seemed like a thing to do, so we did.

"I wasn't the best spouse. I would be home for a few weeks, then I'd be posted to some rathole in the middle of nowhere for months before cycling back for leave, then off again. You know how it goes."

She nodded.

"She didn't like to travel all that much, at least not to battlefield accommodations, so she stayed home. What she did, who she saw when I was gone? I didn't ask, she didn't say, we were good with that. I had a wife, she had a life, it was a fair exchange.

"A couple of years after we connected, we had a son. But she got tired of what a major's income could provide, and she began shopping for an upgrade. She found a general though he was just a stop along the road.

"Our son—Radé—was four when we divorced. We split fourteen years ago."

"You have a son?"

"Had." He paused. Gone this far, might as well spin the rest of it out. "I wasn't much better a father than a spouse though I made an effort to see the boy when I was on-planet, but I wasn't around much.

"Four years after we disconnected, Melinne found a new prospect she liked. Rich man, something to do with food futures, had property all over, a shitload of money. They moved into one of his mansions in Johannesburg.

"I wasn't spying on her, but I had friends who would now and then mention stuff in passing. 'Saw your ex at the opera. She's zipped with a rich guy from Johannesburg,' like that. Life goes on, I didn't begrudge her that. Rich guy for a stepfather, could be worse for my son.

"I was occupied by my career. I let things slide.

"Six months later, I got a call from somebody: Radé was dead.

"I didn't know any of the details. I dropped what I was doing and booked for Earth. I pulled in favors, caught military transports, spaced nonstop.

"I was a hundred parsecs away when it happened, the Zimawali Police Action. It took me more than two weeks to get there.

"I didn't know what had happened when I arrived, only that there had been an accident. A fall. Radé hit his head."

He paused.

"There was nothing I could do. Radé had been recycled;

Melinne had vanished. I thought she was probably afraid of what I might do to her.

"The local authorities ruled it an accident. Terrible, but no one at fault.

"I started to poke around. It turned out that Melinne's lover had a temper and he thumped her when he got irritated. She decided it wasn't so bad a trade, so she stayed.

"There were no direct witnesses to the event, except for Melinne and her lover, and I later came to believe that he— his name was Mandiba—paid her handsomely to go away and keep her mouth shut.

"So there was the official story. But Mandiba had servants. None of them had seen it happen, but they knew. They talked to each other. There were recordings of the man slapping around Melinne on other occasions, and servants who had seen him do it to other women. Somebody heard the child yelling at the man, and his response. There were doctors, emergency-med techs, coroners, recycle techs. A piece here, a bit there, I puzzled it together.

"What I figured out was, six months into their relationship, Melinne's lover was high on some kind of chem and he started beating her. Our boy was eight. He stepped in and tried to stop it. The man backhanded Radé. It knocked him into a marble table, and the edge caught him in the back of the head. Brain hemorrhage. He died the next day.

"The man who killed my son was still there, going on about his business."

Jo shook her head.

"The rules are different for rich men," he said. "Always have been."

He paused again, remembering.

"I felt guilty. I should have been there for my son, somehow.

"Three months later, Mandiba had a freak accident. He was inspecting some property he wanted to buy and he stepped on an old AP mine left over from a local bush war forty years earlier. Blew both his legs off, he died before medical help got there."

She looked at him. "What a shame."

"The local police examined the site carefully. The mine was the right age and kind used in the dustup, and the area known to have been sown with the things. People thought they had all been cleared. Apparently, the sweepers missed one."

Jo said, "And the police figured that it would be hard to find a forty-year-old mine of a certain kind that still worked and plant it in the right place at the right time to make it anything other than an accident?"

"Apparently they did," he said.

"And you never heard from Melinne again?"

"No. I considered hunting for her. She was a loose cannon, she put my son into a situation that got him killed. She would have left a trail of broken relationships behind her. Easy to find."

"But you didn't look."

"No. I figured she would cause herself plenty of grief on her own. And I wondered if I was blaming her for something I hadn't done."

"And here she is all these years later, on the same world." Jo looked at the holographic image. "Still a drop-dead gorgeous woman."

"That she is. She worked at it. She's thirty-eight, going on twenty-two. Exercise, diet, surgery, chem, she takes care of the package."

"You don't think she is here by accident."

"No. If she were living with the richest guy on the planet, it would still be *this* planet, and it's too parochial for her."

"Maybe she's passing through."

"Maybe."

"You think she is here because you are here." Again, it was a statement and not a question.

"If I had to bet on it, yeah."

"Why?"

"That's the question I don't know the answer to. How would she know where I was? Why would she care?"

"Maybe she's tired of looking over her shoulder, worrying you'll show up someday."

"Maybe. And there are too many 'maybes' to suit me."

"Whatever I can do to help."

"She will contact me. And then we'll see."

A priority incoming call bleeped at that moment.

He felt a lurch in his chest . . .

But: No, it was not Melinne—it was Corporate; Alvarez, in OuterZone Operations, leapfrogged from HQ at least three or four links away, but close enough now for a real-time exchange. The miracle of n-space tachyon communications. There was solid science that explained how it worked, but it might as well be magic as far as he was able to follow it. He put the call on the speaker.

"Cutter."

"Colonel. We have a response from Corporate regarding your message about the situation there."

"And . . . ?"

"You are empowered to make an offer."

"How much?"

Alvarez named a figure. More than Cutter would have guessed. He glanced over at Jo.

She shrugged.

"I understand. Terms and conditions?"

"The usual. They pack up and go away, don't come back."

"Masbülc will probably send somebody else. Maybe they'll be better."

"Probably both, but the current crop will likely be in before they get set up, you are already on-site, and we deal with that if it happens."

Never one to take the long view, TotalMart Corporate. Maybe an asteroid would wipe the world out by next growing cycle. Why risk money you didn't have to spend?

"All right. I'll make the offer."

"If they refuse, Corporate would be pleased to see them, ah, negated, soonest."

"I understand."

"Out."

Cutter waved his connection off.

"Well, I guess we better run down an enemy commander and have a chat with him," Cutter said.

– – – – – –

Wink had to use his translator; the fem to whom Kay was speaking either didn't speak Basic or chose not to, and because she assumed he couldn't understand her, he had to keep himself from showing his teeth in a big smile.

"—smells funny," the fem said. "Is that him, or do they all have that odor?"

"They all do. You get used to it," Kay said.

"Odd-looking, too, up close. First one I've seen in the flesh. How do you tell them apart if they are downwind?"

"It's a trick you learn."

"I don't understand why you are here. I have been over this with the other Healers."

"We are looking for something we might have missed. It might help save others."

The fem shrugged. "All right. My mate Cedom came home from work on fourday—he was employed at the Duonde Slaughterhouse, Moon-shift. He complained of a headache and was slightly feverish. He didn't feel too bad. We ate, retired, and he woke up at dawn vomiting blood. The Healers sent a conveyance, he was taken to the South Wall *bolnica*. They gave him medicines, and on sixday, he died.

"Neither I nor our litter—we had just the one, three fems, two males, four seasons old—have shown any signs of any sickness since, and it has been more than two months since Cedom left to hunt on the Other Side. I have his death stipend, and we have family. We get by."

"Did he say anything unusual had happened at his work just before he became ill?"

"No. His primary job was the chop-saw; now and then, he would fill in as a tool sharpener when somebody was off. He was a meat cutter. He showered after work before he left, and there was never a trace of blood or gore on him when he got here, he was always sure to make it so. Not everybody respects butchers, but for those who cannot hunt, they are necessary."

"Certainly they are," Kay said.

"As far as I know, there have been no other illnesses like my mate's at Duonde."

"This is true."

"There is nothing new to say. He came home slightly sick, and two days later he was dead. He was the first to go from this plague, whatever it is. Maybe they'll name it after him."

Even the translator knew enough to shade that last comment with bitterness.

– – – – – –

The restaurant had the high-class look, colorful and clean, only two dozen tables, and Gramps had allowed as how it was the best to be had for Swavi cuisine in Adit, probably on the whole planet. Cutter hadn't come for the food. It was a neutral spot. He had Gramps and Gunny at a table nearby, with Jo and half a dozen troopers patrolling outside. Until the man arrived, Cutter amused himself by trying to figure out which of the other diners belonged to the opposition. He had narrowed it down to four—a hard-looking woman of forty or so across from a muscular, but petite fem, just to the left of the front entrance; and a pair of men who were dressed in softcollar business attire but looked somewhat uncomfortable in those clothes. One of them kept glancing around as if expecting somebody, but theirs was a two-person table.

The opposition's representative arrived precisely on time.
"Colonel. I'm Proderic."

Cutter gestured at the chair across from him. "Please. Just Proderic?"

The man said, "Yes. I hold no military rank, I'm a facilitator. My CO is a retired career army officer; he handles all the field operations."

And not very well. Maybe he was a quartermaster or photon-pusher, but he hasn't demonstrated much ability in the field, Cutter thought. He kept that to himself.

"That salt-and-pepper pair to the right," Proderic said. "Those yours?"

Cutter grinned. So his field guy might be crappy on the ground, but Proderic here had sharp eyes. And that he wanted to play said something. Cutter considered his comments and decided to make a little leap: "And yours would be the two fems left of the door, and the two men to my left."

He smiled. "Not bad, sah."

The waiter came and poured wine into two glasses. It had been ordered before they'd arrived. It was a pale blue. The waiter set the bottle down and left.

Both men picked up their glasses and sipped the wine.

It was dry and crisp, a hint of citrus and legroberry, a Ferling, made locally. Gramps had picked it out.

"Nice choice, I'll have to get a case of this. So, what's Totomo's offer?" Proderic asked.

"You're sure that's why I'm here?"

Proderic's teeth were very white against his tan. "Absolutely. You are better than my guys—I didn't expect TM to send anybody this fast, much less a first-class unit, so I cut corners. A calculated risk—I'll upgrade my guys, if that's what it comes down to. But if your employer wants to pay us enough to go away, we aren't unreasonable."

Cutter nodded. He wasn't a haggler. Yes, he could pinch a tenth coin tight enough to make it squeal, but bargaining back and forth? Not his thing. He named the maximum figure TM had given him. It was going to be take it or leave it.

Proderic nodded. "Actually, it's more than I expected."

"But . . . ?"

"I'm afraid I have to decline."

"You came prepared to do that no matter what I offered, didn't you?"

"Well, you might have come up with a figure I'd have been unable to refuse, but I didn't expect that."

"You wanted to see how much effort TotalMart was willing to put into this."

"Guilty of that, yes. And now I know."

"As you say, it's a fair offer."

Proderic sipped more of the wine. "Yes. But my employer—"

"Masbülc," Cutter cut in.

"I didn't say that. My employer sees this as an opportunity for, um, growth. How about a counteroffer?"

Cutter looked at him.

"We give you, say, half again that much, and you melt your igloos and lift?"

Cutter grinned. "And now we know how much Masbülc values this operation."

"I take that as a 'No'?"

"My employer is a long-standing and valued client. The loss of that business would be major. And even if you came up with a number big enough to offset it? I couldn't. We have a contract. I feel I must honor such. A personal quirk."

"They buy, but they don't sell in this situation, is that it?"

"I don't make corporate policy."

"Ah, well. It was good to meet you. Thanks for introducing me to this fine wine. I'd stay for dinner, but I have some pressing business. A new CO seems to be in order."

"I'd wish you good luck with that, but . . ." Cutter gave him a palms-up shrug.

"I understand. Well, things might still work out, you never know. Colonel."

He stood.

The two couples Cutter had marked as belonging to Proderic stood. He felt good about that—until two *other* single diners also arose: an older woman who looked like somebody's granny and a dark-skinned man who appeared old enough to be granny's father. Good disguises, those. And it made Proderic seem to be a man who crowed *and* zipped his jacket and was letting Cutter know that by revealing his backup team.

Maybe Jo had made them when they came in, or Gramps and Gunny had, but Cutter had missed them.

Interesting.

THIRTEEN

The second Vastalimi to die of the illness was a fighting teacher near the north edge of the Southern Reach. She'd had a place in a village nestled into the foothills, three hundred kilometers away from the slaughterhouse where *Cedom*masc had worked.

Nobody had been able to establish any connection between the two. There was no evidence they had ever met, and as best as anybody could track their movements in the weeks before they died, they hadn't been any closer than the village and the city were to each other.

Neither of them could be linked in any way with Teb, the third to kick off.

The teacher, *Tard*fem, was older, had been a well-known local fighter in her prime, and had a dozen students in her *skola*. She was well liked by her neighbors and the village in general, fit for a fem her age, and had outlived all her enemies. Unmated, and she'd lived alone.

Nobody locally could recall anything unusual in Tard's

life in the days before she sickened. She taught classes, she nodded to people she passed, her place was quiet.

One morning, she didn't show up for class. Students went to find her, and she was already deep in the grip of the malaise. She was transported to the local Healer's but died en route. Must have been pretty tough to be that sick and not go for treatment on her own.

On the flight back from the village, Wink turned it over in his mind every way he could. The only possibility he could see that they could have caught the disease from the same source was that a carrier had been in the city and the village.

If you drew a three-hundred-kilometer circle around both victims, there were no Venn intersections at all.

Nobody seemed to keep records of travel that were particularly detailed. Vastalimi came and went a lot freer than humans tended to do on their planets. When you could just borrow a cart and leave it when you were done, that was loose enough; that there didn't seem to be any carts taken from the village and left in the city, or vice versa in the week before the teacher died?

Had somebody made a round-trip to cause the infection? Maybe there were few enough people in the village to check them all; no way to do that for the bigger city . . .

"Not getting any easier," Wink said.

Kay nodded. "Not yet."

"We are missing something."

"Obviously. But the *Sena* will look, and there are no eyes sharper than theirs. What we missed? They will find."

"You seem sure about that."

"Nothing is certain, but if it is there, the Shadows will eventually uncover it."

"Lot of people could die between now and 'eventually.'"

She shrugged. "We can only do what we can."

— — — — — —

Cutter took a deep breath and exhaled slowly, trying to calm himself.

Across from his desk, Jo said, "She's on her way in."

Cutter nodded. He pulled his sidearm from its holster, pivoted it forward via the trigger guard around his finger, and gave it a half twist, so the butt was toward Jo.

She took the pistol. Raised an eyebrow.

"Yes, I know, I can kill her with my hands, but that would take a little more effort than just drawing and shooting."

Jo shook her head. "You don't have to do this at all. I could talk to her. Find out whatever."

"No. I need to do this."

— — — — — —

He was behind his desk when Melinne came in.

She looked good. Even this close, she could still pass for her early twenties. She was fit, taut, full-breasted, with an athletic swing to her step. Her hair was cut in a buzz, maybe two centimeters long, dyed to a golden bronze that complemented the tone of the chem tan on her exposed, smooth skin. She wore a pearl gray, sleeveless tunic over a sleeveless black skintight, with ballet-style slippers that matched the tunic. No jewelry, no tattoos, nothing else necessary to gild the lily . . .

She sat in the chair facing the desk and crossed her legs. "Hello, Cutty."

He had thought about this moment more than a few times over the years; what he might say, how he might feel. He had gone back and forth in his imagination, which way he would go, icily cool, foaming rage—what his first words would be. Until he spoke, he wasn't sure of what he was going to say.

"Why did you run?"

"Because I was afraid you would kill me. You thought about it, didn't you?"

He nodded. "I considered it. What makes you think I won't do it right now?"

"It's been a decade. If you had wanted to find and kill me, you could have done it long ago. I know what happened to Mandiba."

"He had an accident."

She nodded. "Right."

"Why are you here, Melinne? It's no coincidence."

"No, of course it isn't. Masbülc hired me to talk to you. They want to recruit you to run their corporate military department, starting right now."

He blinked. He hadn't expected that. "What?"

"Apparently, your little army has come up against elements of their little armies from time to time, and yours has always won. They figure it is cheaper to have you working for them than losing battles."

That made sense. When it was cheaper to buy than fight? Buy. "And they thought *you* were the person to convince me?"

She laughed, and for the smallest moment, he remembered how it had been to make her laugh. It had been the most uncontrived thing about her, her laugh, and it had been infectious. It didn't make him want to laugh now, but the memory was there. "I told them that I'd be the last person in the galaxy whose advice you would take. Apparently, their shrinks did a profile based on something and decided it was worth a shot. They gave me a lot of money to try."

He shook his head. "They need to get new shrinks. Is that it? For the money?"

"Mostly, yes. I—we—I never had a chance to say some things. And I was curious. You and I had a short run, but there were some good times." She shrugged. "How have you been, Cutty?"

"You don't get to ask, and you don't get to call me that anymore."

She nodded, sighed. "He was my son, too. I get up every day and remember it. I was young and stupid, and you cannot know how much I regret it. I would have traded places with Radé in a heartbeat, Rick. He . . ." She stopped, gathering herself.

He was tempted to look down at the screen built into the desktop, to check the stress analyzer whose cams and mikes were recording her image and parsing her voice and microexpression, the sensors that picked up her heartbeat and respiration and blood pressure. He could be fooled by a good liar, and she was good, but he heard the ring of truth there.

"He was so brave. Charged in, fist swinging, to defend me. I—" She sobbed, once. "I am so sorry." Tears flowed freely down her perfectly sculpted cheeks.

He could see the scene in his mind, as he had a hundred times before. His eight-year-old son, attacking the man hurting his mother. It was all he could do to keep his own tears back.

There was far too much bottled-up anger in him to release. He felt no desire to walk around the desk and comfort her, the woman he had married, with whom he'd had a son. But he also didn't feel the need to walk around the desk to choke the life from her.

That was something, at least.

It took him a few seconds to find his voice, to keep the emotions from boiling up to overwhelm and drown him. "Tell Masbülc they wasted their money sending you here."

"I told them that before I got here. I'm meeting the local rep when I leave."

"Proderic."

"Yes, that's his name."

"I can't say it's been good to see you," he said. "And I don't think I can ever forgive you. But you don't need to worry that you'll open your door someday and find me there ready to shoot you. Go on about your life, whatever it is. We're done. Whatever your griefs, I won't be one of them."

"You're wrong, Cutty. You'll always be that, until the day I die."

After she was gone, Jo slipped back into his office. She tossed his pistol to him, he caught it and reholstered it.

"You heard it," he said.

"Yep. And she was telling the truth, far as your system and my onboard aug can determine it."

"Doesn't change anything."

"No? You wouldn't consider working for Masbülc once this op is done?"

"That? Oh, sure. Depend on the money, of course, and if TotalMart wanted to match it for an exclusive. But we don't switch in the middle of a contract. If they still want us after we kick their asses here? I'll listen to their offer."

"You figure that Proderic will get himself a better CO?"

"I would in his place. He didn't strike me as stupid."

She grinned at him. "Well, it's been too easy so far, except for the Vastalimi. Hope the new guy can't find any more like her."

She didn't speak to the other part of this; he appreciated that.

– – – – – –

There were a dozen or so Vastalimi on the walk in front of the shops next to the spot where Wink and Kay were about to cross the street. They seemed to be about their own business, but Wink saw a female who appeared to be watching them.

Well, he was a human and unusual around here, but that didn't seem to him to be why she was looking their way.

She sauntered in their direction.

"Somebody coming to say hello," he said.

"I see her," Kay said. "But she's not a fighter; it won't be a Challenge."

"You can tell that?"

"Yes."

The fem arrived and stopped three meters away. She was a bit taller and thinner than Kay, seemed younger as far as Wink could tell, and she wore nothing save her own fur.

"Should I speak Basic?" she asked in their language.

Kay shrugged. "If you need the practice. He will understand if you speak *NorVaz*, *Govor*, or *Jezik*."

"Really?"

"If you have a message to deliver, it is only necessary that *I* understand it. Do you have a name?"

"Call me *Glasni*fem."

Kay grinned. "Very well, '*Messenger*.' Speak."

"There are people who know things regarding your inquires that would be helpful to you. They are willing to share these things; however, they are concerned that they would be in danger if their identities should be revealed."

"I understand. Continue."

"Meetings can be arranged if you agree to terms."

"Which are . . . ?"

"No *Sena*. No one save you and your human should know of this offer. You must be ready to meet with only short notice, and we must be assured of your complete circumspection regarding the matter."

"I understand. I have questions."

"I am not the person to ask for answers. I know no more than I have just told you."

"Very well, then. I will abide by those terms."

"I will tender your agreement to those concerned. Someone will be in touch."

The fem nodded at Kay, but not at Wink. She stood there and watched as they crossed the street.

"Well, isn't that interesting," Wink said, as they approached the door to the hospital.

"In many ways."

"It could be just what we need."

"Yes."

"And it could be some kind of a diversion. A trap."

"Yes. But either way, it is a trail to follow."

"What makes me nervous is the part about nobody's knowing but you and me."

"I can understand that."

"But you agreed to those terms."

"I did. But *you* did not."

He grinned.

"Teeth, Wink Doctor. We are on a public street."

He tightened his smile to lips only. "So if I told your sister about this, it wouldn't bother you?"

"Why would it? You are a sentient being with your own will. You did not enter into any agreement with the fem who named herself Messenger. Nor did she ask it of you."

"They don't believe I might say something?"

"Unlikely. Most of the Vastalimi we interact with will assume that you somehow belong to me and will do as I tell you."

"It does seem that way from what I've encountered here."

"Please do not take it personally, but humans are not held in particularly high regard here. Had they considered you an equal, they would have asked for your agreement. They did not."

"I noticed."

"Which is good. Always better to be underestimated by one's enemy, is it not?"

"Yep. Now what?"

"Now, we go see my brother."

FOURTEEN

"So there's the deal," Cutter said. "Proderic turned out TotalMart's offer of a buy-off, and so we are good to go tactical and do something about them.

"We know where they are." He glanced at Jo, who nodded. The caster she had planted was operational, and it said the cart was still parked at the base they'd uncovered.

Unless Em the Vastalimi had happened across her before she had hidden the bug, in which case it might have been left there on purpose. One had to consider such things.

"So I'm thinking we give them a fat and too-lightly-guarded target and see if they go for it."

Around the table, the others nodded. That would enable the GCES.

The problem with private militaries was that the rules of engagement had to consider civilian authorities in ways that government-sponsored armies did not. ROE for a brigade going into a declared war were different from a corporate unit of fifty engaged with a similar force on an otherwise peaceful planet. You couldn't just stomp in and kill them all without pissing off the local police. The GCES—Galactic Corporate Exception Statute—allowed a fair amount of leeway when it came to shooting at each other, but it was always better if you could show necessary self-defense.

We were, just, you know, escorting a convoy from here to there when the other guy's forces jumped us, and we had no choice.

If you could document that with vids and a photon trail of orders and legal activity, so much the better. If you could show that you were also protecting civilians and locals? Better still.

So if you could lure the other guys into an attack you were set up to deal with? That was the way to go.

"The local military CO is stretched thin, not enough troops, and he's looking to rise in ranks and leave soon, so as long as we don't make too much noise or disturb the locals, we probably don't have to worry about him. We'll have to disguise troop egress, but we'd do that anyway. So let's come up with bait. Kick it around, let's meet again at 1800."

They broke the meeting. Jo found herself with Gunny and Gramps, trying to lay out traps.

Singh was in the yard. Gunny had developed a fondness for the young man, and she looked at the others. "Can we give the kid a lesson?"

"Sure," Jo said.

Gramps nodded.

Gunny waved Singh over.

He didn't walk, he jogged.

Jo grinned, remembering when she'd been that eager to be involved in things.

"Ho, sahs!"

"Singh," Gunny said. "We have ourselves a little strategic and tactical situation, maybe you might help us out with."

Jo allowed her grin to linger just a moment more. Singh's help would be, if anything, minimal, given the wealth of experience among the three of them, but if that's how Gunny wanted to play it, that was okay.

Gunny said, "We are going to knock Masbülc's dick into the dirt, but we want them to think it's their idea."

Singh nodded. "Yes, sah."

"How you figure we should go about such a thing?"

Singh considered it. "Some kind of lure into a trap."

"That's good," Gramps said. "What do you reckon would work?"

Singh thought about it some more. "Well, what they are after are those purple vegetables, yes? Either grabbing them or destroying them. So doing it at the source, in transit, or at the destination would be their choices. The source and destination are the most well guarded, so in transit. They have tried that and have been repulsed, but it is still the easiest of the three. Give them a convoy that is somehow vulnerable. What about shipping cargo by water? A barge up a river, a ship via a local sea? Such vessels are more constrained in their movement and easier to target, yes?"

Gunny grinned, like a proud mother at a bright child. "Why, that's a good idea, Singh."

Jo played along: "But won't they suspect a trap?"

Gunny said, "Actually, we make the barge the decoy. It's too easy, so they will suspect it's a trap, and will look around to see what we'll be covering up. Ah like it."

Gunny said. "Remember Meko?"

Both Jo and Gramps grinned.

Singh looked blank.

Gunny said, "Meko was a guy we met during a dustup on New Java, a local, worked security at some entertainment arena. He was old—older even than Gramps here. Retired military. He liked to stop into the local pub where old Army guys or SoFs hung out for a beer now and then."

Singh nodded.

"We got the story from the pubtender one evening after Meko had his one beer and left.

"Meko was quiet, laid-back. Average-looking, not real big. Nobody'd look at him twice in a crowd.

"He was a religious man, Ah don't remember which one he was into—was he Hindu?"

"He was a Zarathustran," Gramps said. "They are monodeistic, all about truth and order, as I recall. He always wore a little cap whenever we saw him."

"Right. Anyway, he spent a fair amount of time going to his temple or church, whatever. One evening after the service, he was walking home, a trio of local thugs who'd been doing strong-arm robberies decided he was a viable target."

Gunny said, "So they rolled up on him in a cart, hopped out, and gave him the speech, give up your money, or we kick your head in."

Singh nodded. "I think I see where this is going. This was unwise, yes?"

"Oh, yeah. Meko was retired military, but not just any military, he'd been a blue hat."

"A Ghost Lancer?"

Gunny grinned real big. "Yep. Ghost Lancer, a hand-to-hand combat instructor, and a veteran of scores of down-and-dirty campaigns. Uniform wasn't big enough to hold all the medals and ribbons and patches he'd earned. Those kind of guys are tougher than a rhino-hide bag full of granite. You probably couldn't pick a worse man to fuck with.

"Pubtender said there was a traffic cam or building security cam caught it. Three guys surrounded him, six seconds later, all three of them were on the ground in need of serious medical care. Two of them didn't last until it got there, and it was wasted on the third, who croaked on the way to the hospital. Meko didn't have a scratch."

"And lo, order was restored," Gramps said. "Amen."

Singh nodded.

"Gunny's point here," Gramps said, "has to do with underestimating an enemy. Sometimes, best way to sell something is to let people sell themselves. If the Masbülc troops think they've figured this out on their own, if they believe they caught us hiding something? They'll be more inclined to go for it."

"I'm not sure I see the connection with the story of the Ghost Lancer," Singh offered.

Gunny grinned really big. "Well, our old drinking buddy Meko? That benign look of his was an act. He liked to use his skills—you don't get into the blue hats unless you are into serious violence. Since good predators can usually tell each other, something in the eyes, the way they stand or move, Meko went out of his way to look like he was prey. He walked a route where he knew there had been previous attacks. He pretended to be foolish, because an attack was what he wanted. A chance to keep the rust off."

"Ah. Most devious."

Gunny said, "Taking something at face value, making a snap judgment at first glance can get you into deep shit. Hip shots are faster, but aimed are more accurate."

"Unless it's Gunny doing the shooting, in which case it doesn't matter," Gramps said.

"Was that a *compliment*, old man?"

"Slip of the tongue. Forget I said it."

They smiled at each other.

– – – – – –

Kay called her sister. "How goes the investigation?"

Leeth said, "We have *Sena* sifting reports, investigating on the streets. It goes as well as it can, given how little there seems to be to it."

"Anything of substance?"

"Not yet. Even if there was, I wouldn't tell you. We don't need an amateur getting in our way."

"I am charged by our brother to look into this."

"From the *medical* side. I represent the law, and my agents will handle matters *criminal*."

Kay waited a beat, then said, "I see. Wink Doctor would have a word with you."

"Really? Why?"

"I'll include him in." She nodded at Wink, who thumbed his own com to life.

"*Sena* Leeth," he said. "I have some information you might find interesting."

He told her about the street meeting. She listened without interrupting until he was finished.

"Well done, Wink Doctor. And compliments to you, Sister, for observing the letter of an agreement, if not the spirit."

"'Spirit' is a nebulous term," Kay said. "It means different things to different people. Do the *Sena* enforce the law or the spirit? If an adversary makes a foolish error, it is her concern, not mine."

"True. You will keep me apprised?"

"That claw rips going and returning."

There was a long pause. Finally: "We do have some leads, I can tell you that much," Leeth said. "Skimpy as yet."

"Such as . . . ?"

"Such as not enough to tell you until we have more. Will you teach the *Sena* how to follow a scent?"

Kay didn't speak to that.

"There may be nothing here with this messenger, Kluth. Someone winding your stem just to watch you dance."

"And maybe not."

"Let me know if you are contacted by these people."

"Not I," Kay said. "Wink Doctor might feel a need to com you again."

Leeth whickered.

They discommed. Wink said, "Your sister is tight-lipped."

Kay shrugged. "It goes with the job. I will prod, and she will parry, I expect nothing else. If she and her agents can find the answer, no one will be more pleased than I—it will reflect well upon the *Sena*, and my sister's victories are mine.

"But an answer must be found, and it might fall to us to

be the ones to find it. We won't ignore anything that crosses our trail if it might lead us to our prey."

"So we sit around and wait to be contacted?"

"I think we won't have to wait long. If they weren't ready to talk, they wouldn't have gotten in touch with me."

Wink nodded.

Kay continued: "My sister will investigate the messenger who approached us. I expect that within short order, she will know who the messenger really is and where to find her. She will probably hold off on contacting her until we see if those who sent her have anything of substance to say.

"Leeth's first loyalty is to the *Sena* and to law and order. She might be tempted to come along and hide in the bushes, to keep an eye on things."

"Worried about her sister?"

"Maybe. But if it turns out this plague is Vastalimi-made, despite Leeth's belief otherwise, she would position herself to catch the perpetrators. And I don't want them frightened off. They were specific, no Shadows. Harder to track a bird flown than one on the ground. She doesn't want us bumbling into the path of her investigations; that gate swings both ways."

"Your show. But maybe I could leave a message that won't be delivered until after the meeting is over? We come home in one piece, I cancel it. If not, it gives her a place to start looking."

Kay considered it. "Leave such a time message for Droc but not for Leeth. He will be more circumspect in his actions, and if the time comes he feels the need for *Sena*, he can contact Leeth."

"Got it."

FIFTEEN

The trap was set, and the Cutters were about to spring it. It had been laid out using the basic idea Singh had offered: A barge was loaded with a secret cargo in such a way that any opposing military with half a brain and the barest intelligence unit could not have failed to notice it. As it left the dock headed downriver for a seaport five hundred klicks away, there was no air support, and only one boat with a few soldiers acting as escorts, an easy target.

Too easy a target, and if the Masbülc mercs didn't look at it askance, they'd have to be completely stupid. Cutter thought that they would upgrade their CO, and anybody worth his component elements wouldn't be in a hurry to go for the bait. They'd look around.

The convoy of wheeled vehicles, for which more efforts had been expended to load and get it rolling secretly, was on the move, using narrow, back roads. The convoy had a few more guards, but not enough to stop any real effort to take it. And the work to keep it secret was enough, maybe, to convince somebody that was the intent.

They had sat down and worked it out to the nth detail, and their main force of ground troops, eighty strong, and just shy of the legal limit, was already in place. Cutter and his staff, with Singh, were taking a hopper to a hidden staging point. The attack, were it to be a surprise and successful, could only be launched through a narrow window, and that's where CFI would be, waiting. If the Masbülc fly buzzed in, they would swat it.

Nancy, the best pilot they had, flew their hopper, and they kept it low and slow as they headed for the stage.

His field team wore shiftsuits, which gave them advantages, and the slow ride rocked them into a semidoze, at least it did Cutter. He wouldn't be leaving the hopper, nor would Formentara; they'd be monitoring the action from there. He would rather be in the thick of it, but Jo was too good an XO to allow him to take the risk most of the time. Now and again, he could coax her into letting him into the action, but that happened less and less. He understood. Commanders were supposed to lead from the rear; getting killed was bad for the business.

Singh was a newbie but not totally green. He had gone with them on sorties on Ananda, demonstrated his courage and a basic skill, but he need seasoning, so they kept him close. After his initial action and kill, the team had talked about their first hot actions, mostly to help him get past it.

Eventually, most of the team had stepped up to tell their tales, then or later.

They had been interesting stories. Wink, Jo, Gunny, Gramps, even Kay. Cutter hadn't heard some of them directly, but public spaces in his camps were usually under electronic surveillance. Say something in the yard, chances were somebody could hear it if they wanted to bother. Word got around.

Cutter hadn't told his story. He hadn't thought about it in a long time.

Not that he could ever forget it . . .

- - - - - -

It had been his first time in the field after basic, so long ago and far away, a little police action against a private militia that had gotten too feisty and had started stepping on civilian toes.

Cutter's light-infantry rifle platoon had been part of A company, with two other companies, B and C, set to surround a sixty-solider enemy unit and either capture or take them down.

Cutter was in Second Squad, run by an old sergeant, Ali Muhammad Ali. The ten-person squad was a mix of a couple of old hands and mostly newbies, and the platoon leader had been a shavetail second loot straight out of some university ROTC school who thought he was Robert E. Lee, George S. Patton, and Lead Foot Franklin McGruder all rolled into one. A man who used the words "glory" and "honor" a lot in much of his conversation.

Their assignment was to guard a narrow road leading from the main field of battle, and that would have been easy duty—the road bottlenecked between two old buildings just past a bridge over a narrow but deep river, there was plenty of cover, and all they had to do was line 'em up and knock 'em down if anybody tried to leave that way.

It was a cool fall day, but the trees still had most of their leaves, and Sergeant Ali set Cutter and the rest of his squad behind bullet-stopping brick and permaplast walls. Cutter was a rifleman, but set to feed ammo for the light machine gun being run by Corporal Omar, who was on his second tour.

The other two squads were placed, the com units seemed to be working just fine, and the main action was going to take place three klicks away, on the other side of a patch of woods, so probably, Ali said, they wouldn't see anybody, and maybe not even hear much of the engagement. The militia was outnumbered, outgunned, and if their commanders had the sense Allah gave a jackboot, they'd surrender PDQ, Ali allowed.

Cutter figured their captain gave them the job because it was the least likely to get anybody killed, and he'd have been right, except that Lieutenant Savoy Oslo Brinkley—and yeah, it didn't take the unit thirty seconds to latch onto the man's initials—wasn't content to do what he'd been ordered to do.

Thirty minutes after the push started, it seemed to be over. Ali had unauthorized access to the other two companies' opchans, and he gave the squad a blow-by-blow.

Apparently, however, a dozen or so of the enemy managed a retreat to escape being captured, and nobody seemed quite sure where they had gone. There weren't any sats footprinting the area, and a wind blowing through the trees messed up the motion sensors or some shit.

Lieutenant Brinkley, who shuffled about, but mostly stayed with the Third Squad, came to where Ali, Omar, and Cutter were.

"Some of the enemy combatants have escaped the net," he said.

Ali, who already knew this, nodded as if it were news. "Sir."

"I think we need to go collect them."

Ali cast a quick glance heavenward—Brinkley didn't catch it—and said, "Sir, if they come this way, we'll have them. They can't wade across that river, they'll have to use the bridge, and come right up the road."

"No, they could spread out along the riverbank there, and it would be hard to capture them."

"Our field of fire covers that pretty well, Lieutenant. They won't get far if they try that."

"We want to capture them alive if we can, Sergeant."

Ali didn't say anything to that.

"They could be valuable sources of intel. So I think it best if we move across the bridge and set up in the woods, there and there." He pointed.

"Sir? I don't see what the tactical advantage would be—"

Brinkley cut him off: "That's why *I'm* the officer, and *you* are the sergeant.

"First Squad will take the point, you will follow them, and Third Squad will bring up the rear."

"Begging the lieutenant's pardon, sir—"

"This isn't a *discussion*, Sergeant Ali, it is an order. We move out in two minutes."

"Yes, sir."

After Brinkley left to speak to the other squads, Ali offered a string of what sounded like Arabic curses. He shifted into Basic and ended with the phrase "shit-for-brains asshole photon-pusher who couldn't find his dick with both hands!"

Cutter said, "Is this a problem for us, Sarge?"

"Nah, just a boneheaded move by a glory hound who wants to polish his brass. It won't matter if we are on this side or that, thirty of us set against a dozen stragglers running to save their asses, we get them either way, but trying to capture them if they do show up might get some of us killed. Don't matter what SOB says, if you see somebody and they point a weapon in your direction, you cancel their ticket, you understand?"

"Yes, Sergeant."

"Good. All right, let's get ready to move."

First Squad was three-quarters of the way across the bridge and Cutter's unit ten meters onto the structure when the shooting started.

Apparently, the remains of the militia were not interested in capturing anybody, and smart enough to know that an exposed bridge was a great place to kill your enemy.

First Squad dropped prone and returned fire, but they were wide open, and the militia had a light machine gun and somebody who knew how to use it.

Cutter saw half the men ahead of him catch rounds and go down, and the hosing kept on.

Cutter's squad shot back, too, but all they could see were muzzle flashes—the militia troops were in the trees.

"Back it up, back it up! Move!" Ali yelled, as the deadly rain spewed past them.

Omar took a round in the throat and fell. Ali bent and grabbed his arm, and Cutter moved over to help—

There was a lot of noise, and time skewed crazily as men screamed and continued to fall.

The fog of war, they called it, insanity loosed—

They were all out in the open here, no concealment, much less cover, and they had to get off the bridge, or they'd get slaughtered—

"Keep going! Across the bridge! Keep going!"

Cutter looked to see Brinkley, waving them on with his sidearm.

Was he out of his fucking mind?

"Fuck me—!" Ali yelled.

Cutter turned, and saw the sergeant go down. A splotch of spreading darkness appeared between the bottom edge of his dorsal armor and the hip plate, centered over his spine—

Cutter had a moment of tachypsychia: Time slowed to a crawl. Sound went away.

There was Brinkley, standing in front of him, waving his pistol. Men were going around him, like a stream around a rock, he was silently bellowing, trying to exhort the remaining members of the squads to go across the bridge, which was already blotched with the dead and dying, and each second more of them joined the fallen.

Brinkley lashed out with his sidearm, hit somebody across the side of the head, knocking him down—

Cutter looked at Omar and Ali. Omar looked dead, and Ali's legs were paralyzed, he could tell. He let go of Omar's arm and grabbed Ali's armor handle and started dragging him—

—Brinkley was suddenly there in front of him, pointing his gun at Cutter.

Sound came back:

"—let him go, get back across the bridge! Now! God-dammit, *now*!"

Cutter had his left hand on Ali's armor handle and his assault rifle in his right hand. He didn't think about it. He reacted. He shoved the weapon forward and triggered it. The recoil rocked it in his single-handed hold, but he was so close he couldn't have missed. The bullet ricocheted off the lieutenant's armor just over his sternum and angled upward, hitting beneath the chin. The lieutenant's helmet lifted from the impact as the round blew through his skull and pierced the helmet.

The man collapsed, brain-dead before he hit the deck.

He dragged Ali off the bridge, and one of the other sergeants got the rest of the platoon under cover.

Of the thirty troops, six were killed and twelve more wounded, but the remaining soldiers were enough to keep the enemy from risking the bridge.

Ten minutes later, Baker Company arrived and wiped out the militia.

In the hospital later, Cutter went to visit Ali.

"Hey, Sarge. Sorry about all this."

"Are you kidding? I'll be here three months while they knit my spine back together, feeling up the nurses, plus another three for rehab, and then two weeks leave with six months back pay. Me, I'll be getting tanked and laid in a posh jukery while you and the squad are getting your asses shot off in some hellhole. Advantage: Ali, all the way."

Cutter chuckled. "Right."

"I owe you, Cutter. Lot of guys would have left me there."

"Would you have been one of them?"

"Hell, who knows? Maybe, maybe not."

"Listen, about the lieutenant."

"That craphead snake-sucker? What about him?"

"Well, you know, how he . . . died."

Ali looked him square in the eyes. "How he died was, he took an enemy round during the engagement. Couldn't have happened to a more deserving asshole, in my considered opinion."

"Sarge—"

"No, Cutter, don't say anything else. Maybe you didn't see it, but I was looking right at him when it happened. It was an enemy round zipped across that bridge and took the man out, only thing it could have been. *That* is how it went down, you understand?"

Cutter nodded. "Thanks, Sarge."

"For what? Send me a vid of them pinning the medal on you. You're a hero, Cutter. You saved a lot of soldiers with your action. Not just me and the guys on the bridge, but anybody SOB would have commanded later."

He hadn't felt like a hero. He'd been scared shitless. But the next few days had been unlike any other. The air had been sweeter, food tasted better, and everything seemed brighter and more imbued with . . . something. He understood the phenomenon, of how almost dying made you appreciate what life had to offer. And it was a potent drug, that feeling. Battle was not glorious. But surviving it? That was.

— — — — — —

It must have been in the air, the memories of first encounters with death. Cutter, half-dozing, heard Singh say something to Jo he couldn't quite make out.

Formentara muttered something in return.

Jo said, "Excuse me?"

Formentara said, *"Neca eos omnes. Deus suos agnoscet."*

Cutter understood that one: Kill them all, God will know his own . . .

Singh looked at Formentara. "You aren't a combatant. You don't kill people."

"Did I say that?"

They looked at hir.

"I'm not a soldier, that's true. But that's not to say I don't have my own story."

"Want to share it?" Gunny asked.

"Sure. Why the hell not?"

They waited expectantly.

— — — — — —

"I grew up on Oceanica, in the big spaceport city Lalau. We lived in the slum district called Papauaa—that translates to 'sty.'

"The summer I turned thirteen, I caught the attention of Limanui, the port's largest flesh peddler.

"The man had three hundred whores working the streets and docks for him, and many of them had not entered into the work voluntarily.

"He was rich, and he was connected. He owned police, judges, politicians, port officials, even the local Army commander was in his pocket, and nobody in Lalau told him no.

"He had a thing for *mahu* not yet of age, and when he saw me, or more likely an image of me somebody showed to him, he wanted me.

"The man could have just had one of his thugs grab me and deliver me to his bed. But the flesh seller was a sadist. It was not enough to simply collect me and rape me; he wanted to season the experience with my terror.

"He commed me. Told me who he was and what he was going to do to me, in great physical detail, and the day and hour it was to happen. And he made it clear that there was nothing I could do about it except to get used to the idea. In a ha'month, he said, I would be his and he would use me every which way, then put me to work at the docks as a whore.

"I was thirteen, my parents were working poor, we had no clout and no recourse. If I told them and they tried to stop it, they would simply be removed, maybe killed. And

I had a younger brother and sister, and I didn't want them to suffer.

"I thought of running, catching a ferry to one of the barrier islands, maybe even stowing away on an orbital lifter, but I realized the first time I went outside our plex that Limanui was having me followed.

"Running wasn't going to happen. Hiding wouldn't work.

"I could maybe get a weapon and try to resist, but against his hired thugs, I would have had little chance.

"I could have killed myself, and I considered it. It was my fallback option.

"What I had going for me was I was smart. I shoved my panic down deep and thought about all the ways I might save myself and my family.

"A deadline looming for rape and slavery does wonders to spark the imagination.

"Once I hit upon an idea, I did the research. I found what I needed, how to do it, and I thought about the best way to effect it.

"My cousin's wife was a clone tech, she worked in a lab making prosthetic implants, most of her work in recreational dentition."

Off of Gunny's look, zhe said, "She made dress teeth. Cosmetic things—fangs, oversizers, jeweled, like that."

Gunny nodded.

"I went to see my cousin-in-law, told her what I wanted and why. She didn't want to do it, but she understood how limited my options were. I was family, so she agreed to help."

"I was accosted on my way to school by Limanui's thug on the date promised. He took me to his master's mansion. I was stripped, searched, made to shower, and led into Limanui's bedroom to await his pleasure.

"He was a big man, fat, beefy, and he expected to find me quivering with terror when he arrived, and that's what

I showed him. He inspected me, turned me this way and that, poked at me, and commanded me to kneel before him.

"I did, crying and begging, which only made him more rampant. He grabbed my head and shoved his penis into my mouth.

"I had already snapped the protective tip off the implanted canine tooth by the time that happened, and the act of biting triggered the tiny hypodermic injector inside, the needle being made of the same ceramic as the tooth so it wouldn't show on a metal scan.

"I didn't have to bite hard at all. Just a little nip.

"He backhanded me hard enough to knock me sprawling, but it was too late. The blue-spider venom I had extracted was under enough pressure so it blasted into his flesh. The needle was on a spring, and it retracted enough so that I wouldn't stick myself on it even though there wouldn't have been any poison left in it by then.

"Before he realized he needed help and could call for it, the venom took him down.

"The blue spider's poison is a fascinating substance—it's both a smooth-muscle paralytic *and* it causes blood to clot.

"My rapist was unable to move, and, after a few minutes, his blood began to thicken. Either his heart infarcted, or a pulmonary embolus blocked a lung, maybe a stroke, any or all of them. It didn't matter to me which.

"He died.

"Once he was gone, and I was sure he was too far to bring back, I opened the bedchamber door, and screamed: 'Heart attack! He's having a heart attack! Help!'

"When the medics showed up, I left with them. I was unarmed, small, they didn't even consider that I had done anything to cause it. By then, the guards didn't care, they were already wondering about their next job.

"Who would notice a tiny wound on a man's prick if they weren't looking for it? An exam wouldn't reveal the

presence of spider venom unless they were specifically looking for that; and so the cause of death was obviously
natural.

"Even rich men kick off from heart disease. Happens all
the time.

"Oh, yes. I recall the first one I killed. It's one of my
fondest memories."

- - - - - -

Nobody had anything to say when Formentara finished.

Hell of a story, hirs.

Nancy finally broke the silence: "Males, Fems, and
Other, we have arrived at our destination, and I hope it won't
be anybody's final one. Local weather is sunny, visibility
twenty kilometers, right at human body temperature out
there, but it's a dry heat. Mind your step as you depart the
hopper, try not to run into the trees, and thank you for flying
Nancy Air. We hope your flight was a pleasant one, and we
hope to see you again real soon."

"You heard the fem," Cutter said. "We're on the clock.
Go. Formentara and I will save your seats for you. Try not
to get your clothes all dirty."

SIXTEEN

Wink was across the table from Kay at the cafeteria when her com buzzed. "*Kluth*fem speaks."

She looked at Wink, pointed at her ear.

Wink activated his com, set no-talk to the same channel. He had it tied into his translator, which was good, because the speaker used the native language.

"—will speak with you. Today, one hour. You may bring your human, no one else."

"Agreed."

The voice—Wink couldn't tell if it was the messenger or not, though it was feminine—said "I remind you of your agreement: No *Sena*, tell no one else."

She rattled off a series of coordinates that Wink didn't understand but that Kay obviously did.

"We will be there."

The com ended.

"Here we go," Wink said. "They didn't say anything about my bringing a hidden pistol."

"No, they did not. Though it would probably be best if you didn't shoot anybody until we find out what we can."

"I'll put in a timed message to Droc. How long should I set the delivery delay?"

"Two or three days."

"That long?"

"If they plan to kill us, chances are we will be dead sooner, and it won't matter to us. If we die, speed won't matter. Droc will call Leeth eventually, and she will find our killers no matter how long it takes. If the meeting is legitimate, that will give us enough time to perhaps circle around and track them."

He shrugged. "Your show."

"Include the coordinates in the message," she said. "Let's finish eating and go, no hurry."

Forty-five minutes later, using a cart, they arrived at the meeting place. Their cart was trackable, and its PPS locator sig would be recorded somewhere if anybody went looking for it.

Which they probably wouldn't, and not for a couple days if they did.

It was a warehouse, in a block of dozens just like it, a squat, single-level building of cheap, off-white preplast, no windows, a rectangular box forty meters by sixty, three meters tall.

There were Vastalimi about, going into and coming out of other buildings. Assorted cargo carriers rolled or fanned by, but their designated structure seemed quiet.

"We didn't beat them here," Wink said.

"Of course not. Whatever they have in mind, they were already set up when they made the call."

Wink resisted the urge to loosen his pistol in its waistband holster or touch his knife's handle in the SOB sheath under his short tunic.

They alighted from the cart and walked across the street. The air had a sharp odor, smelled like some kind of solvent.

The door they approached slid open automatically as they reached it. Kay walked through the entrance as if she owned the place, no hesitation.

Nobody shot at them, leaped from hiding, or otherwise tried to do them harm.

So far, so good . . .

The place was almost empty. There was an office kiosk, the rest of the building, well lighted by solar pass-throughs, held a square table and four chairs. Two of the chairs were occupied by Vastalimi, one male, one female. Neither stood as Wink and Kay approached.

The male gestured at the chairs.

Wink glanced at Kay.

She took the chair to the left and sat, not looking at him as he moved to occupy the chair on the right.

The female spoke, using her own language: "You may call me *Broj*fem. This is *Dvah*masc."

The translator gave it to Wink: Number One and Number Two. Cute.

"You know who we are," Kay said. "You have something to say to me?"

Number One said, "You left our world years ago, and your decision then was smart. We understand why you returned but better that you had not."

"You called us here to tell us things we already know?"

"You are involved in matters deeper and wider than you comprehend. Best for you and your family if you quit the hunt."

"People are dying from an incurable illness, and that includes some of my family," Kay said. "And we both know, by your calling me here, that this is unnatural, so it isn't an unfortunate happenstance but intentional. If you have knowledge of this, better for you to share it now."

"Or what, fem?" Number Two said.

Kay looked at him. "As agreed, *I* have not told the *Sena* of this meeting, but you should know that they are aware of the problem and investigating it. The Shadows' claws carve exceedingly fine."

"The *Sena* do not frighten us," Two said. He smiled. "We know who your sister is."

One said, "Our offer: Leave now, quit your investigation, and live."

"I will not quit."

The Vastalimi exchanged glances.

Two said, "I told you."

"Nothing lost in trying. You should learn that taking the easy path is not always a weakness."

Wink's urge to pull his pistol was overwhelming, and fuck it if it was improper. He carefully allowed his hand to centimeter toward the weapon's butt . . .

"Touch that weapon, and you die, human," One said.

Now she spoke Basic.

"Unless you are a lot faster than I know Vastalimi are, I'll get one of you, at least. Kluth won't be sitting on her hands, either. I like our odds."

"You didn't think we were *alone* in here, did you, human?"

"Wink," Kay said, "leave it. There are three more of them covering us. One in the ceiling, one in the office, another behind the exit to the left. They will have guns."

"Very good, Kluth," One said. "One doesn't expect a Healer to have such sharp senses."

"Sharp senses, but dull wits," Two said. "Now you are nothing but a captured pawn, and you just walked in here and let us take you."

"Did I?"

One said, "Remove your gun, human, and drop it. Carefully—twitch wrong, and you'll be spiked—The People know how to shoot, too."

Wink pulled the pistol from its holster and gently put it on the floor.

"Have you any other weapons?"

"No."

"Put your coms onto the table. Your earbuds, as well."

Both of them did.

"Good. Stand and follow us."

Wink and Kay did as they were told.

— — — — — —

"Relax, Singh," Gramps said. "Everything is on schedule."

"I am okay, sah. The plan is sound."

"And won't survive first contact with the enemy," Gunny said.

They had their helmet face shields up and were off com, to make sure nothing leaked for the Masbülc unit to hear. If their intel was correct, and Formentara was the one getting it, so it damn sure was correct, there were a couple heavy platoons moving in, sixty troops, with some light APC and carts and a couple of drones. More than enough to knock over some big vans full of vegetables, stupidly guarded only by a squad.

"When they get here, we'll give them a chance to lay down their weapons and surrender," Jo said. "Once we get them in our sights, of course. In case they make the wrong choice."

"Do you think they will surrender, sah?"

Jo shrugged. "Probably not. They are paid to fight, not to give up, and they will likely assume it's some kind of trick by a force they think they have outmanned and outgunned. In their place, I'd need to see some proof. Any luck, by the time they see enough to convince 'em, we'll own them."

"You are all so calm."

"No, we ain't," Gunny said. "We just have more practice looking that way."

Jo said, "There's the pulse from Formentara. Ten minutes. Helmets down and lock and load."

"I don't understand that term," Singh said. "Shouldn't it be 'load and lock'?"

"That's yours, Gramps," Gunny said.

"It predates modern weaponry," Gramps said. "Ancient

flintlock rifles were put on half cock before being charged with powder and shot. You locked an external striker in this position to prevent an accidental discharge. The command hung on even after the weaponry changed."

"Do history afterward, Gramps," Jo said. "We have company coming to call."

"Copy, that." He flipped his face shield down.

— — — — — —

They sat on the bare floor, backs propped against the wall on either side of the room's only door. Unlikely that somebody would step in and give one of them *their* back, but dumber things had happened. They had padded Kay's claws with some kind of locking gloves and slippers, hands and feet, but they had not bothered to search him, which he still found amazing, so he had his knife.

He had told Kay this, and she'd shrugged it off. "You told them you were unarmed."

"And they *believed* me? No search?"

"The idea of *two* handguns probably wouldn't occur to them. Vastalimi who own any sidearms figure one is sufficient. I expect they wouldn't consider you a threat even if they knew you had a knife."

Wink shook his head. "And you don't think they are listening to us?"

"Why bother? We are locked up. Nothing we can *say* will change that."

"You really don't think about things like humans do."

"Why would we?"

"And you don't want me to get those off you?"

"Not yet. We need more information."

After a time, Kay said, "I have not told anyone offworld why I left. Given the circumstances, it seems fair that I should tell you."

"I'm all ears," Wink said.

"There was a male named Zolo. He was old, well respected,

a hunter's hunter. A longtime Council member, and, by all accounts, a scrupulously honest politician. He developed an illness and was hospitalized, diagnosed with Red Fever.

"This is an uncommon and often-fatal sickness, an opportunistic viral pathogen that sometimes takes hold when a patient is injured or debilitated. The virus is common, most of us carry it, and it is harmless most of the time, kept in check by normal flora and fauna.

"Zolo, hunting alone deep into a reach, apparently twisted a knee and broke an ankle chasing prey. It took him two days to limp home, during which time he apparently succumbed to the viral infection.

"He was not my patient. The diagnosis was made, the treatment commenced, and his condition was considered grave.

"I had patients in the *bolnica* wherein Zolo was undergoing care. I knew his Healer slightly, a fem of considerable skill. She was doing what could be done, the prognosis was not good, and Zolo, who was in and out of a coma, had said his good-byes to his family and friends.

"Old people die, and Red Fever has a high mortality rate. Death comes, one shrugs, that's how it goes.

"Of a morning as I was making my rounds, I passed Zolo's room—he rated a private space—and chanced to glance in as I walked by. I got a good look at him in his bed."

She paused. "Do you know why my brother asked me to come home?"

"I understood that you were considered an excellent Healer."

"Yes, and mostly for an odd reason. Do you know the term *intuicija*?"

"No."

"It means something like 'clear sight,' though this is an idiomatic use. It is a relatively rare phenomenon among Healers. There have been theories put forth as to its cause, but no one knows for certain why or how it works. What happens is, a Healer can look at an ill patient and immediately know what the problem is."

"Augenblick," he said.

She regarded him, head turned to one side. "I don't know this term."

"The blink of an eye," he said. "A word used among humans for the same medical abilities. One of my professors had it; he could now and then walk into a room, look at a sick person, and *know* what was wrong with them."

"Ah. I did not know that humans could do this."

"So you have this ability."

"Yes. It is erratic, unpredictable, and infrequent.

"When I saw Zolo, I knew that he had been poisoned." Wink nodded.

"I spoke to his Healer. She thought that I was mistaken. There was clear evidence of the viral pathogen in Zolo's system, in sufficient amounts to be considered the clinical illness."

"But secondary to the poison?" Wink offered.

"That is what I offered. The Red Fever was a complication but not the primary cause. Because the diagnosis was made immediately, nobody thought to look for anything else.

"So the question became, if he was poisoned, what was it?"

"And," Wink added, "if it was accidental or deliberate?"

"That was something for the Shadows to worry about," she said. "My concern was for the patient. However, the idea that somebody might have intentionally poisoned Zolo was a matter of some delicacy. He had powerful enemies and powerful friends, and the balance between various factions in the Vastalimi government and industry was—and still is—precarious. Family, pack, they are all entwined and sometimes complicated. A step this way, a half step that way? There might come a collapse that could ruin thousands, send dozens to prison.

"A small stone tossed into the sea there might swell to a tsunami there."

Wink nodded. "Lot of that going around among humans, too."

"As a Healer, my concern was for the patient. I was young, sometimes righteous in my views, and I insisted that a search for the poison be done. Maybe he was too far gone, maybe the fever would kill him, but it was possible that the poisoning could be treated and if so, that might make the difference. And later, the Shadows could sort those who had done what and mete out appropriate justice."

She paused. "Poison scans came back negative, at first. A few days later, Zolo went to hunt on the Other Side. But I had raised the question, and there were people who had good reason to wish that it had not been raised. An old Vastalimi had gotten hurt and developed Red Fever and died, that was the story they wanted everybody to believe, and there was no place for a young Healer ranting on about poison; they didn't want anybody digging through that offal.

"So whispers began. Evidence disappeared. Zolo's body was quickly cremated, pursuant to a request that nobody remembered him making.

"It was made clear to me that if I stayed on Vast and continued to prattle on about poison, stirring up muck that did not need to be stirred, that I and my family would be made to suffer. My relatives, say, would suddenly be Challenged every time they stepped outside. The chances of our having fatal accidents would rise. Doors that had been open in this business or that would close. If, however, I were to find that I wished to pursue opportunities offworld? There would be no repercussions to my family for my mistaken view that one old male had been poisoned."

Wink shook his head. "That's fucked-up."

She shrugged. "I was in the wrong place at the wrong time. The best thing was for me to leave, so I left.

"We have an expression," she said. *"Tzit dogoditi se."*

He raised an eyebrow.

"Shit happens."

"I hear that." Then, "Wait, you said, the poison scans came back negative *at first*?"

"I had some friends who could keep their jaws closed who would help," she said. "I had some tissue samples. There were trace amounts of *sivotro* in the plasma. Not a substance that occurs naturally as such, distilled from a kind of rare earth, debilitating and fatal in tiny amounts. A minute dose could certainly put a person into a state where an opportunistic pathogen could step in and complete the job."

"So you had real evidence."

"Which would have been as useful as spitting into a windstorm and caused my friends no small grief if they were willing to stand up and offer it. No point in asking them to do that, there were too many forces who would claim the test had been altered or faked."

"So you were screwed."

"Tzit dogoditi se," she said.

He hesitated to say it, but having heard this much, Wink was curious, so he did: "And how does Jak fit into the story? Other than his uncle."

She blinked at him. "Why would you think he does?"

He said, "I sat in the *bolnica* cafeteria for meals every day, surrounded by Vastalimi who didn't realize I could hear and understand most of what they said." He tapped at his ear, indicating the missing earbud. "I think it amuses them to talk about us, with me sitting right there smiling and looking like a dull ape.

"Jak's name has come up a few times."

She whickered softly. "Always a mistake to underestimate you humans.

"Jak. Jak and I shared sleep mats, on our way to becoming mates when this happened. He was in medical administration at the time, which is how we met, in the *bolnica*.

"Naturally, when this happened, I told Jak all about it.

"His counsel was to pack up and lift, leaving Vast behind. He would, he said, miss me beyond measure, but it was the best thing for all concerned."

Wink didn't say anything.

"At the time, I thought he was the voice of reason. It was later that I realized his motives might be less concern about me and my pack than for his own fur. His association with me would put him at some risk, more so were I to stay on Vast. There might be some liability for the *bolnica* were it determined that a highly respected Vastalimi's treatment was in error. Jak had ambitions, and a mate in disgrace would be a stumbling block to those.

"In retrospect, that was one of the best things to come from all of this, that Jak and I did not become legally mated. I believe I would have eventually come to realize what kind of person he is, but it might have cost me dearly in time and energy before I did.

"Even a killing storm waters the grass."

Wink nodded. He would have said something else, but Kay snapped her gaze away from him at the room's door. He never heard the footsteps approaching before the door opened.

It was Two. He held a pistol. "Step out, Kluth, and move slowly and carefully. Twitch, and you die. Human, you will stay here."

Kay stood. She flicked a glance at Wink, then moved out.

The door shut behind her.

He waited for a moment, then stood, walked to the door, put his ear to it.

Nothing to hear.

He had already examined the lock, and it was simple, old-tech, obviously installed in a hurry from something they had on hand. No knob had been left on the inside, but the latch was a simple spring-loaded bar that snicked into place when the door was closed. No electronics, nothing. Even a simple dead bolt would have been much better, but without tools, the spring latch would have been sufficient. With Kay's claws being padded, she wouldn't have been able to get at the latch, or to rip through the door or walls, and human fingers wouldn't do the trick, so their captors would have had it covered.

He could open it. He had already told Kay that, but she had said they should hold off for a while, to wait and see what happened.

Now seemed like a good time.

— — — — — —

The Vastalimi might be all about honor, but for Wink, honor was tied up with survival. The female guard with her back to him might kill him and Kay if she got the notion, and while they'd taken his pistol, he had his knife.

That still amazed him. They asked him if he had any more weapons, and either they believed him when he said he didn't or didn't consider him dangerous if he did. *Human? A threat? Please!*

He had the knife in a saber grip, ready. Opening the door had been easy, all of six seconds, to stick the point into the latch and slide it clear. No guard watching it.

Skulking through the building was a little harder, but he had taken his time. They had better hearing and senses of smell to go along with the superior vision. Quiet and careful was necessary.

The guard was concentrating her attention elsewhere, her own pistol holstered, and she didn't hear or sense him coming until too late. Her turn at the last quarter second actually helped him—the tip of his blade sank in between her fifth and sixth cervical vertebra and her motion made the cut for him, all he had to do was hang on to the knife.

She fell, cord severed, paralyzed from the neck down.

There were advantages to being a surgeon, and knowing where to cut was one of them. And this was a good technique by its nature.

No longer any threat there.

He took the pistol from her nerveless fingers. It was not a model he knew, but the operation seemed simple even enough: He stroked the magazine-eject panel, a double-touch. The magazine dropped into his other hand. It held fifteen darts. They were probably poisoned, maybe with nonfatal shocktox, but that didn't matter. He reinserted the magazine. A green diode lit on the pistol's butt. No external safety—must be in the trigger itself.

Now. He needed to go find Kay and pot some kidnappers. With any luck, they'd eat darts before they knew what had hit them.

He considered the downed guard. He had no scruples against killing an enemy, which this one certainly was; still, it wasn't necessary. The cord could be fixed, and eventually she'd regain use of her body below the cut though it would take several months, were she a human. He and Kay would be probably long gone when this fem became functional.

Then again, the injured Vastalimi had been part of kidnapping them, and likely set to kill his friend once they'd tortured her for whatever information they thought she had.

Dead enemies didn't come looking for you later.

He moved to the side to avoid the arterial spray, leaned down, and nicked both carotids, zip, zip, easy as that. The Vastalimi's expression, not something he was all that adept at reading, seemed surprised. He said, "If you are captured by the enemy, don't let them give you to the humans. We aren't quite as harmless as everybody thinks. Take that with you to your Other Side."

He wiped the blade off on her fur away from the pumping blood flow. Sheathed the knife, and stood.

Without a com, he would just have to do it the old-fashioned way and find Kay himself. And shoot anybody who got in his path.

He was done being the quiet and docile human here. It was time to break shit and raise hell.

SEVENTEEN

Jo was ten meters ahead of the others when the enemy mercs realized they really were being attacked by a superior force. She was running every useful aug she had, she had the suit, and she was fast, but they weren't blind, and at least a few of them had decent combatware on the clock.

It didn't matter for the first one, she was too far ahead of his response curve. She fired her carbine, one shot, and the tiny rocket impacted with his breastplate armor and blew a hole through it, shattering his sternum and rupturing the heart beneath it. He never got a round off—

The second soldier whipped his own carbine around and triggered a burst, but Jo was already in the air in a high, forward flip over and *above* the incoming, tucking tight for speed, and coming down heels first onto the man's shoulders, knocking him flat.

Her proprioception aug let her land in perfect balance. Damn, that was great!

Before he had a chance to recover, she fired two

rounds into his body, and he was done, too, and KMA, friend—

Carbine fire from behind her took down the next merc, and Jo had time to see the impact of the round on his face-plate as it blew up, along with a goodly part of the head behind it.

Gunny, taking head shots because she could?

More fire from both sides. A round glanced off her shoulder plate, denting the soft ceramic but not punching through. The ricochet screamed away into the forest, dopplering into silence.

Another incoming small-arms round blew past her head, two centimeters away, maybe, and whistled as it went.

The temptation was to hose, to spray-and-pray, and chances were at this distance that would do some serious damage, but it was never a good idea to run your weapon dry in a fire zone unless you were sure you had taken all the enemy out. Given the terrain and conditions, it would be hard to tell if there were shooters hidden and waiting for a weapon to click empty.

Jo indexed a short figure—looked female—and did another double tap. The figure spun and sank to the ground, triggering off a long burst of full auto from her weapon but pointed too high to hit any of Jo's team.

"To the left!" Singh yelled.

Jo was already aware of the three mercs in that quadrant, but they were scrambling for cover and not aiming as they threw rounds in her general direction. She dropped low— panicked fire tended to start high and climb higher—and aimed low, sweeping her weapon from left to right, targeting legs just above the tops of their midcalf boots. The boots would be armored, but between the knee and boot, a lot of people didn't bother, considering that too small a target to worry about. Not that overlap-joint armor would stop what she was throwing anyway, but still—

Now she let the carbine run full auto. She had a sixty-round magazine, and she'd used only four rounds, she could afford ten or fifteen on a sweep. She moved it in a short arc, relaxed her finger on the trigger—

All three went down with shattered shins and knees—

Jo came up, sprinted, and hurdled the downed mercs, looking for the command cart—

Behind her, her team grabbed the three wounded mercs who might have the wherewithal to keep resisting even with their legs shot out from under them. They'd give them field first aid and try to keep them alive.

"Down!" Gunny yelled, and Jo dropped prone, skidding on the damp ground—

Somebody ahead opened up with a light machine gun, the hard chatter of a 10mm spewing jacketed hail in her direction but passing over her at chest height.

How had Gunny known?

She saw the muzzle flashes, but not the gun itself, fifty-plus meters ahead, shrouded by the dense woods.

She indexed the flashes. No more mercs in sight, might as well finish off the mag.

Jo hosed the target until the carbine ran empty. Some of her rounds hit something hard enough to create sparks. Didn't see that often, even with jacketed.

Somebody screamed. The fifty went quiet.

She tapped the electronic eject button twice and shoved a fresh magazine into the well. It seated and whined, and the round counter lit: 60, then blinked off. Probably she should tape over that, lot of troops did, so the LED wouldn't give them away, but it wasn't likely anybody would see the brief green flash, and besides, it wasn't as if anybody was going to be worried about shit like that now . . .

Say, did you see that little green light?

Why, no, I must have missed it while I was busy watching a fucking assault team spray bullets at us!

She heard a motor start. That would be the command cart retreating.

Jo came up and sprinted, her augmented muscles and nervous system driving her body to a speed the best unaugmented runner who ever lived couldn't begin to match.

—there, just ahead and to the left, *there* was the cart—!

The cart's gunner was gone and the fifty pointing skyward, but they might have a bot shooter, so she couldn't assume the gun wasn't in play anymore.

Her carbine would punch through some body armor, but not the stressed plate on a command cart. Wouldn't hurt the solid-body tires, either, and she didn't want to use a grenade on it because she wanted the CO alive if possible. She'd have to stop it somehow.

The road was dirt, packed down from use. Jo pulled a grenade, thumbed the safety up, and tapped the timer. *Four . . . three . . . two . . .*

She threw the grenade over the cart. It arced, fell, and went off just as it reached the road five meters in front of the vehicle—

The blast threw up a blinding shower of dirt and blew a half-meter-deep, two-meter-wide crater into the road.

The driver instinctively veered to the right, the turn sharp enough to tilt the cart. The low center of gravity kept it from going over—until the back wheel slipped into the grenade's crater. That did it. The cart tipped, rolled, landed on its side, engine roaring, drive wheels on the passenger side spinning—

"Gotcha, asshole!"

Gunny ghosted into view, carbine held ready. "We all done back there," she said, "five by five." She looked at the cart lying on its side. "You get us a prize, Jo?"

"I believe so. Let's go see."

From her earbud, Cutter's voice: "Aren't you done out there yet?"

"We decided to stop and have some lunch before we came home. Fighting makes you hungry, Rags."

"So I dimly recall."

"Maybe next time," Jo said.

"Yeah, sure."

– – – – – –

The building was larger than the warehouse in which they'd been captured, with individual rooms. Kay's claws were top and bottom still bound, but the bigger problem was the sturdy chair into which she was securely strapped.

One and Two were in the room with her, and Two kept popping his claws in and out in anticipation.

"What say, Kluth?" he said. "An ear membrane first? An eye?"

Kay said, "What does it matter? You'll kill me soon enough. Being blind or deaf when I die? So what?"

"Brave talk. We'll see how long it lasts."

One said, "Yes, you die, but you can make it hard or easy, your choice. We can dart you. We can slash your neck arteries, and you can bleed out, relatively painlessly."

"Dead is dead. Why should I make your task any easier?"

One shook her head. "You understand we need to know everything you know and that you will tell us eventually."

Kay was listening intently. Nothing yet.

"Eventually, the universe goes cold and collapses to start anew."

"Unlike my comrade, I get no pleasure in another's pain. Tell us what we need to know, swear it is true, we'll make it quick."

"Fuck your father."

One looked at Two. He said, "They were right—we might as well be talking to the chair. But she will change her song." He snicked out his forefinger claw and waved it back and forth. "I bet I can jab this finger into a tender spot and wiggle my talon enough to make you scream like a cub."

She told him where he could insert that finger.

He laughed. "Oh, I shall enjoy this so much!"

Kay finally heard the sound for which she had been listening. "No, you won't. Two only, please," she said in Basic.

Both of the Vastalimi looked at her. Two frowned. "What?"

The door opened behind them. They turned to see what the guard wanted, only it wasn't the guard—

Wink fired before he stepped into the room. The male Vastalimi who called himself Two took the dart in the throat. He spasmed, fell, and jittered on the floor.

"Kay wants you alive," Wink said to the female, "but I don't have any problem killing you. That'll bring my total up to five for the day. Free her, or I'll fucking shoot you and do it myself."

Once Kay was out of the chair and on her feet, she said, "Unbind my hands."

One nodded, but her claws popped out and she lunged for Kay—

"Wink, don't—!"

Wink fired three times—*pap-pap-pap!*—and the fem went down—

"Tzit!"

Wink came over to help Kay free her hands and feet.

"There will be a magnetic key in her belt purse."

Wink nodded, opened the small case, found the key. He freed Kay's hands. She took the key and bent to remove the slippers.

"I wanted this one alive," she said.

"Sorry. I wanted *you* alive."

"She knew that. It's why she did it. Any of the other guards survive?"

"Not any I saw. I stabbed one, shot two others. Far as I can tell, that's all there were in the building."

"Done is done. We'll have to collect or follow whoever comes to check on these."

"You think somebody will?"

"Yes. They will wonder why nobody has checked in. Someone will come eventually."

"Should we call Leeth?"

"No. Nothing has changed. We still need to know who is behind this, and we need a trail. We'll find a place to hide and watch."

— — — — — —

The officer in the captured command vehicle was a captain, and while Cutter didn't recognize him, the man was an experienced ex-Army man who had some common experiences.

"Captain Tharp."

"Colonel."

"You want a drink?"

"Sure. Whaddya got? Beer?"

Cutter nodded. He pulled a plastic stein from the bin, peeled the top off. The release of pressure foamed the liquid, and the chiller built into the base cooled it quickly.

Tharp sipped at the brew. "Ah. Thanks."

"You're welcome. So, are we going to be able to talk?"

"Usual protocols," Tharp said. "I can't give up any tactical stuff, no real intel. You know how it goes."

Cutter nodded. "I respect that."

"That was well played, your trap. We thought you'd screwed up, that decoy barge was so obvious."

"Win some, lose some."

Tharp nodded. "Yeah, you kicked our asses pretty good. What's the drill, Colonel?"

"Nothing mighty. You go back to your new CO, tell him he's now outgunned and outnumbered, and that if he pulls out, we won't chase you. Two-hour window, so nobody has time to import any new troops. We'll channel the wounded to local hospitals, collect the dead, and put them wherever he wants, all within legal RoE. If not, we roll over you."

Tharp nodded.

"Think he'll go for it?"

Tharp shrugged. "I don't know the guy, he just got here, but he's old-school, and he seems to know his shit. It doesn't take a weatherman to see which way the wind is blowing. If he's as good as I think, yeah, he'll sign a Term-of-Surrender and beat a strategic retreat. Doesn't mean somebody won't come back when the ToS clock runs out."

"Crop will be in by then, and gone. Won't do Masbülc any good."

"Masbülc?"

Both men grinned.

"Finish your beer, Captain, and I'll have somebody drop you at your camp."

"I don't expect you'll need directions?"

"Nope."

Tharp raised the half-empty stein. "Always nice to do business with an old pro, sir."

Cutter nodded. Yes, it was.

They'd have to stick around for a while, make sure Masbülc didn't try to hustle another SoF unit in or spread this unit around to go guerrilla, but Cutter didn't think they would. It was all about timing, and this ship had essentially sailed. A few more weeks, they'd be done here and off to the next job. As easy as anything they'd done lately. That was good.

EIGHTEEN

Wink said, "You still don't want to call your sister?"

"No. Nothing has changed."

He nodded.

They were in an empty building that allowed them a view of the one in which they had been held. Wink had made a run for supplies, food and water and a couple of padded mats upon which to sleep. Kay didn't seem to mind the bare floor, but Wink preferred some padding these days.

It had only been a day since their escape, not quite that, but they were set up for at least another two or three, should it take that long, after which he could make another supply run.

As it turned out, that wasn't going to be necessary.

A cart arrived at the building under surveillance, and a quartet of Vastalimi alighted. They were all males, and three of them were obviously muscle; they were large, moved well, and were armed with handguns.

One of them carried a backpack.

Those three approached the entrance with care, while the fourth one held back, watching.

Hickory, Dickory, and Doc . . .

The trio split—Hickory and Dickory went inside, Doc stood near the door, waiting. They had handheld coms, and the one by the door used his.

After three minutes, Doc nodded at the one who was obviously the boss, and the two of them entered the building.

The theory was that they'd have a look at the dead Vastalimi and do something about them. Haul away the bodies themselves, or call somebody. Either way, they'd depart eventually, and somebody being careful could follow them if they happened to have their own cart parked nearby, which Wink and Kay did. After that?

Well, to make *smeerp* stew, first you have to catch a *smeerp* . . .

After twenty minutes, the four exited the building, hurried to the vehicle, and drove away.

Wink and Kay ran to their own cart. Something bothered Wink, but he couldn't put his finger on what it was.

"They'd didn't try to remove the bodies," Wink said.

"Maybe somebody is coming later," Kay said.

But when they were only a half klick or so away, there came a loud explosion from behind them.

The backpack. None of the four carried it back out, that's what he'd noticed. "Want to bet that's why they were in such a hurry?" Wink said.

Kay nodded. "A large bomb obscures a lot of evidence."

NINETEEN

A few more days, week, maybe, this would be wrapped up, a snoozer of a job. Jo preferred more action and uncertainty, but the odd easy stroll was good for business and morale. If you got paid, got leave, and none of your friends were killed, there was something to be said for that.

She was in the gym, working on her tumbling. She was practicing a front flip with a walkout. She came down, then caught sight of Singh in the doorway.

"What's up, Singh?"

"Gunny sent me, sah, to tell you that you have a visitor."

"A visitor?"

"Yes, sah."

"And the visitor is . . . ?"

He shook his head. "Gunny told me to tell you that she is making popcorn."

Jo frowned. What was he talking about?

She wiped her face and neck with a towel. "Well, let's go see."

A couple of nervous-looking newbie guards stood on this

side of the gate with their carbines at low ready; outside the gate stood Mish, the Vastalimi.

Jo walked over.

"Em."

"Jo Captain."

"What can I do for you?"

"My unit has packed up and is awaiting transport to ship in orbit, but you and I have a match to finish," Em said.

Jo nodded. Of course. She should have expected this.

She glanced around.

Gunny, Gramps, Formentara, and Rags stood in the shade of the Op Center behind her, leaning against the wall or standing with arms crossed, watching.

Gunny waved.

"Popcorn," Jo said. She shook her head.

"Let our visitor in," Jo said to the guards.

"Captain?"

"Open the gate. And put those carbines away, you won't need them. If Em here had evil on her mind, she could have come over the fence and taken you both out, and neither of you would have gotten a useful shot off."

The two guards glanced at each other nervously. One of them tapped a shirt pad on his left shoulder. The gate slid open.

Em walked through.

"Same as before," Em said. She looked around.

"If you win, you walk away, nobody bothers you," Jo said.

Em whickered. "*If* I win?"

Jo smiled back. "Yeah, I suppose that is unlikely."

Now the whicker turned into a deeper laugh. "I like you, human. I don't say that much about your species."

"And yet you work with us."

"I get to see the galaxy, and the prey can shoot back. Keeps it interesting."

Already in her workout tights and her muscles warm, Jo said, "You want to loosen up?"

"Not necessary."

"Pardon me if I'm unfamiliar with the proper ritual," Jo said. "Do we need to make our declarations again?"

"The match began at our base, it is not yet done. No need to repeat anything." She lowered her center of gravity. "When you are ready."

Jo raised one hand in a hold-it gesture, and called out: "Em and I are going to dance. If I lose and can't get up? She walks away, nobody stops her."

She looked at Em. "They'll honor it."

Em nodded. She edged closer.

Jo relaxed and settled a bit lower in her own stance. Normally, a Vastalimi would open with a leap, but since they both had experience with how each other's species fought, Jo wasn't banking on that. If Em moved within her range, which was greater than that of an unaugmented human and not quite as great as a Vastalimi's, Jo would attack, but her training with Kay had shown her that augmentations notwithstanding, she was still slower than Kay.

Technique that depended on speed went to the faster fighter.

Technique that depended on power went to the stronger fighter.

If you were slower and weaker, you couldn't go there; instead, you used form and position. If your skills with those were good enough, you could beat faster and stronger fighters all day. If—

Em danced in, not a leap but a stutter step designed to draw Jo's response—

Jo didn't bite. She held her position, waiting

Em turned the attacking step into a bias move, skirting Jo's range and bypassing to Jo's left—

Jo shifted her weight forward and V-stepped to cut the distance—

Em saw it and lashed out with a low side kick—

Jo stopped, and her proprioceptive aug nailed her balance

perfectly. Em's heel was two centimeters shy of her knee. *She's on one foot—*

Jo sprang, tucked into a tight ball, and did a half somersault, opened and snapped her right leg out in a thrust kick—

Em didn't expect that. She dodged to her left but not quite enough, and Jo's foot slapped into Em's right shoulder and knocked her off-balance—

Em went with it, threw a backflip, a loose pike. Slower than a tuck, but faster than a layout to a stance, and more stable—

Jo charged, feet churning, knew she'd get there in a left lead, and had her right knee coming up when she was close enough—

Em saw the knee coming, knew it would be too hard to block and she wouldn't be able to dodge—

Got you—!

But Em fooled her—she came in, hopped up, and put her lead foot onto Jo's knee, and used the force of the strike to leap high into the air and *over* Jo's head. She'd land several meters away behind Jo, that was brilliant—

Except that Jo realized it in time and as Em took off, Jo caught her right ankle with both hands and held on—

Em's momentum was great, but Jo got a good grip, and her weight was more than enough. Em's flight stopped, turned into a fall. She tried to kick with her other foot to get loose, but Jo twisted and dropped, hung on to Em's ankle, and Em flew outstretched facedown onto the ground—

Em managed a bit less than a quarter turn, to land not quite on her face, but not quite on her side.

It was rather like swinging a heavy flail and slamming it onto the ground.

The force was terrific. Enough to knock the breath and most of the consciousness from the Vastalimi.

Jo let go, scrabbled over the fallen Em, and snaked her arm around her throat.

Stunned as she was, Em managed to grab at the choke.

She also extruded her claws, which bit deeply into Jo's forearm—

Too late. Jo's pain dampers kicked in; the carotid hold did the trick. Em went out, the claws retracted, and Jo rolled away. Her arm oozed blood from where eight of Em's claws had pierced it, but all the wounds were on the dorsal side, and no big bleeders had been cut. Easy to glue shut.

After a few seconds, Em regained consciousness. She sat up, turned to face Jo.

"Your match," she said. She noticed the bleeding. "I apologize for the extrusion. It was reflexive."

Jo nodded. "A fair fight."

Em shook her head. "They won't believe this around the fires. Probably serve me better not to speak of it."

"I won't tell if you don't," Jo said.

Em whickered. "A fair match and an honorable opponent."

Jo got to her feet, watched Em do the same.

"Going to rejoin your crew?"

"I think not. My contract was for this engagement only. Might you have an opening here? It seems I have things to learn."

Cutter seemed to appear as if by magic next to Jo. "You're hired," he said.

Em looked at him, then at Jo.

Jo nodded.

"Terms?" Em said.

"We can discuss those, but whatever you were getting before, we'll match."

"Even though I was defeated by a human here in front of you?"

"Jo's not your average human."

"So I have seen."

"Colonel?"

Rags turned. Gramps stood there. "We have a message you need to hear."

The image was compressed for delivery across the parsecs, and when it expanded, it was a little grainy and fuzzy until the computer program rectified it, but the Vastalimi centered in the frame was clear enough in his speech.

When he was done—it was a one-way only—Cutter and his crew looked at each other.

"That's Kay's brother?"

"We have no reason to believe otherwise," Cutter said. "He's telling us what Kay told us before she left."

"Well, shit," Gunny said.

"They have been missing for a couple of days."

"Reckon somebody collected 'em?"

"Or killed them," Jo put in. "In which case, there's not anything we can do."

Em, who had been invited in to see the message, said, "If there was a point to be made by killing them, then it is likely their bodies would have turned up already."

"So if they are still alive, we might be able to do them some good," Cutter said.

Gramps said, "It's three weeks and some from here to there. We might be really late to the party."

Cutter looked around. "Not if we take The Chomolungma Shortcut."

Gramps blinked. Nobody else said anything.

After a bit, Singh, the least-traveled among them, said, "What is this shortcut?"

Jo said, "Back in the late twentieth and early twenty-first centuries on Earth, there were commercial companies that offered a climbing adventure for tourists, an ascent of Mount Everest. That name comes from the man credited with surveying the hill's height. All the locals who could see it from different regions had their own names for it: It is also known as *Sagarmatha*, *Zhūmùlǎngmǎ Fēng*, and *Chomolungma*.

"This is the tallest mountain on Terra and visible for a long way on a clear day.

"At 8850 meters, achieving the summit was, until modern times, a dangerous trek. Weather can go from sunny and mild to stormy and well below freezing in an hour. Recreational climbers had to spend a period of weeks to acclimate themselves to the decrease in oxygen, and even then, supplemental tanks were carried and used by nearly all those attempting an ascent.

"More than a few people died attempting the climb, from exposure, from altitude sickness, from falls, sometimes from exhaustion.

"If you were on a team essaying the trip, and you were seriously injured, you had no recourse for rescue. Aircraft at the time could not safely come and fetch you, and if you fell and died, climbers would simply step over your body, not having the physical ability to pack you down."

"Nice," Gunny said. "Not a 'leave no soldier behind' philosophy, is it?"

"Part of the assumed risk," Jo said. "You knew going in what would happen if you broke your leg or ran out of oxygen, and tough titty.

"The mortality rates were, until the tours were regulated and safety measures made mandatory, about one climber in a dozen. Even after that, one in thirty-five wound up fatal. Plus there were some serious cases of frostbite and altitude sickness."

"Not really good odds," Gramps observed.

"People wanted to take the risk, they still do. There's a restaurant on the peak now, you can fly in, eat ersatz-yak burgers for lunch, and be back at your hotel that afternoon. But people still climb."

"People are crazy," Gramps said.

"No question," Jo said.

"You seem to know a lot about this, sah."

"Well. Yes. I'm crazy, too."

Singh looked at her.

"I made the climb once."

Gramps shook his head.

Jo continued: "When it works, the trip through the peculiar hyperspace called the SST—the Super Subquantum Transit—results in an incredibly fast trip. You can cross half the galaxy in a few days. We still don't know exactly how it works, or why, only that it does.

"Except that one ship in ten that goes in doesn't come out again. *That* is why it is called The Chomolungma Shortcut. It is a high-risk exercise."

She looked at Cutter. "Colonel?"

He said, "So here's the deal. Wink and Kay are in trouble on Vast. A standard hyperspace lane will take us three weeks to get there, by which time they might well be good and dead. If we risk the Chomolungma, we can drop back into NS in seventy-two hours and maybe do them some good.

"Or not. We could get there too late even so. There is a one-in-ten chance we won't make it at all.

"It costs a fucking fortune to hire somebody crazy enough to make the trip. Nobody knows what happens to those ships that don't exit. Maybe they are still in the warp, maybe they came out in some alternate universe, maybe they were vaporized as soon as they entered. So if you don't want to risk it, now's the time to take some R&R."

Gunny laughed. "Who are you talkin' to, Rags? Not any of us. We laugh at Death."

Cutter grinned. "I had to ask."

"With all due respect, the fuck, you did."

Em said, "You would do this for a comrade?"

Cutter said, "In this case, yes. Two weeks ago, we couldn't have left, but we are done here."

"I have found the right humans. Count me in."

"All right. Pack it up. We'll take the shortcut and see what happens."

— — — — — —

"So, where are we?" Wink said.

"Southeast part of the city. A neighborhood of people who are well-off."

"I can see that. Nice dwellings."

"We won't be able to stay here for long," she said. "Rich people are more concerned with losing their possessions. Someone will notice us parked here and wonder why."

Wink nodded. The van had dropped the one they thought was the leader here, and he had gone into a house. They had decided to let the others go and to check this one out.

"So, recon?"

"Yes. But you stay here. Humans won't be common, you'll be noticed. I will be, too, but if I don't stay long, it won't matter."

"Think this is the guy doing it?"

"If not, he is a thread that will lead us further on. And no, I don't want to call my sister."

"What about your brother? He might be worried about us, too. It's been more than two days. He will have missed us."

"Leeth will be monitoring his communications. Droc will survive not knowing.

"I'll be back in a few minutes. Try not to be noticed."

She stepped out of the cart.

— — — — — —

"We are spacing in *that*? That ship looks older than dirt," Gunny said.

Gramps said, "Nah, I believe we created dirt first, then this. But not long after."

Gunny shook her head.

Jo could understand the reaction: The ship did look as if it had been sideswiped by an asteroid and only partially repaired. The hull was dinged and pitted, and there were rainbow patterns that made it look as if the stressed stack had been annealed and retempered. It hung there in the vacuum like a relic from another century, an eighty-meter-long lozenge with rounded and melted edges. She couldn't make out the name at this distance unaided, but a tag floater under the image identified the vessel as the *Elfu Mwaka Valco*.

What did that mean? Jo wondered. "Abandon all hope . . ."?

Formentara said, "I guess the owners figure if it disappears in the Chomolungma, it won't be that much of a loss."

"How much did you pay for our passage again, Rags?" Jo asked.

Cutter shook his head. "Enough so we could probably buy that ship, tear it down, and rebuild it."

"And for that much, what do we get?"

"The pilot has taken that ship into the Void and come out more than a score of times."

"Great. So he's overdue to not come out?"

He held up one hand in Jo's direction. "He's what's available. You are a volunteer, remember."

It was just the seven of them: Rags, Formentara, Gunny, Gramps, Singh, Em, and herself—they'd left the unit back on Far Bundaloh with Lieutenant Atkins in charge. Atkins was an old hand and should have no trouble making sure the harvest was finished before he packed it up and went home.

Cutter said, "I believe I'll go visit the fresher. I don't want to die with a full bladder."

He wandered off.

As they stared at the vessel via the orbit port's viewscreen, Singh leaned over to Jo. "Pardon, sah, but I have heard the colonel referred to by the name 'Rags' several times. Does this have some special meaning I should know?"

Jo grinned. "Gramps tells the story better. All those decades of practice."

Singh looked at Gramps. "Sah?"

The older man smiled. "Ah, yes, the warnom. I wasn't there, you understand, but I have it from somebody who was.

"It was during the Nchi Uprising, on Earth. The colonel was a buck sergeant leading a DGF squad.

"Nchi was one of those short-lived countries on the African continent, used to be Kenya, Uganda, one of those near Lake Victoria. You were a mapmaker in that part of the world back then, you could always be assured of a steady income, the names and borders changed so frequently.

"Um. Anyway, the local warlord started slaughtering the residents, and it slopped over into the country next door. Cutter's DGF—Detached Guerrilla Forces—unit was relatively close, stationed on Comoros, an island in the channel between Mozambique and Madagascar, and somebody decided it was a good idea for the GU to stick its nose into the situation.

"They figured a couple of platoons of the galaxy's finest waving their hardware would scare the warlord enough so he'd stop shooting.

"Surprise, surprise, they were wrong. Guy was apparently crazy, and he threw everything he had at them. The end was never in question—the Galactic Union Army is never outgunned, certainly not by some pissant thug in the backwoods; however, there was a communications snafu, and Cutter's squad was cut off from the rest of his platoon and surrounded by a goodly chunk of the warlord's army. Dozen rifle toters against maybe a hundred Nchians, armed with everything from assault rifles to vehicle-mounted machine guns and mortars.

"Cutter called Support for a salvo of smart missiles, but somebody dropped the ball on that, and they were getting the crap shot out of them.

"They were in a town that recycled and refabbed a lot of clothes for export, cotton, hemp, natural fibers, like that. Cutter led his squad past one of the garment-recycling factories toward what looked like a thin spot in the enemy's lines.

"They were almost there when somebody in Missile Support finally woke up and sent a spray of rockets in their general direction. The rockets did clear out a nice gap in the line, but one of them strayed and hit the recycling plant, blew it to kingdom come.

"There were apparently tons of old clothes waiting for the refabber slung in all directions, and a big smoldering clump of them fell right on top of Cutter and buried him.

"When the action cleared enough to see, Cutter had vanished.

"The enemy troops on the ground were closing in, and the GU squad was still looking, but they couldn't find their sergeant.

"Now, what you need to know is, these Nchians were a superstitious bunch. They had a legend regarding mythical ancient creatures of the forest they called the Matambaa. According to the stories, these creatures were immortal, manlike, shaggy, covered with moss and whatnot, and if one of them caught you, you'd get dragged straight to their version of Hell to be tortured for all eternity.

"So Cutter, buried under a two-meter pile of shredded, still-burning fabrics, dug his way out, more pissed off than scared, cursing up a storm.

"Just as he cleared the pile, all wrapped up in smoking shirts and sheets and the like, beating at them with his hands to try and put out the remaining bits still on fire, the half dozen Nchians running point arrived.

"They saw him. One of them yelled, 'Matambaa! Matambaa!' and the six hit the brakes, spun around, and hauled ass.

"Cutter's squad was near enough to catch the action, they saw the fleeing soldiers screaming in terror as Cutter appeared.

"As it turned out, in the Nchian language, 'matambaa' means 'rags.'"

Singh grinned. "Ah. That's a good one."

"Might not be true," Gunny said. "But you never let truth stand in the way of a great story . . ."

They looked at the ship hanging there in space.

"Ten to one in our favor," Formentara said.

"We've gone places where the odds were worse," Jo said.

"Gravity always wins in the end," Em said.

— — — — — —

The pilot who met them at the transfer lock was a raffish-looking man of maybe thirty. He was average height, had longish hair, and was well built under a thin, white, long-sleeved shirt. Over that he wore a sleeveless vest, with dark silk pants tucked into ship-soft jump boots, and he had a pistol slung low on his right hip. The holster looked like leather, or a pretty good imitation of it, a warm and dark brown, and there was a strap near the muzzle that looped around his leg just above the knee.

He glanced at Em, and if seeing a Vastalimi board his ship bothered him, Gunny couldn't tell it.

Gunny looked at the holster. Come on. Guy must think he's some kind of fast-draw expert, strapped down that way.

The weapon puzzled her. The butt looked to be some kind of dark wood, inset into a bright blue frame. Was that metal? The piece had a kind of stretched-open S-shaped shiny rod jutting out a couple of centimeters from a rounded section above the butt. External hammer. The trigger guard, trigger, and that back piece all appeared to be the same kind of bright blue material. The rest of it was covered by the holster.

"Interesting weapon," she said.

"You must be 'Gunny,'" he said. "I am Mão Unico, at your service. Here, have a look."

The gun appeared in his hand almost as if by magic, and Gunny resisted the sudden urge to draw her own weapon. Too late . . .

She revised her opinion. He *was* fast.

He twirled the sidearm around in his grip and extended it to her butt first.

She didn't know what it was, but she could see it was either a real antique or a good copy of a cowperson weapon, right out of a prespace historical drama.

"A revolver," she said. It was heavy, probably twice the weight of her own pistol.

He grinned, showing nice teeth. "Good. Almost nobody gets that much."

"It's steel. How did they achieve that color? Anodizing?"

Unico said, "Not anodizing, it predates that. It depends on the polish beforehand. The polish, and different metals, give you various shades. The metal is put into an oven and heated, with the color coming from a fuel mix of charcoal—that's partially burned wood—and types of animal bone. It's not just decorative, but also helps protect the metal from further oxidation. This particular weapon also predates stainless steel, so it needed a coating to slow rust."

"Really? Predates stainless?"

"Yes. It is a Colt Pocket Model percussion revolver, .31 caliber—that's just under 8mm. The octagonal barrel is four inches—about ten centimeters—long. Made in NorAm circa 1849.

"Not the original finish, of course, I redo it myself every couple of years. I could plate it with a modern protectant, but that would be cheating."

"In 1849? That's old-style dating from what, three hundred years before spaceflight?"

"Close enough."

"What kind of ammunition does it use?"

"Originally, it was a deflagrating chemical propellant called black powder. Predates smokeless gunpowder. I could make the original, but it's messy and creates a lot of smoke on ignition, so I use a substitute called Pyrodex."

"Look at her, she's like a child in a candy kiosk," Gramps said.

"Hush, old man. Go on."

Unico said, "Each of the chambers in the cylinder—there are five of them—is like a miniature cannon. While the weapon is assembled, you measure the proper amount of propellant into each chamber, muzzle pointed skyward. Then you push a lead ball down on top of that—I don't use lead, of course, but a malleable stacked ceramic that approximates the density and weight. There's a little rod under the barrel there, see, a lever that lines up with the chamber. That forces the ball tightly against the propellant. Once that is done, you put a dab of grease on top, to prevent accidental chain-firing and to oil the rifling. The final steps are percussion caps, which can be put on via this slot."

He pointed.

"Here let me show you how it breaks down for cleaning."

She handed the weapon back to him. He did something with a control on the side, and the barrel came away. He removed the cylinder and showed it to her. "See, each of the chambers has a small copper nipple on the back, just there, and the nipples each have a tiny hole bored through it. A cap—that's the little copper thing, there—fits over the nipple.

"To fire the weapon, the hammer is cocked, which rotates a loaded chamber underneath it. When the hammer strikes the cap, it ignites, sending a spark through the nipple into the chamber, where the Pyrodex ignites and blows the ball down the barrel."

"Hard enough to do damage?"

"Kill you as dead as the best dart gun made. Velocity somewhere approaching three hundred meters a second. Sights are rudimentary, but it is as accurate as many combat sidearms out to fifty meters."

Gunny shook her head. She'd seen and handled smokeless-powder weapons, there were still plenty of those around, but never anything this old. "God, that's—that's *archaic*! How long does it take to reload that cylinder?"

"A few minutes. The second-fastest way is to carry a spare already loaded. It can be replaced in a few seconds."

Gunny was still amazed. "Ah can't believe anybody carries something like this! Five shots? Ten, if you are lucky? What if you run into more enemies than that?"

"Well, there's this . . ."

He came up with his other hand holding a 6mm dart pistol he must have hidden under his vest. "Faster than a reload is a second gun."

Em whickered. "Two guns? Devious lot, you humans."

"That is the absolute truth," Jo said.

"Maybe later you can shoot it," Unico said to Gunny. "I have a range in the cargo bay."

"I'd like that," she said. "Assuming we live that long."

TWENTY

When she returned to the cart, Wink Doctor was slumped, keeping, literally, a low profile.

"These are the most uncomfortable seats I can dredge up from recent memory."

"Not built for humans," she said. "The designer probably never expected one would use it. If it makes you feel better, I don't find it comfortable, either."

"So, what's what?"

"I was not able to see much directly. I connected to our borrowed com's search function and determined that the dwelling at this address is listed as belonging to someone named *Frow*masc. A background search on him says that he is an importer of offworld electronic components used in trash-compacting control systems."

He nodded. They had not found their own coms, nor their earbuds, but the dead Vastalimi had a couple of coms they weren't using.

"My. That sounds . . . exciting."

"On the face of it, it is rather dull; however, there are

reports, unverified, that *Frow*masc's company might be importing things other than common electronic parts, including certain recreational chemicals that are illegal here."

"Ah. The man who came to check on a kidnapping and who caused a warehouse to be blown up is a criminal? Imagine that."

"We should move this vehicle to another location."

She waved her hand over the control panel. The cart's engine came online. "We need to park somewhere we can see the dwelling's entrance but far enough away from here so we won't be noticed by the same set of neighbors."

"Another surveillance."

"Yes. Either Frow will go somewhere, or somebody will come to visit him, and we will have another trail to follow."

"Works for me. Was there any reason this guy might be responsible for the illness?"

"Nothing apparent. Save that he was involved in our capture and covering up the deaths connected to it, and we are investigating the cause of the illness. That appears to be more than coincidence."

"Yeah, I'd have to say it seems as if somebody doesn't want us to go down that path."

The day had been sunny but a bit cooler, so they didn't have to find any shade to park in, but there were heavy gray clouds in the distance and moving in their direction. Rain coming, Kay knew, and with some lightning. This was good for them—The People did not mind rain all that much, but it would cut down on those who'd be out and about, so it might be safe to stay in one spot longer.

If a neighbor approached and asked why they were parked there, Kay would offer that the cart had malfunctioned, and that they were waiting for a repairperson to arrive.

Wink would be a brow-raiser, of course. Locals might be used to seeing a cart in need of repair now and then, but one with a human in it? Not so much.

Still, there was a trail here, and short of backing off and calling in her sister, Kay could not see another way to stay on it.

They would just have to see how it went. With luck, it wouldn't take too long for something useful to happen.

They were still in motion, looking for a spot to stop the cart, when Wink said, "Hello?"

"What?"

"We got company."

Kay glanced at the rearview camera's feed. Indeed, a vehicle, larger than theirs, had arrived at the Frow dwelling.

"Never a dull moment," Wink said. "He must have called somebody."

The new arrival was pointed in their direction. Kay pulled to the side of the street and stopped a couple of blocks away.

A pair of males they had not seen before alighted from the vehicle, a gray, six-passenger fan-wheeler. Such carts rolled where there were roads, and if water travel was necessary, could retract the wheels in favor of repeller fans. Kay hoped that wouldn't happen since their cart did not have that capability.

The two males went to the dwelling, out of sight.

A minute later, they returned, with, presumably, the one she had identified as the dwelling's owner, *Frow*masc.

Such an assumption could be wrong, of course. That he was staying in the house did not necessarily mean he was the owner of record; however, that was not as important as seeing what he did.

"Crouch," she said.

The gray cart rolled past them. She allowed it to get a block or so ahead, then pulled out to follow them.

There were tricks to following prey that might be looking over its shoulder for pursuit. The first was not to let them see or hear or smell you. The second was, if you had to get close enough so you might be spotted, to present a nonthreatening image. Crouching to look smaller, appearing to be uninterested in the prey and about other business, turning away. One could also trail on a parallel, or sometimes in front. A good hunter learned about her prey and did things to avoid spooking it.

Tracking one of The People in a vehicle presented some problems more difficult than hunting a grasseater on the flats for one's next meal. In a city with other vehicles, smell was useless, one had to be a sight hunter, so parallel tracking was difficult. The vehicle could turn, and if you couldn't see it, it might be too late to recover once you noticed.

The same thing could happen if you were too far behind or too far ahead. There were rules for operating carts, and while one could break those, there would be times when traffic flow would impede the ability to maintain visual contact with the prey.

One had to be far enough away not to draw notice but close enough to stay with them.

After a few minutes, Kay realized they were heading toward the northern edge of the city. They had passed through the warehouse district and were approaching the Mountain Road, a four-lane street that led northwest to the Gray Mountains. They were less mountains than gentle, rolling hills, but the highest natural point within a hundred kilometers. Traffic flow was moderate, which gave Kay enough cover, but they needed to be alert so as not to miss the gray cart exiting when it did.

There were a lot of gray carts, Kay realized. She had not noticed such a thing before.

"Looks like we are going for a ride in the country," Wink said.

"Indeed."

"How are we on fuel?"

"The cell is three-quarters of capacity. The meter says we can travel for six hundred kilometers."

"Hope they aren't going any farther than that."

"Unlikely on this road. There is an intersection ahead. The western turn leads to the Inland Sea, only fifty kilometers away. The eastern turn winds to the hills, and they are but thirty klicks from here. They could be going along the coast or past the hills, but this is not the ideal route—there are better paths."

"Maybe they are trying to see if anybody is following them."

"Possible, but who would be?"

"Us?"

"Were I them, I would not think so. We were kidnapped and managed to escape. In their fur, I would assume we had gone to ground, or to the authorities. They will probably have some way of knowing the latter—word would get out if the *Sena* were hunting kidnappers, and that won't have happened. In their place, I wouldn't think that we would circle around behind them."

"Maybe they are smarter than you," Wink said. He smiled.

"I doubt that. Were they, they would not have taken us as they did. They would have fed us enough information to keep us busy and unsuspicious. They showed their fangs too soon. This was not a smart move."

"Well, they didn't expect us to get away; if we hadn't, we'd be dead now."

"But that we are not means their revelations were a mistake."

"Good point." He chuckled.

"Something funny?"

"An old Terran joke. In the entertainment vids, heroes are often captured by villains, and the villains, being overconfident, often make that same error—they tell the captured hero things they don't expect him to be able to use since they plan to kill him. But he escapes and has the information to use against them."

"And . . ."

"The joke is that the first rule in the School of Villain Training is that you never tell the hero anything; you just kill him and be done with it."

"That would be smart. Criminals, however, seldom seem to be such, at least in my limited experience."

"Let's hope these people continue that."

- - - - - -

"I am showing all couch fields green," Unico said. "Can I get confirmations, please?"

"Green," Cutter said.

This was followed by a chorus of like responses from the others.

"We are good to go," Unico said. "Stand by for the jump. Me, I customarily take a deep breath about now, just for luck. In three . . . two . . . one . . ."

Cutter felt that familiar ripple effect as the ship went into warp, as if a cold wave had passed through his body . . .

After a moment, he heard somebody exhale.

"Well, we're still here," Formentara said.

"Thus far," Em allowed.

"Fems and males, we have achieved entry into the Super Subquantum Transit. You are free to move around the ship; however, please keep your safety field lit while you are in your seat as we here in the pilot's chair do, in the event of unforeseen turbulence."

"What is he talking about?" Singh asked.

Gunny shrugged. "Got me."

Gramps said, "It's terrible how the young people today have no sense of history. Our pilot is offering the traditional instructions given by airship pilots to passengers in pre-spaceflight times."

"Sure, you know that 'cause you were *there*," Gunny said.

"Experience is the best teacher, Chocolatte."

"Uh-huh. I bet if we cut you in half, we'd find rings, just like a tree."

"Only on the part that gets hard as wood," Gramps said. He smiled.

Gunny shook her head and laughed.

Point to Gramps, Jo thought.

Unico was only a few meters away at the ship's controls. He stood, stretched, and ambled back to where the others were also starting to move.

Singh said, "What happens now?"

"All things going well, we cruise along for the next 71.5 hours, then line up for our exit back into n-space. Should put us within spitting distance of Vast. We dock, you catch a dropper down into the gravity well, and I see if I can find some more passengers who want the thrill of a lifetime."

"You aren't worried about the odds?" Singh asked. "I mean, if you have made scores of such transits and the chances are one in ten that you won't come out during one, doesn't that make you nervous?"

"Nah, not really. I think the odds clock resets with every jump."

Gramps chuckled.

"What's funny, ancient one?"

He regarded Gunny. "Back in the airship days on Terra, there was a period in which political terrorists would sometimes blow up passenger craft. Somebody would sneak a bomb into a piece of luggage or somesuch and it would go off, destroying the vessel.

"So a frequent traveler, who was worried about this possibility, asked the ticketing agent about this. What, he wondered, were the odds of his getting onto a craft with a bomb on it?

"'Oh,' the agent said, 'very low. Maybe one in a hundred thousand.'

"The traveler thought about that for a moment, then said, 'Well, I fly a lot and those don't seem like good numbers.'

"So the agent said, 'Okay, here's what you do. Next time you travel, bring a bomb with you in your luggage. Chances of your getting onto a plane with *two* bombs on it are a couple million to one . . .'"

The humans laughed.

Em said, "I don't understand the humor."

Gramps said, "It goes to the inaccuracy of statistics. Statistics say a man with one foot on a hot stove and the other on a block of ice is, on average, comfortable."

"This also makes no sense."

Jo said, "You know the one about the young fem Vastalimi who breaks her leg, catches on fire, and falls into an abyss when she tries to trip her brother?"

Em grinned. "Yes. That one is funny."

"Ever tell it to a human?"

Em thought about that for a few seconds. "Ah. I see what you mean. Humans do have a strange sense of humor."

"There you go," Jo said.

— — — — — —

The ship had a small gym and a couple of treadmills. Gramps was on one, Gunny on the other. Though he was mostly a desk jockey these days, he did try to keep fit.

He shook his head.

"What?" Gunny said.

"Just thinking about technology."

"About the time when your mama invented the wheel?"

"That goes without saying, Chocolatte, but a little closer to home than that."

"Such as?"

"Consider how we live. We came from primordial slime, spontaneously achieving life, and within a billion years, give or take, we evolved into complex beings who came up with science and machineries that allowed us to climb into boxes and zip across the galaxy. Moving through places where no human could live for more than a few seconds unprotected, to stand on worlds beyond our wildest imagination even a few hundred years ago."

"Civilization, old man. Is that the slowest speed the tread-mill has?"

"I'm in no hurry. Burn the same number of calories over distance if you walk or run."

"But you have so little time left."

He shook his head. "You think we are civilized in any meaningful way?"

Off her look, he continued: "I mean, we have the high-tech toys, the ships, the hardware, the ability to make seven-league boots seem like nothing, but look around. What do we do for a living? You and I? We fly to new worlds, we dig in, we unship our weapons, and we spend a lot of time kill-ing our fellow creatures, humans and others."

Gunny blinked. "So?"

"So for me, the mark of a civilized species would be they don't destroy each other in wholesale numbers. They would, you know, figure out along the way that sentient life is rare, precious, and whenever possible, they'd find a way to spare it. Our tools have outstripped our ethics. Instead of figuring out ways to lift ourselves to the next level, we have just come up with better ways to kill each other."

She shook her head. "Ah'll be damned. A philosopher. Ah'd never have thought it. What brought this on?"

He shrugged. "Always been there."

"And yet, here you sit, having just left god-awful Far Bundaloh where we punched holes in the opposition, on our way to Vast to help Wink and Kay, ready to punch holes in anybody there who gets in the way."

"Yep."

"No, uh, contradictions in your mind?"

"Plenty of 'em. It's like the whole grand-illusion thing, Maya. It might all be smoke and mirrors, but whatever it is, I'm part of it, and I have to recognize the boundaries and operate within them. I put down my gun, I don't solve anything, I just get unilaterally disarmed and become an easier target. I don't know how to wave my hand and make the notion of guns something we toss away as irrelevant."

She shook her head. "Amazing. Just when Ah think Ah have you pegged, you say shit like this."

He smiled at her. "My years of experience will keep you guessing, child."

She waited a few seconds. "So, assuming we don't get killed out here in the Void, or after we land, what would you do if you decided to walk away? Ever thought about it?"

"I have. I sort of don't see it as likely, but the notion has crossed my mind."

"And . . . ?"

"I'd like to retire to some semitropical world where there are thunderstorms and warm nights and open a school."

"Teaching . . . ?"

"Stuff I've picked up along the way. How to stay alive when the shit hits the turbo. What money is and what it does. Funny stories about the planets I've been to, what I've seen and done."

"The Old Man's Academy of Hard Knocks?"

"Yeah, something like that.

"Or, I could open a pub."

She chuckled.

"What about you?"

"Me? Like you, Ah ever figured Ah'd make it that far, to retirement. Expect Ah'll step slow at the wrong time, run up against some dead-eye, hot-hand kid who'd beat me to the draw and plink me before Ah get her."

"What if you get lucky, too?"

She considered it. "Maybe Ah'd ask for a job at your academy. Or bouncing at your pub."

"You'd be welcome, Chocolatte."

She looked at him. "Well. Let's see if we get that far."

"There's that."

"Me, Ah'm gonna have my ten klicks in pretty soon here, so Ah'm gonna go take a shower."

"Don't use up all the hot water."

"Ah don't see why not—time you get done crawling your 10K, it'll be heated up again. Ah could take three or four showers, a nap, and watch a few vids."

"Slow and steady wins the race."

"Hell they do."

"Depends on what you are trying to get to. Times when long and slow are better than short and fast."

She grinned. "You talk a good show, don'tcha? Ah'm gone."

TWENTY-ONE

Twenty-nine kilometers outside the city, there was an exit road leading east, and the gray cart used it.

"There they go. Do you know this area?" Wink asked.

"Not well."

"Let me get a map up."

Wink lit the PPS and figured out how to get a map centered on their location on the holographic screen. It was harder because the language was Vastalimi and the cart's translator was slow on visual input. Eventually, it sorted that out, but it took nearly fifteen seconds.

He shook his head.

"Now what?"

"Any civilized planet, a com and the internets will synch. I could ask for a map in Basic, and it would just give it to me."

"You have the correction, right?"

"Finally."

"You humans have no patience. It's a wonder you ever survived as hunters long enough to achieve anything."

"We ate a lot of fruit and roots."

"I'm sure you must have. And had many species of prey laughing at you as they escaped."

"Tell that to the Vastalimi who captured us."

"Point taken."

He looked at the map. Their subjects were half a klick ahead of them, still enough traffic to cover them, albeit the road was now only two lanes.

"There are several public roads or private driveways along this stretch for the next several kilometers. Hold on, switching to orbital view . . ."

They drove in silence for several seconds.

"Come on, you slow piece of crap . . . Here we go . . . There are a small number of what look to be country estates—large dwellings, big lawns, like that. I have the computer's interpolation views at treetop height. Spendy-looking places."

"I recall before I left Vast there was some development out this way designed to appeal to rich people. We do have some of those who don't mind being extravagant in their living styles."

"Most of these are information-blocked, no more than a grid number or address. Some of them have interesting names: Razor Ridge, Hunter's Vista, and . . . what does 'Limit Backpack' mean?"

"*Kraj Naprtnjaca?*"

"Yeah."

"It means your hunting bag is full."

"Ah. I sense a theme."

"Rich people can still hunt," she said, "but more often than not, they don't have time for it. They sometimes compensate by naming their mansions something that offers to the world that they are still interested in chasing prey and blooding their claws.

"It may also be that the dwellings were built on the sites of old hunting lodges, and the names kept."

"Well, unless they plan to drive through, I'd guess they are going to visit one of these rich folks' homes."

"That might prove interesting," she said. "What could possess somebody with great wealth to enter into the business of infecting Vastalimi with some kind of fatal illness?"

"We can ask them that."

"That might prove difficult. Wealth carries a certain status, and rich people are treated differently by the law than those who are poor."

"My, my, another thing your people share with mine."

"If we can determine who Frow goes to visit, any approach to question them will have to be circumspect."

"Can't just knock on the door and demand to know what the fuck is going on?"

"No. Likely our bodies wouldn't be found if we tried."

"Ah. So what do we do?"

"Using such knowledge, we might be able to question *Frow*masc in a more effective manner. Should that give us useful intel, we could then get official help."

"Finally put in a call to your sister."

"Yes. The rich have their shields, but the *Sena* can go anywhere if they have sufficient reason. We would need to give it to her."

"Works for me."

"Let's see where they go. Once we know that, we can return to Frow's dwelling and perhaps prepare a surprise for him."

"I like that one, too."

- - - - - -

"Welcome to Raptor's Roost," Wink said. "Which is about all I can tell you about it, the name."

"It's enough. There are records detailing who owns it and the Shadows will be able to obtain them. Even they will have to be cautious in their approach, but an accessory to kidnapping, attempted murder, and blowing up buildings will merit investigation even if it must be done with care. We need to gather a little more information first."

"Back to *Frow*masc's place?"

"Yes. We will speak with him and see if he can shed some light on our problem."

"I am certain he will be eager to help," Wink said.

— — — — — —

At Frow's, they gained entry via Kay's kick to the door next to the simple lock.

"No alarms, security?"

"Few of The People bother," she said. "Even the rich ones. Burglary is not a major problem."

Wink shook his head. Always fascinating how different races thought, and here another example.

"Hope nobody saw me."

"More likely smelled you, but humans kind of smell like rotting meat, so maybe they'll let it go."

The residence was nicely appointed, the furnishings expensive as far as Wink could tell. Some animal heads were mounted on the walls, most with big, sharp teeth.

Nobody home.

They closed the door and managed to cover most of the damage.

"His bodyguards might come in with him," Wink said.

"Probably not," Kay allowed. "They didn't before. If they do, you have my leave to shoot them."

Wink smiled. "You will intercede with your sister for me when she comes to arrest me for vastalimicide?"

"It will be self-defense and unavoidable," she said. "Not criminal."

"Even though we broke into the house?"

"A small thing, in the grand scheme of things."

He smiled. "Should we poke around?"

"If you want. I don't expect Frow will have left anything

incriminating lying about to be found, but I suppose that is possible."

Curious, Wink did a quick search. For all that the furniture and paintings and sculptures looked spendy, there wasn't really a lot of stuff here. It was spare, more empty space than not.

As Kay had said, there weren't any flashing signs pointing to evidence. The computer was lit, but nothing his translator saw leaped out screaming "Dig here!"

It was the better part of three hours before they heard the vehicle arrive.

Wink rolled his shoulders and neck to loosen them, pulled his pistol, and stood next to the entrance, out of direct sight.

"Something is wrong with this door," Wink's translator picked up from a speaker in the entryway.

Frow stepped into the room, saw Kay five meters away in front of him.

He was talking to somebody—

Sure enough, the bodyguards had come with Frow, and they were right behind him. So much for Kay's notion.

They must have caught Wink's odor because all three turned to look.

Wink pointed his pistol at the bodyguards. "Move slowly and drop your weapons."

The nearer guard moved, instead, very fast. He snatched his pistol from its holster—

Shit—!

Wink had the advantage, and before the guard could get the pistol pointed his way, he got a round off, no problem, *pap*—! A head shot—

He swung to cover the second guard, who had cleared his pistol—

Only the guard didn't even try to get the muzzle pointed at Wink. He pressed his pistol against the back of Frow's head and pulled the trigger—

There was a muffled *whump!* as the compressed gas blew the dart into Frow's skull—

Shit, shit, shit—!

Too late even though Wink had already fired his own weapon twice more, hitting the second guard in the neck and face.

The male collapsed. Dead on arrival.

Kay came over to stand next to Wink. They looked down at the three corpses.

"Well," Kay said, "that was instructive."

"You think? What lessons did you learn, O wise one?"

"At the sign of a threat, the guards first reactions were to kill Frow, even at the cost of their own lives. Someone did not want Frow talking about this, and they had the means to subvert his guards into killing him if that looked likely."

Wink nodded. "Yeah."

"Not what I'd hoped for, but more than we knew before."

"Now what?"

She sighed. "Now we call Leeth. This trail ends here. She will have to make a run at the owners of Raptor's Roost. Maybe she will have something else by now."

TWENTY-TWO

"This is about as good a ship's shooting range as Ah've ever seen on a vessel this size."

Unico smiled. "Well, I spend a lot of time on the raptor; might as well enjoy the comforts of home as best I can."

"Raptor?"

"The ship's name—*Elfu Mwaka Valco*," he said. "Translated, it means, 'the Valcon of a Thousand Years.' Valcons were small raptors, akin to kestrels and hawks. The previous owner was something of a religious fellow, and the name comes from some ancient Terran warrior cult. Easier to keep the name than screw around with all the reregistration shit."

Gunny shrugged. No big deal.

The range was narrow, barely room for two side by side, but with holographics enough to approximate CQ combat, at least eight meters.

Unico removed his relic from its holster and laid it on the bench. "We'll need hearing protection," he said. "It makes a bit of noise when it goes off." He handed her a pair of ear cups and put a pair on himself.

Gunny adjusted the cups. She could hear as well as usual, but there was a cutout circuit that would trigger within a couple of hundredths of a second at a loud noise.

"Go ahead. The front sight should be level with the top of the rear notch, and at eight meters, it shoots a quarter meter high, so hold low."

"Show me," she said.

He grinned at her. "Worried that it might blow up?"

"Thought crossed my mind."

"I've fired it a couple of hundred times," he said.

"So you say."

He grinned wider. "Woman after my own heart. Step back a bit, there is some flash from the cylinder gap to the sides, it can burn you if you aren't wary."

Gunny moved a half step behind him.

He thumbed the hammer. There were clicks as it locked into place. He stood with his right foot forward, body turned sideways. He aimed at the man-shaped holographic target, holding the pistol with one hand, arm extended almost straight . . .

BOOM!

Even though the suppressors cut the sound down to a safe level, she could feel the pressure wave from it and could see the recoil make the weapon bounce a bit in his hand.

A sudden cloud of whitish gray smoke filled the air in front of the muzzle, partially obscuring the target.

A few seconds later, the smoke cleared, drawn up into exhaust fans. A pulsing blue dot showed where the round impacted on the target, dead center in the chest.

Unico looked at her and raised an eyebrow.

"Set that thing off in an unventilated room, you couldn't see what you are shooting at for follow-up shots."

He nodded. "The original propellant smoked even more. There's a story about a famous bad man. He was in a pub, playing some kind of card game, and there was a disagreement. The bad man and another of the players pulled their pistols and fired at each other. After two or three exchanges, they couldn't see each other across the table, but they kept firing. The bad man—I believe his name was Doc Hollandaise, fired an entire cylinder, five or six rounds, and missed his target from two meters. Wounded a couple of bystanders, though."

She nodded in return. "Ah can believe that."

"Want to try it?"

"Oh, yeah."

Gunny took the revolver, hefted it. It was still a heavy sucker.

"You can use both hands. I like to play with the old single-hand stance."

Gunny said, "That one seems like a handicap outside a meter or two."

"Yes and no. Less steady a hold, but it came from the old dueling days. Two men, each with a single-shot pistol, stood ten to twenty paces apart and fired. Standing sideways presented a narrower target than facing the other shooter."

Gunny held the weapon in her right hand, moved her left over to clasp the right, used her left thumb to cock the hammer. Took some effort to lever it back. She kept her finger off the trigger, the thing didn't have a safety. She aimed. Moved the gun, aimed at a different spot. Went back to the original position. She had a feel for it now.

She said, "But if your opponent could shoot and hit anything, sideways would let him punch a hole through both lungs if the ball had sufficient velocity." She didn't look at him, but lined the sights up. She took a deep breath, let it out . . .

He chuckled. "Point taken. But in those days, medicine was rudimentary. A solid hit to the torso with a large-caliber dueling pistol was often fatal, or resulted in an infection that killed the victim shortly thereafter. One lung or two, didn't matter."

"Those guns accurate enough to make head shots at twenty paces?"

"Some of them were."

"Then it would be up to the shooter to do her job right." She took another breath, let half of it out, held it . . .

She fired, recocked the weapon, fired again, then a third time. The smoke was so thick, despite the exhaust fans, that she couldn't really see the target after the second shot, so she was relying on muscle memory.

The smoke cleared.

"My," he said. "Mozambique Drill. And the last round fired blind. Impressive."

Gunny smiled, put the weapon down on the bench. The first two rounds keyholed, just a hair above where Unico's round had hit. Her third shot had hit the target's head, eye level, three centimeters to the right of center. Well. The trigger was kind of stiff, so she pulled it a little. Easy to fix, once you knew.

"You just shot better than I can with my own gun."

For her part, Gunny was surprised the gun was that accurate. But she shrugged it off. "Ah have a knack," she said. "If it throws something, Ah can usually shoot it okay. But Cutter is better."

"Really?"

"Yeah. Some kind of magic, only way Ah can explain it. Outshoots me every fuckin' time."

— — — — —

They found an empty cart. Kay gave it a destination.

"*Shan*masc again?" Wink said.

"The same."

"I thought the kid made it pretty clear he wasn't involved in his late uncle's business. That his monies were clean."

"So he said. My sister has just allowed this is not strictly true. There is not enough evidence to proceed to an arrest, but young Shan is apparently less candid than he offered."

"Ah. And she will attend to the late Frow?"

"She will."

Wink nodded. "Got it. All right. So we go and have another chat with Shan."

"Yes."

"And what do we think he might be able to tell us?"

"If we knew for certain, probably we wouldn't need to speak with him. I have been given to understand that there are, among the enemies of the late Teb, those with connections to assorted medical schools. Criminals are often in sudden need of Healers who aren't in any hurry to report certain kinds of injuries, or those who may be willing to do things upstanding Healers won't. The story is, that smart operators will sometimes sponsor students for various kinds of training that might come in handy later. LawSpeakers, Healers, Accountants."

Wink nodded. "Makes sense. And medical schools have access to the kind of equipment and research that might be used to create a killer bug."

"Just so."

– – – – – –

Kay could see that Shan was jittery.

He had outdone himself in foppery—a freshly trimmed hair pattern, some bright dye, finger rings, bracelets on his wrists, biceps, and ankles. He had dressed for show.

There weren't any servants about, just the young Vastalimi, and he was trying to control his breathing, but not quite managing it.

He was excited about something, and as he led them to a patio with a large, clear area, Kay realized what was going on.

She shook her head. Fools and younglings . . .

To Wink, she whispered, "Stand by with your pistol."

"What's up?"

"Not certain, but be ready to wave it about, just in case. Just don't shoot him."

"Always ready for action, that's our motto. Let me know when."

"Why don't you go sit in the shade," Shan said to Wink, "while I have a private word with Kluth? Pour yourself a drink."

Kay gave Wink the slightest of nods.

Wink headed for the shade of a fan tree, whereunder there were chairs and a table, upon the latter of which were a decanter of wine and glasses. The tree was easily fifty years old and not native to this area. Must have cost a fair amount to have one that big transplanted here.

Shan turned to face her, three meters away.

He might as well have erected a bright, flashing sign announcing his intent.

"Don't," Kay said.

Shan blinked at her. "Don't *what*?"

"Offer a Challenge."

"What makes you think I was going to?"

Kay shook her head. "Your stance and your energy. And your . . . *accoutrements*."

That caught him off guard. "My what?"

"You are *bukvan*," she said. She waved at him. "You have gone to great effort and no small expense to groom yourself. As if you wanted to showcase it. You did not do it for me. Where are the cameras? You planned to record it, didn't you?"

He looked surprised, even crestfallen. "How did you know?"

She could hear his disappointment at being caught out.

"Because this is not my first summer back from the veldt."

"So. You are *old* and maybe *afraid* of my offer of *prigovor*?"

Was this youngling trying to bait her? Please!

Kay knew that if she laughed, it would enrage him, and he would feel honor-bound to go through with a Challenge no matter what. She wanted him alive, and he might be good enough that she'd have to kill him if the claws came out.

So she played to his ego because she didn't need to assert her own. "Maybe a little bit. I have heard that you are a formidable fighter."

"This is true. However, you're the fem who beat Vial, who, while also somewhat past his prime, was still considered by many to be a great duelist."

"And?"

"And, it would seem such a fem would not feel threatened all that much by somebody with only a few Challenges to his credit, no matter what you might have heard about his theoretical prowess."

Hmm. Sharper than she figured, and he wasn't going to let it go that easily.

She nodded. "A good point. Still, perhaps we could defer our dance to another time. Right now, I have bigger challenges to deal with, the deaths of many of our people. Once I tend to that, I'll be happy to come back and let you take a swipe."

He considered that for a moment. She could almost hear him thinking: *If you live that long.*

He said it aloud: "If you don't get killed first. As I understand it, you have been loping along the edge of Death's border since you came back to Vast, and He has tried for you more than once. If you die, I won't ever know if I could have taken you."

Kay considered her response. Would offering more nutrition to his ego do it? If she could convince him she was really worried he would win?

No, that probably wouldn't work. She didn't believe it, and she wasn't that good a liar.

The truth wouldn't help, either. If she said, *Well, I am certain I could claw you dead and bloody, then wipe the flagstones clean with your corpse*, that wasn't likely to help things. The young sometimes had massive egos.

Technically, she could refuse, he didn't have extraordinary grounds for *prigovor*, and she was exempt from the rest. Of course, he might decide to attack anyway if she declined, thinking that he could lie to the *Sena* afterward and tell them it was a fair Challenge. Not much hope he could fool them, but the young were often shortsighted. Went along with the ego:

If one in a thousand can fool the Shadows, why, then, that would be me, and I am going to live forever anyway...

"You forgot my human," she said. She made it appear as if she were combing her neck fur, but what she did was flash the human jive for "gun."

"What about him?"

"Cast a look and see for yourself."

Wink was outside Shan's peripheral vision, ten meters away. The young male turned his head slightly.

Wink held his pistol in one hand, low, the muzzle pointed at Shan's torso. He waggled it a little.

"What is this?"

"Why, it's a *gun*," Wink said. "And you know us humans, we can all shoot the nuts off a buzzing sackfly at this range. You do something stupid—and by 'stupid' I mean pretty much anything at all other than just stand there—I'm going to spike you."

Shan's outrage was large as he turned back to face Kay.

"This—This—is *monstrous*! Have you no honor at all?"

"Less than I did at your age. Hear me, Shan: My mission is of major import, life or death for perhaps thousands, and personal delights such as you offer must follow far behind. I have neither the time nor the patience for anything that stands in my way.

"We can talk. You can help me, and when I'm done, I will return and you can offer *prigovor* and we'll see who can do what. With your help, I might survive to do so. If, on the other hand, I get killed, maybe some of the blame will rest with you. And as you said, you'll never know.

"What do you really want to do here, Shan? It is your choice."

Steam was not actually rising from his head, but she could almost visualize it.

Finally, he said, "All right! I'll help you. But only if you give your word you will stand ready to accept my Challenge when you finish your mission."

"Done."

"Tell your human to put away his weapon. We can talk."

Kay inclined her head in Wink's direction. "Wink? If you would?"

"Sure thing."

Shan turned to see.

Wink did a fancy twirl, spun the pistol on its guard around his finger, one direction, then the opposite, tossed the spinning pistol free into the air, caught it, and tucked it away in the holster over the small of his back.

The offhand expertise to do that five-second routine must have taken many hours to achieve.

He returned his hand into view, then suddenly reached back, snatched the pistol free, whipped it in front of himself, then did another spin, this one with the gun held sideways, parallel to the ground, before he tucked it away again.

He showed Shan his teeth.

Now Kay did smile. Wink had just shown Shan that he was adept with the handling of his weapon and could get it back into play in a hurry.

Shan looked disgusted, but he was also impressed, Kay could tell.

"Fine. Let us move into the shade," he said.

- - - - - -

Wink realized as they were talking why Kay had him pull his piece on Shan. The young male had been about to Challenge her. She didn't want him dead until she got what she came for, and Wink didn't doubt she could beat Shan, probably with one hand tied behind her.

Always pragmatic, Kay.

"Somebody created this pestilence," Kay continued, "and why they did remains a mystery. However, there aren't that many places where such a complex thing could be done on-planet. And the kind of person who would *do* such a thing would eliminate many possibilities."

"And this concerns me how?"

"You speak of honor. How honorable is to inflict a horrible death on hundreds when you are only after one, or maybe a few?"

"You know this to be so?"

"We do not know it for certain. But it has started to seem more likely. There are, I am given to understand, three things necessary to prove in the commission of a crime: means, motive, and opportunity. We have the first, at least some of it. And that second part, motive, usually ends up being one or more of but a few choices. Financial or personal gain; redress of injuries, real or imagined; emotional instability; madness.

"The most common motive is gain, either money or power. Maybe that is not the case here. Revenge might do it, though it seems a long and complex way of achieving it. Certainly one could argue that wholesale slaughter of one's fellow beings requires at the least emotional instability and even madness."

Shan looked at her. "You lecture like one of my professors. I don't need to know all this."

"But you *do*. If you are to live long and prosper as a member of our society, ignorance will not serve you."

He shrugged. "I can pay people to know such things for me."

"And can you pay someone to know when and what to *ask* of your hired help?"

"What do you want from me, fem?"

"Names. People you know who might have the means and motive to, say, kill your uncle."

"And hundreds or thousands more just to throw off suspicion? I don't know anybody that evil."

"Maybe not. Tell us who might come closest to it. We will determine the rest."

He shook his head. "These are the kind of people who will claw first and ask no questions until you are unable to answer them. Cross them, and you won't be able to return for my Challenge."

"I have stayed alive this long with serious people trying to kill me. You have seen recordings of Vial fighting."

"Yes."

"He might have been past his prime, but do you seriously think you could have beaten him?"

"I believe I might have defeated him."

"I *know* I did. The names. I promise I will do my utmost to survive."

He sighed. "All right."

He looked at Wink. "Maybe you might show me how to do that gun-twirling thing you did? My skills in that arena could use improvement. My teacher isn't a human."

Wink grinned. Had to like this kid, really. "Sure, why not?"

"Shan," Kay said.

"Yes?"

"Tell none of these people that we are coming."

"Why would I?"

"I don't know, but better that you do not."

"Fine. As long as you come back after this is all done."

"You have my word."

"Then you have mine. I will tell no one."

— — — — — —

Heading away in the cart, Wink said, "You think this is going to be a good direction?"

"Maybe. But at least it is a direction, and it feels more right than not."

"Leeth's idea?"

"She has certain constraints, even given the severity of

the situation. We are not bound by these in the same way. If we find something of use, Leeth can figure out a way to follow it up. Once the *Sena* have a trail, there are no hunters better able to track and catch their prey."

"Okay. So we go and stir some shit up and see what happens."

"Just so. Let me call Droc and Leeth and tell them of our progress."

But when she got through to Droc, he had news. Wink's com was connected to Kay's, and he heard it, too. Droc had found something weird in the patients.

"We should go and see him first," Kay said.

"I'm good with that."

TWENTY-THREE

Formentara said, "This is really a much more sophisticated ship than it appears from without."

"How so?" Jo said.

"Computer, control systems, life support, recreation, you name it, everything is top-of-the-line completely integrated, state-of-the-art."

"Huh."

"And disguised. The boards look like antiques, but they are spin-leveled, there are all kinds of functions you wouldn't know were there by looking at them. Ship looks like a junker, but it's an illusion."

"Interesting. Wonder why?"

Formentara shook hir head. "I think maybe our Commander Unico wants to be underestimated. That antique weapon he sports is backed up by a modern pistol. His devil-may-care attitude might lead folks to believe he's not very bright. That would be a mistake, and maybe a fatal one. Smart tactics."

"Good to know.

"Unico says we'll be transiting back into normal space at 1800 hours. If we don't pop like a soap bubble or vanish into some n-space side pocket or whatever, we'll be in the vicinity of Vast pretty quick."

"Yeah, another world with nothing for me to do except sit around and stare at the walls."

"You should get a hobby."

"I *have* a hobby. It requires electricity and technology."

"They have those on Vast."

"Not so I noticed."

Jo laughed.

– – – – – –

"Here, look at this," Droc said. "We isolated it, and it seems odd, but it doesn't seem to be inimical in any way."

The holographic projection floating in the air showed tiny particles that enlarged when Droc waved his hand.

"See, they appear to be small-virus-sized bits of organic material—there's the breakdown, carbon, sterioisomers of this and that, skeletalized atoms, nothing that should cause illness, even at much higher concentrations than this."

Wink and Kay exchanged glances. Wink said, "Where did you find it?"

"Marrow," he said. "In the bones of the feet. It didn't trigger any alarms when we did spot it. It is not harmful in any way."

Wink said, "What would it take to *be* harmful?"

Droc looked at him. "What do you mean?"

"I mean, assuming that you could add something to this . . . substance. What would make it pathogenic?"

Droc shook his head. "Who can say? Any number of things. But there isn't anything else in the patients' systems we can find that would have done that."

"Wink?"

He looked at Kay. "What if we are looking at a combination of things? A bipartite agent that combines *inside* a patient to create a synergistic effect? Alone, this doesn't do anything, but mixed with something else, it creates a causative agent?"

"Enzymatic?" Kay said.

"Maybe, I don't know."

"Droc?"

"Possible, but again, there's nothing in the patients to show such a thing."

"What about waste products?"

"Urine, feces, perspiration?"

"Maybe even exhaled gases," Wink said. "Something that *was* in the patients but *isn't* anymore. Did what it was designed to do and was excreted."

Droc and Kay looked at him.

"That's diabolical," Droc said. "Who would think of such a thing?"

"Humans have used variations of it for centuries," Wink said. "Two chemicals in separate compartments, mix them together, all kinds of useful effects. Light, heat, explosives, even medications."

"We have lab results for those tests. We can check."

"Might be a good idea."

- - - - - -

And in the end, that's what it was. Simple, yet clever. Two different agents were used, both of which were harmless, but when combined, created an effect. Once the systems were damaged . . .

"See, here, that is a metabolite for a plasmodium, a carrier that can be absorbed through the skin. Probably the victims walked through it, which is why it shows up in the tarsals."

Vastalimi did not ordinarily wear shoes.

"And there, in the urinalysis, that small waste product, almost below the test's ability to notice, that is the metabolized dregs of . . . well, we aren't exactly sure from what it was extracted, but extrapolating from that, then mixing the source with the sterioisomers and scaffolding, we come up with, at least theoretically, an agent that could produce reactions that would attack major organ systems. Once the process has started, it doesn't reverse."

"So it isn't contagious," Wink said.

"No. Somebody manually administered it to make it look like a vectored illness, but essentially, it is a recombinant toxin. Not a pathogenic life-form at all."

"Somebody went to a lot of trouble to do this," Kay said. "Such a process is complex and complicated. And would seem to be administered personally, a direct connection, the way the deaths have occurred. Somebody sprayed the stuff where it would be walked upon. That would explain some of the families who contracted it."

"We're still no closer to figuring out who," Wink said.

"Actually, that's not so. The technology necessary to create and produce such a thing is not common on our world. It gives us other avenues we can pursue," Kay said. "As does knowing how it was probably administered."

"We know how, but still not why," Wink said.

"Nor who," Droc added.

"We have the names Shan gave us. We need to go and talk to them."

"Gonna tell your sister about this?"

"No need to bother her." She looked at Droc.

He shrugged. "She won't hear it from me."

– – – – – –

In the cart, Wink said, "We are getting closer, aren't we?"

"One hopes. There is something odd about this; I cannot quite grasp it, but it niggles me."

"Niggles?"

"Is it an incorrect use of the word?"

"Got me. I've never heard it before."

"It means 'a small annoyance.'"

"Lessons in my own language from a Vastalimi. Great. How smart am I?"

"Compared to what?"

He shook his head. "A rhetorical question. So you think this guy will talk to us?"

"Given the choice between us and the *Sena*, yes."

"I have his bio here, on the infoweb. A lot of it seems to be speculation, not a great deal of hard information. Seems that *Rill*masc's claimed occupation is listed as 'Hunting Guide.' And apparently business must be going like an X-ray pulsar because he owns a lodge on a big patch of land near the western edge of *Travnjaka*, the Great Grassland.

"Judging by the scale, you could entertain a couple score people in the place without them feeling crowded. Big house."

He brought the holoproj up larger. She glanced at it.

"There is an advertisement for hunting safaris, which include lodging and all the amenities. Expensive, these hunts, but even so, when your land is measured in square kilometers, you have to be leading a lot of folks out into the grass, unless land is cheap."

"It's not cheap. Look up the value of that parcel."

He fiddled with the computer. "Ah. Yeah. Another rich Vastalimi."

"We have a few.

"Rill's would have been gained mostly through criminal activity, I don't doubt," she said.

"I don't see any direct links to—ah, wait, here we go . . ."

"What?"

"Apparently our friend Rill is a patron of Healers. He endows a scholarship each year at some place called VHU."

"That's the central Healer school. I studied there."

"On a scholarship?"

"No. I worked my way through doing various menial jobs."

"I understand; that's how I got through medical school myself. Sort of."

She glanced at him.

"I was a fair cardplayer," he said. "Gambling helped with the tuition—I won more than I lost."

"A useful skill."

"Risky. Where I went to school, the locals didn't like to lose. Big winners sometimes wound up dead or vanished."

"Why does that not surprise me? That you took such risks?"

He grinned.

"So Rill has a medical tie-in."

"Which could be no more than coincidence. Two or three steps out, probably most Vastalimi have medical connections."

He shrugged. "That's what we are going to find out, isn't it?"

"Enter the search term 'Lazov,' followed by a colon and Rill's name."

Wink did so.

The hologram bloomed. "Wow. There's a lot more information here."

"Which must be taken advisedly. This is the underground version of the net, and much of the information found here is based on rumor as much as reality. Vastalimi do not gossip as much as humans, but there is some."

He nodded. Read silently for a moment. "Speaks to his criminal activity. Smuggling, gambling, drugs. Also says he likes particularly challenging prey and hints that some of those are illegal imports, rare animals not native to Vast."

"Crooked on one end, crooked on the other," she said.

"You don't expect him to roll over and confess."

"Certainly not. What he says will be circumspect. We will be looking and listening to how he says it."

"That will help?"

"It might."

– – – – – –

Formentara found hirself sitting next to the Vastalimi fem as they prepared to exit the warp. It would be a few minutes yet; Unico was doing his thing at the ship's controls.

Jo sat to her other side, the others strapped into seats around the cabin.

Formentara said, "So, how is it you came to be working for a mercenary army if you don't mind my asking?"

Em shrugged. "It's not that interesting a story. We are not as curious a species as you humans, but I had an itch to see the galaxy. Vastalimi have a wide range of skills, but among your kind, we have value as fighters. At home, I was average. Out there?

"You know the old joke? How many Vastalimi does it take to change a biolume?"

Formentara shook hir head.

"'Change it? Easier to claw down the wall and let the sunshine in!' There are places where that attitude is appreciated."

Formentara grinned.

"Relatively few of us take to interstellar travel. We aren't particularly xenophobic though most of us tend to stay close to home, save for vacations or short trips of necessity.

"I wonder why Kluth left. From what I understand, she was a good Healer, a useful skill here. She left years before I did, and there was some kind of scat about it. I never heard the details, but the impression was that she had little choice."

"Didn't tell us, either," zhe said.

"I look forward to meeting her."

"You still have family on Vast?"

"Such that it is. My sire fancied himself an expert hunter, but was less adept than he thought. He was run over by a herd of cud-chewers who stampeded the wrong way. This is considered a less-than-honorable way to meet one's end. He died when I was a cub, leaving only two litters behind. Half of those didn't survive *Seoba*. You know the term?"

"Yes, a ritual trek in late cubhood. Kay told us about hers. You roam a big grassland, no tools, hunting for a couple of months. A coming-of-age thing."

"Apparently, some of my siblings inherited our father's slowfootedness. The survivors, six of them, grew up to become fairly normal citizens. Nobody rich or famous, no major criminals, working at low-to-mid-level occupations. Those to whom I was the closest didn't come back from *Seoba*.

"My mother found another mate, one who wanted his own offspring. My mother supplied him with six litters in six seasons and died of a complication during the birth of the seventh litter. Her spouse is not unpleasant, but we have no depth in our relationship. My half siblings have their lives, and I know none of them particularly well.

"As a young adult, I had a liaison with a male with whom I was to formally mate. A week before that was to happen, he stepped crooked in a Challenge and lost. After his death, I had little to keep me there."

"Shit happens," Formentara said.

"We have that saying, too.

"And what of you? You do not smell like the others. There is a level of complexity in you they don't have."

"I am *mahu*. My nature is . . . not as straightforward as that of most humans. We are androgynes, sometimes called pan-genders, and relatively few in number. Our physical appearance is such that sexual identity is not immediately apparent."

"You all look alike to me," Em said. "Wasn't for smell, I could barely tell you apart."

Formentara chuckled.

"When Leeth said that finding Wink Doctor and Kluth would be difficult, you and Cutter Colonel exchanged significant looks. Why was that?"

"Good catch," zhe said. "Our troops have implanted trackers. These have a limited range, and are normally inert, but within a few hundred kilometers, a coded ping will activate the device, and I can locate it."

"*Kluth* allowed this?" Her tone was amazed.

Formentara shook hir head. "Actually, she didn't. We sneaked one into her. It was technically legal, according to her contract. Unfortunately, she figured it out and had us remove it."

"I don't doubt that. You have done this with me?"

Her tone took on a certain quiet menace.

"No. Kay made it pretty clear that Vastalimi didn't hold with such things, so we learned that lesson. But humans tend to be less concerned. Wink has an implant. Find him, we should find her, assuming both are still alive and together."

"Ah."

"As soon as we can shake our minders, if we get any once we arrive, we'll go look."

"We will have watchers, and a klatch of humans won't be easy to hide on Vast."

"We have you to help. Inside a closed vehicle, we should be able to move around without drawing too much attention; there are ways to disguise our scents, as well."

Em shook her head. "You think of things that wouldn't occur to most of us. You are a most devious species."

"Absolutely true, that."

"Getting ready to exit," Unico said. "Take a deep breath and with luck when you let it out, we'll be back in normal space. In five . . . four . . . three . . . two . . . one . . ."

TWENTY-FOUR

*Rill*masc was big, bigger than most Vastalimi Wink had seen so far. He was half a meter taller than Kay, taller even than Wink by several centimeters, and had the build of a sprinter, muscular and taut.

"*Kluth*fem the Healer and the human Wink Doctor," he said, his voice not as deep as Wink would have guessed from his size. His Basic was almost without accent. "Do come into my lodge."

Interesting that he answered the door himself, and that he knew who they were.

"This way."

He led them down a long hallway with a high ceiling. The waxed wooden walls were adorned with trophy heads of various animals, including what looked to be a white liger. Not a big cat you'd find outside of a preserve or a zoo, and certainly not roaming around on Vast.

A lot of the heads had sharp and long teeth, and they were showcased in snarls.

The hall ended at a large room with an even higher

vaulted ceiling, and more animals, head and in some cases, the entire creature, as well as rugs, chairs, and couches covered in different skins.

No doubt that this was a hunting lodge, and Wink suspected that Rill had taken all these animals himself.

He wondered about it aloud: "All your trophies?"

"That spitbear, to the left, next to the airwall? A brother took that one. I had it stuffed and mounted to honor him—he died fighting the bear. The rest of them . . ." He shrugged, but the grin was revealing. A proud male, strong, fit, and adept, and well aware of his prowess. Wink knew the type.

Wink *was* the type . . .

"Sit, if you like." Rill waved at the chairs and couches.

"We'll stand," Kay said. "We don't want to take up too much of your time."

"Some refreshments?"

"Thank you, no."

Rill said, "How may I assist you?"

"You know who we are, I assume you understand our mission?"

"You are investigating the disease that has killed many of The People."

"We are."

"A terrible thing. What makes you think I can offer any help? I'm a but a humble hunting guide." He smiled, knowing they didn't believe him.

"You apparently do quite well at it," Kay said, looking around. "Well enough to endow a medical scholarship at VHU."

"Ah. I see. You think I might have a tame doctor who whisked this plague up in a test tube, then inflicted it upon my enemies?"

"Teb was the third to die."

"And I grieved not at all for the sister-*jebangje*, turd-eating, back-clawer that he was. But if I had wanted Teb dead badly enough, I would have done it personally."

He raised one hand and popped his claws out and in, to demonstrate that he could do that.

"If you could have gotten close enough. It is our understanding that Teb was a cautious sort. Getting next to him wouldn't have been easy."

"I didn't care enough to try," he said. "Nor would I be so sloppy as to cause the deaths of so many others—including if I am not mistaken, your parents and several of your siblings?"

Wink digested that. Rill had taken the trouble to find out about her parents and to use it as a barb. Interesting.

"I would not think you to be that sloppy," Kay said, ignoring the part about her family. "But smarter people than you have done more foolish things."

"You have my word as a hunter that I had nothing to do with Teb's death, nor those of any others infected with the disease. Not my style."

She nodded. "I'll accept that. Any suspects you'd care to point us at?"

He grinned, a fast flash of teeth, too quick to be thought a real threat. "Oh, I have plenty of enemies I would sic you on if I thought it would cause them grief, but again, I wouldn't waste your time. You are sure that the cause is unnatural, aren't you?"

"We believe it to be so."

"I wish you success. I know a few people who died from this. Most of them not the most untarnished of citizens, but it is, I am given to understand, a most unpleasant death. I prefer to see my kills done cleanly, without suffering."

Before she could speak to that, Rill looked at Wink. "Are you adept with the weapon you have hidden behind you on your belt, Wink Doctor?"

"I'd like to think so."

"Interested in a wager?"

"What kind of wager?"

"You leave here on foot. Go in any direction you choose,

take your weapon with you. I'll give you an hour's head start, then track you. When I find you, one of us kills the other. I'll be armed only with these." He held his hands up and popped his claws out, then back in again. "If you win, I'll have my estate transfer a million New Dollars into your account."

"And if you win?"

"What will it matter? You won't care."

Wink looked at Rill. "Let me ask you something. Do you have a, uh . . . private trophy room? One with heads you only allow a few special visitors to enter and see?"

Rill whickered. "Oh, very good! Quick and sharp, so much the better! What do you say?"

Wink thought about it for a moment. Armed with his pistol and knife against claws? He could take this guy . . .

"I am tempted, but I have bigger goals in mind."

"I understand. When you are done with your bigger goals? The offer will still be on the table. You strike me as a real challenge, and I've run out of those lately. And I'll show you my private trophy room . . ."

– – – – – –

In the cart, Wink said, "You believe him?"

"Yes."

"Because he swore as a hunter?"

"Because he is what he is. I don't doubt he would kill an enemy in a heartbeat, but not from hiding—he is too full of his own pride." A short pause, then, "You considered accepting his challenge, didn't you?"

"Well, a little. Million noodle's a lot of money."

"But that's not why you'd have done it.".

"No."

"The trophies you saw?"

"But they weren't armed with a gun, nor as smart as I am."

"The former is true. Had you accepted the offer, I would think the latter was not."

"You'd bet on him?"

"I am not prone to make such wagers."

He waited a second, thinking about her answer.

"I'd be interested in seeing his private trophy room," he said.

"As I imagine the *Sena* would be interested. I suspect they could solve a number of disappearances and murders based on what they'd find there. I also suspect that if the Shadows ever come to look, that room will go up in a white-hot flash, leaving no usable evidence behind.

"Besides, by the time you saw the room, you wouldn't be in a position to appreciate it."

He nodded. Another road not taken. "So, who's next on our list?"

— — — — — —

The seven of them prepared to step into the port's lock on Unico's ersatz-rattletrap ship. They were only eighty thousand kilometers above the surface of Vast, but the drop would take a while; something to do with limited orbital space.

It was more than lucky that they had Em along; none of them had any firsthand knowledge of Vast, and even the best research at a remove was no comparison to having a native guide.

Interesting, sometimes, how those things worked out.

"There are many ways to die on our world," Em said, "and many of them are violent. Best you try to avoid irritating The People, and if you do, be prepared to do battle . . ."

She gave them some rules and social mores, including a quick-and-dirty lesson in Challenges and how best to avoid them, and how to use a weapon if somebody did want to rip your throat out.

It sounded like a dangerous place to Jo though she wasn't particularly worried. She could imagine that Wink had been rubbing his hands when he arrived here, thrilled at the prospect. The man camped on the stoop to Death's butcher shop frequently, and he would risk his life for all manner of reasons she thought fairly trivial.

Not that she didn't sometimes do the same. Some neuroses ran really deep . . .

She and Wink had enjoyed a hot and brief sexual congress after the job on Ananda, but she didn't see any future in that—neither of them was looking for anything more.

She liked him, and he was part of their team, as was Kay. If they had been taken out, then the rest of them were going to find and make whoever did it pay.

Attack one Cutter, you attacked them all.

Formentara said, "Not many augmentation parlors here."

"It is not a thing The People do," Em said.

"Naturally. You keep taking us back to the stone age, Colonel, my skills are going to atrophy down to nothing."

Rags grinned at hir. "I really don't think that's likely. I expect you could sit alone in a dark room in a desert in the middle of nowhere and still exercise your mind just fine."

Zhe grinned back at him. "Well, genius does find a way to amuse itself."

Jo said, "Okay, we are good to go, right?"

Everybody seemed to be ready.

Unico said, "If you ever need another hackney through the Void, let me know." He looked at Gunny. "Nice shooting with you, fem. I'll practice some so I can keep up with you next time."

"Good luck with that," Gramps said.

They stepped into the lock.

– – – – – –

The dropship took its sweet time getting them down. Six and a half hours? That was unheard of most places. You plugged into a standard orbit, fell into the gravity well, and were on the ground in ninety minutes, maybe two hours, tops.

Gramps shook his head.

"What?" Gunny asked.

"As you never tire of pointing out, I'm not gettin' any younger."

"Well, it's got to be faster than taking a skyhook. You remember those, right?"

"Actually, I do, and this is not much faster than those."

— — — — — —

When they finally entered the port proper, the place was, not surprisingly, thick with Vastalimi. Jo tried not to stare, but it was impressive seeing that many at once.

All of them faster, stronger, deadlier than she was. It was humbling.

She didn't like the feeling.

Em said, "And here come the Shadows."

Jo glanced at her.

"The purple dye on the shoulders and the strapped side-arms. Our police, the *Sena*. There are four of them, and you seldom behold that many in one place unless there is big trouble. They are here for us."

"Why, what did we do?"

"We came to Vast. There are few humans here, and most of The People have probably never seen half a dozen of you in a clot like this. I think the Shadows are here to make sure we—by which I mean you—don't cause a riot."

"We aren't looking for trouble."

"Doesn't mean you won't find it. There are more than a few Vastalimi who would just as soon claw you as look at you—though in your case, that might be a fatal mistake."

Jo nodded.

One of the purple-shouldered fems moved to intercept them. She looked fit and moved well. And familiar . . .

"I am Leeth," she said. "Kluth is my sibling."

Sister who's a cop. Another thing Kay never got around to telling us. Jo shook her head. They hadn't told anybody they were coming, a tactical decision, but of course, a cop would have access to information about incoming visitors once the ships arrived.

Rags stepped up. "I'm Cutter. Is there word from her or Wink?"

"As it happens, yes. They were kidnapped but managed to escape."

"Sheeit, you mean we came all this way for *nothin'*?" Gunny said. She tried to sound arch, but the relief was obvious to Jo. All of them would feel that way. They were soldiers, and as such, had developed padding on their emotions—comrades died in battle, you couldn't let it overwhelm you. Still, Wink and Kay were, well, not just comrades.

"So why aren't they here instead of you?" Rags said.

"They continue to investigate, seeking the cause of the malady. As of now, we don't know exactly where they are, only that they were alive and well when I heard from them yesterday."

Rags glanced at Formentara. Zhe smiled, and Jo knew why.

"I will convey you to a place of safety and we will wait to hear from Kluth."

"All due respect, we might be able to help with their investigation."

"First you would have to find them. It's a big planet, and you have no idea where they are."

"We can locate our own when we need to do so."

"A nice ability. You'll notice we don't have a lot of humans here. That would also be a problem—you won't blend in.

"Meanwhile, if you will come with us, we have a transport waiting." She turned and walked away.

Gunny leaned over to Gramps. "I bet she is sudden death with that pistol. Look at the rig, how polished that handle is from use; half the checkering is worn off."

"Good, she can do our light-fightin' until we get to our ride."

With two of the *Sena* behind them, and Leeth and the fourth in front, they moved through the terminal. Crowded as it was, people got out of the way as they approached.

Jo noticed and said so.

Em said, "Lot of things can get you in deep shit here; fucking with the *Sena* is at the top of the list. They can arrest you, decide if you are guilty, and execute you on the spot, at least for some acts. Nobody will blink if they do. Best not to put yourself in that situation."

"That's a lot of leeway to give a police officer."

"It's not an easy job to get. You have to be highly trained, skilled, and vetted. Your performance is reviewed frequently."

"Got it," Jo said.

Well. Whatever else it might be, "boring" didn't seem to be a particularly useful word for visits here . . .

— — — — — —

The next two stops yielded no more information than had the visit with Rill. Nobody offered to let Wink become the most dangerous game, nobody was particularly obnoxious, but they were not particularly helpful. Yes, they knew about the disease. No, they had nothing to do with it. It was a terrible thing.

Kay was inclined to believe them. Not that Vastalimi didn't lie, certainly they did, but nothing in the demeanors of those they had interviewed leaped out and called attention to itself as outright fabrication.

Humans, it was sometimes said, would climb a tree to tell a lie. Vastalimi needed what they thought were good reasons.

Something about this whole line of inquiry felt wrong to her. It was perfectly reasonable to look for connections to people who had the expertise and equipment to generate the fake pestilence. And her less-formal questions might get responses that *Sena* absolutely would not get. Still, it didn't feel as if she was on the quarry's trail.

She said so to Wink.

"So, what do you want to do?"

"We can try one or two more and see if anything comes up."

"Okay. Next on the list is one *Jares*masc, ostensibly an artist, who arranges assassinations through *prigovor*, at least according to the rumor net."

"Let us go and speak with him," she said.

"Going to call your sister?"

"Why would I? We have nothing new to report."

He shrugged.

TWENTY-FIVE

"I am *Droc*masc," the Vastalimi said.

Of the humans, Jo was likely the only one who could see a family resemblance among the three siblings. It was in the carriage, the facial features, maybe even the voices. It was plain to see with Droc and Leeth standing side by side, and had Kay been here, she would have fit right in. Of course, Jo had spent a lot of time with Kay.

Droc looked at Em, who rattled off something in their language. Jo had but a few words of that, and hadn't lit a translator, but it was apparent there was some kind of formality involved in the greeting. Interesting, since Kay had never been big on ceremonial greetings, considering them a waste of time.

"Leeth tells us that you have found a cause for the disease?" That from Rags.

"With the help of your medic, Wink Doctor," Droc said. "He saw a trail we had not seen."

"Bet he loved that," Gunny said.

Droc continued: "The agent is not natural, nor a pathogen

per se, but a kind of complicated poison that creates a toxin. The body's defenses cannot overcome its own reactions. This lessens the worry about an epidemic."

"But makes it a crime," Leeth added. "For which the perpetrators will be found and punished."

"This is what Kay and Doc are doing?" Jo asked.

"Yes. They follow leads."

"And you don't know where they are?" Rags said.

"My sister prefers to do things her own way. She has not informed me of her movements, save generally. She will probably check in within a few days, at which time I can tell her that you have arrived."

"Or we can go look for her ourselves," Cutter said. He wondered: If Kay had called her sister, wouldn't Leeth have her com number?

Maybe she just didn't want to give it to her . . .

"That would not be the wisest path. You are unfamiliar with our laws and social mores. Wandering around on your own could put you in no small amount of danger."

Jo saw all of her team grin at that though they kept those expressions close-lipped.

"We have Mish here as a native guide."

Leeth looked at Em, rattled off a spate of Vastalimi, of which Jo caught three or four words.

Em responded, her tone deferential but not overly so.

"Still," she said, switching to Basic, "half a dozen humans will cause a stir wherever they go. I would prefer that you keep an escort should you risk traveling around the city."

Cutter said, "Of course. We don't want to be part of the problem."

Jo held her grin. They had no intention of allowing a tail to stay with them when they went looking for Kay and Wink. And if the local cops believed they would, that might make it easier to lose them.

"We will take you to a place where you can stay," Leeth said.

Formentara said to Droc, "Any progress on a cure for the toxin?"

He looked at her. "No, nor do we expect any. The goal is to catch those responsible and stop them from doing further harm. Those who have already been infected are dead or dying, and other than palliative care, there is nothing to be done for them. By the time we know, it is too late. *Tzit dogoditi se*."

Jo knew that phrase, she had heard Kay use it several times. *Shit happens.*

She glanced at Rags. He gave her the tiniest of shrugs.

Hard people, the Vastalimi.

Kay and Wink arrived at another big house, not as rustic as the hunting guide's but large enough to get lost in. They were admitted by a servant and led down another tall and wide hall into a big room, again with vaulted ceilings. They really seemed to like that here.

Instead of stuffed trophy animals or their heads, however, the hall and walls were home to paintings, with sculptures on stands here and there, including a couple of busts of Vastalimi, as well as quarter-sized statuettes of The People. All carefully lighted to show them to their best advantage.

"You suppose all this art was done by Jares?"

Kay shrugged. "Who can say? They look enough alike to have been rendered by the same hands."

"They any good? They look pretty good to me."

"They display a mastery of the craft. That statue of the pair of running *vepar*? Very dynamic and just slightly exaggerated anatomically, for effect. That twice-life-sized painting of the *div macka*? The big cat? It looks almost alive, the colors are vibrant, electric, and it is as good as any such illustration I have seen. This artist knows exactly what he is doing."

"Thank you," came the voice from behind them.

Wink turned and saw something he had not seen before:
A fat Vastalimi.

Not morbidly obese, but certainly carrying fifteen or
twenty kilos of excess weight, most of it in the belly and
hips. Huh. He hadn't really thought about that before, but
now that he saw this one, it struck him: These people were
in better shape than any other intelligent species he'd been
around.

Jares caught Wink's look. "I am Jares. I don't hunt as
much as I once did. Too much sitting in front of a canvas
or a mound of clay these days. Makes staying fit hard.

"Please, sit, have some refreshments. How may I assist
a fem with such good taste in art? And a human? I don't
suppose you'd consider posing for me? I haven't had a chance
to sculpt a human before."

Kay said, "I suspect you know who we are and why we
are here if our experiences of late are any indication."

Jares whickered. "Yes, that is so. Certain of my . . . ah . . .
colleagues have contacted me. Let me echo them: You are
growling at the wrong burrow, Kluth. None of us would do
such a terrible thing."

"This from a Vastalimi who arranges assassination by
Challenge?"

He whickered again. "*Allegedly* arranged such assassinations, dear fem. If the Shadows had proof, we wouldn't be
having this conversation because I would be dead. Besides,
my work has gained a certain favor among collectors; it
provides all that I need or want. Even if I *had* once engaged
in such illegal activity as you suggest? Those days would
be behind me."

He looked at Wink. "I expect I could get a hundred thousand ND for a statue of you, maybe more. Pose for me, you
can have half of what I get."

Wink shook his head. A human could make a good living
on this world, assuming he lived long enough to collect the
money . . .

"Are we being recorded?" Jares asked.

"Not by us," Kay responded.

"Then let us be candid, dear fem. Whoever has unleashed this plague upon the people is a monster. Those of us who have, from time to time, trodden upon paths less—shall we say—pristine, in realms not strictly legal, have certainly done things that most would shun. But even we have our standards, our ethics, and no Vastalimi in my acquaintance would lower him- or herself to such a vile depth.

"It is perhaps natural to assume that those who pander to vices—drugs, sex, gambling and the like—would be where to seek one who'd inflict wholesale death upon his or her fellows: If you want a serpent, you go to where the serpents slither. However, in this case . . . ?"

"Your reasoning seems specious. Kill one, kill a hundred, it is only a matter of numbers."

"Really? Then consider it from a different stance: It would be extremely bad for business. Such a heinous crime, if it has been determined that this is the case, will draw the most vigorous response from the *Sena* anything has drawn in my memory. They will turn over every rock, poke into every crack, dig up every buried bone looking for the perpetrators. Nobody who sells a cloudstik, accepts a wager on a game, sends out a paid companion would be safe from scrutiny. And in the looking, other things would certainly turn up that many would prefer to stay hidden.

"Who among us would call that down upon him- or herself? How stupid would you have to be to *not-know* what a scatstorm you'd create?"

Kay nodded, and Wink found himself also doing so. Yeah. Somebody smart enough to create this killer infection and get it out there was not going to be categorized as "stupid" . . .

"We have taken up too much of your time," Kay said, as she came to her feet.

"Not at all, dear fem. In this matter, I am as willing as

any Vastalimi to help." He looked at Wink. "If you remain on our world for a time, please consider my offer to become my model. It would be my honor to have you as a subject. Three-quarters of our fee?"

"I'll think about it."

"Excellent!"

As they walked away, Kay said quietly to Wink, "Better than your last offer."

"I'm not sure of that. Jares seems to have a big appetite. Who knows what he might do after the sculpture got done . . . ?"

She whickered.

— — — — — —

"So are we gonna go find Doc and Kay?"

"Oh, yeah, Gunny, we are," Rags said. He turned to Formentara. "No bugs?"

"No."

Not "None that I can find." Just "No."

"Okay. Here's the deal: Em, can you secure a vehicle large enough to haul us around without being visible? As soon as possible?"

"Of course. It might be tricky to make sure the *Sena* don't know about it, but I still have some contacts here who can help. We will need at least two—we leave in one, go to a hidden location, and switch to the second. The first can continue on to lay a trail—Vastalimi are very good trackers, none better than the Shadows. If we bring that one to a place nearby where they might see it? They will be looking for that."

"Good. We'll need a diversion for the watchers to get going. Gramps?"

"How about Ah take care of that part?"

Gramps looked at Gunny: "You still pissed off at me for shooting that APC on Far Bundaloh, ain'tcha?"

"Look up 'killjoy' in the pedia, there's a picture of you," she said.

"I thought you said that was next to the entry for 'dirt.'"

"Different picture, but still you." She smiled. "Singh can help me, he needs to learn some more about the fog of war."

The young man smiled at her. "Sah."

"Fine," Cutter said, "you can create the diversion. Formentara, can you rig up something so they think we're still here?"

Zhe stared at him as if he had turned into a giant roach. "Excuse me? To whom do you think you are talking?"

Cutter grinned. "It was a joke."

"Not funny," zhe said.

"Your reaction was," Jo said.

"Remember that next time I tune you up—I might decide to give you a nervous tic."

"Let's move it along," Cutter said. "We have colleagues to find."

— — — — — —

"Now what?"

Kay said, "Something is wrong here. Jares said it: This is too large a hammer to squash gnats. Some of the worst criminals would happily torture an enemy to a long and painful end, but none of those who have been killed by the infection seem important enough to justify such a wide-ranging attack."

"Maybe one of them *really* pissed somebody off?"

She shook her head. "It does not make sense. It is too complicated—a couple of missiles that would take out a compound? Simple. If you wanted to hide it, you could fire a score of such rockets at different targets to cloud the investigation.

"Vastalimi tend to be more direct about such things."

"But we don't know that whoever did this was after just one person. Maybe they are crazy, and they just wanted to create a panic?"

"Vastalimi don't panic. *Tzit dogoditi se*. We all know this."

"Doesn't rule out 'crazy.'"

"No. There are those who are mentally disturbed. And if it is truly random? That will make it almost impossible to find them. However, it does not feel like madness. There is a purpose here. Find out why, we can uncover who."

"Brings me back to my question: What now?"

"There is one more possibility about which I have been thinking. You know the phrase that Demonde Gramps sometimes uses? 'Follow the money'?"

"Yeah?"

"Perhaps somebody has made a profit from this infection, the deaths."

"Who? Undertakers? Insurance sellers?"

She shrugged. "I cannot say, and while the idea of somebody's doing this for money seems particularly outrageous, especially for a Vastalimi, it is something to be considered. We might be looking for a different kind of criminal altogether."

"You need to call your sister in on this?"

"She would be able to find out such information, she'll have access to banking records. However, there are others with access to these data."

"Anybody you know?"

"Yes. I'll put in a com to Jak."

"Jak."

"Yes."

"Just to make him dance because you can?"

"That would be but an additional benefit."

He chuckled.

TWENTY-SIX

"We about ready?"

Jo nodded. She accessed her aug and its chronometer. "Five minutes from . . . now."

"Formentara?"

Zhe looked at the tracker zhe held in hir hand, half the size of hir palm. "I got Wink located. He's way the hell and gone away from here, 394 kilometers to the northeast."

"You tried his com's opchan?"

"You enjoy insulting me, Colonel?"

Rags grinned.

"If they are on com, they are way out of range, assuming they are even using any of the usual bands or their own equipment."

"Just checking."

"You should check on people who need it."

Em said, "Our vehicle should be on-station. The escape window will be small and will close quickly."

Rags nodded. "Everybody set?"

They were.

－－－－－

Gunny and Singh crouched behind a power transformer that routed energy for the area. The device, the size of a small van, was marked with a danger sigil, but there was no barrier around it, no fence, nothing.

Singh had remarked upon this: "But is this not dangerous? Anybody could wander over here and accidentally hurt themselves. Or do as we are about to do."

"Yep. Ah asked Em about it. She said they don't spend much time and energy protecting stupid folks from themselves. The symbol for danger should be enough."

"What if a passerby cannot read the sign?"

"Tough shit. Improves the gene pool."

He nodded. "I understand that people sometimes take that to extremes. I remember a shipment of carbines we imported once. There was an imprint on the barrels, warning users not to point the muzzles in unsafe directions."

She chuckled. "Has to do with legal liability. You'd think anybody smart enough to pull a trigger would know what the gun was for, but apparently there are some who aren't. Not that they'd be smart enough to read the fuckin' warning and understand it, either, but there you go. All right. Let's move."

The two of them came up and moved away from the transformer.

They kept to the shadows, and there were plenty of those. They didn't see anybody else on the street as they headed for an alley nearby.

"Two minutes," Gunny said quietly.

"Stet that," came Cutter's voice in her earbud.

"So here we have the basic ingredients in the art of distraction," Gunny said to Singh, as they walked toward the rendezvous point. "When in doubt, wait until dark, turn off the lights, and blow shit up. Gets people's attention *stat*."

"Sah."

"Now, since we aren't in a hostile situation with regard to our hosts here, we don't want to cause a lot of damage. So the popper shorts out a switch on the transformer, don't cost much to fix, but the neighborhood gets dark. Well, dark*er*, since they keep things kinda dim around here anyhow.

"And the light and noise from the spew-rocket draws their attention since it'll be the only thing to look at, come the sudden darkness."

"And while they are looking at that, CFI sneaks away," Singh said.

"There you go. And Formentara will have rigged up something so they hear voices and see things behind the window shades. I expect it won't take 'em long to catch on, but by then, we're long gone, and we haven't done much damage and probably broken no more'n a couple of minor laws."

"Still, I cannot imagine they will be happy with us, the Vastalimi police."

"You step onto a mat for a sparring match, and the other player smacks you in the nose, whose fault is that? You know what he intends to do, and you know what to do to prevent it. He hits you? You need to be better."

"Sah."

"Not our job to make 'em happy. They supposed to be watching us, so if we get away, and they miss it? Their fault. Everybody knows how tricky humans are."

Singh grinned. "Yes, sah."

She accessed her timer. "Got about a minute. Best we move along."

— — — — — —

The laser rocket had been programmed to emulate a series of explosive-artillery airbursts a couple of hundred meters up. It wouldn't fool anybody for long, but the flashes and attendant *booms!* set to go thirty seconds after the transformer shut off power would be impossible to miss—and you wouldn't be able to tear your gaze away for the duration. Like humans, Vastalimi eyes were attracted to motion, and a light in the darkness? They'd have to look at it.

All they needed was thirty seconds to get clear, and once that happened, Jo knew, they were golden.

Even a suspicious cop who suspected a diversion would be off-balance for a minute or two, plenty of time to be long gone.

Yes, there could be some minor legal consequences, but that would be dealt with later.

"Stand by," Jo said, "Five . . . four . . . three . . . two . . . one . . ."

The lights went out. She accessed her visual aug. The ambient heat residual and warmth generated by the others and herself was enough to navigate by, and it would be brighter outside with the city glow.

Jo took a couple of deep breaths and oxygenated her system more than it already was. In thirty seconds, the sky would light up to the southwest, and the two Vastalimi watchers they knew about would look that way and wonder what the fuck was going on.

There was always a chance something could go wrong. Maybe somebody out walking the local equivalent of his dog, or a drunk in an alley, an unexpected bystander in the wrong place at the wrong time? No way to be a hundred percent sure of any operation, but the odds were in their favor. And that's what you had to play, the odds . . .

"Stand by," she said again. "Coming up five . . . four . . . three . . . two . . . one . . ."

The rocket was supposed to go off a thousand meters away and a couple hundred up. Jo had done the calculation on how long it would take the sound to arrive—three . . . two . . . one . . .

Boom! Boom!

"That's us, people. Asses and elbows."

— — — — — —

They were in the middle of nowhere, night heavy upon them, and Wink was tired of riding. They had not passed a vehicle coming their way for twenty kilometers, and there was nothing to either side of the road but empty fields and distant hills.

"We could continue on to find lodging," Kay said. "There is a small town an hour farther ahead."

"It's a warm night," he said. "And I bet I can find a soft spot on the ground more comfortable than this damned cart's seat. Unless you need a bed?"

She whickered.

"We have any food left?"

"Some," she said. "Enough to get by for another day or two, nothing fresh."

They found a place to pull the cart off the road near a field with grasses growing a half-meter high.

"Anything we need to worry about in the way of insects or predators?"

"Local insects probably won't know what to make of you, nothing poisonous, and there's nothing dangerous large enough to sneak up on us we won't hear before it gets close."

"Assuming you aren't too heavy a sleeper," he said.

She whickered.

They walked out twenty meters from where they'd parked the cart, tramped the grass down in a ragged circle, and lay on it. The ground wasn't that hard, and the grass padding made it comfortable enough. They lay on their backs, looking into a clear night sky, with unfamiliar constellations dotting the darkness.

"So . . . Jak?" he said.

"Yes. He concerns himself with wealth. He will have ways to find out what we need to know. I'll call him again in the morning."

"Hmm."

"What does that mean?"

"Nothing."

"I think it does."

He propped himself up on one elbow and looked at her. It was dark, but there was enough star- and moonlight—the double moons were visible, one full, the other just a sliver—to see her clearly.

She mirrored his pose, a meter away.

"Well. It seems that you might not be done with Jak altogether. Past him having information we need, I mean."

She blinked at him.

"You think I harbor feelings for him?"

"Yes."

"I am past caring for Jak."

"But not yet indifferent."

"I don't take your meaning."

"He screwed you over. You had a long time to live with that, and while I don't think you feel anything like what you did before you left Vast, the anger is still there."

"So?"

"Not saying that you aren't justified in feeling it. Only that until you get past hatred and anger, you aren't done with him. There is a connection still. It gets severed when you no longer feel anything toward him at all."

She didn't say anything for a time. Then, "I see. Is this the voice of experience?"

"It is."

"Ah. And will you tell me the story?"

"Probably. Another time."

He lowered himself to his back. She did likewise.

He heard a noise, it sounded like a short series of coughs, not close.

"What was that?"

"Gray bear taking prey," she said. "Not close."

"I thought you said there wasn't anything big enough to be dangerous out here."

"I said we'd hear it coming. Besides, the bear has taken prey. It won't be hungry for a while."

He grinned into the night. What an interesting fem Kay was . . .

"A question?"

He looked at her. "Go ahead."

"You are first among our company in the willingness to take risks that might end in your injury or death."

"Yeah?"

"Why is that?"

He shrugged. "I don't know. It's always been that way."

"Always?"

"Far as I can remember. There's a rush connected to it, striving and surviving. An intensity of sensation afterward. Nothing like it."

"Interesting, You cannot recall the first instance?"

"Nope. I can't. I—" He stopped.

Of a moment, he could.

"Leilani Zimmer," he said. "Man."

"I don't understand."

He looked at her, but what he was seeing was his own past with a new clarity.

She raised an eye ridge in question.

He nodded, and told her that story.

— — — — — —

Leilani Zimmer.

She was sixteen, nearly two years older than he, and if she had noticed he was alive, he couldn't tell. Drop-dead gorgeous, Leilani was, with short, curly hair puffed into a tight electrostatically held cap, lush in the breasts and hips, the first-string left striker on the clubball team at their school.

Like most boys his age, Tomas Wink walked around in a cloud of lust, shedding testosterone like a summer dog losing its winter coat, and Leilani—Elzi, to her friends—passing by was worth an automatic erection. Hard enough it would hum.

He had no chance with her, not a prayer. He wasn't a jock; he was six centimeters shorter; and not that great a student. Not rich, not in with any of the smart sets, not handsome, your basic fourteen-year-old tweek. A face in the crowd.

He actually recognized her voice when he heard her scream since he went to all the clubball games and knew it from her yelling at her teammates.

"No! Get off!"

He was crossing the yard behind the school, where the back gate opened into the park, and he turned the walk into a run.

"—asslick nodick! No!"

Tomas homed in on the sound, and with the voice, there came a slap.

"Slit! Hold fucking still!"

A break in the carefully groomed trees, and there they were: Leilani, on her back on the ground, her shirt ripped open, her shorts pulled down around her knees.

Sitting on her belly about to backhand her face again, Mars "Stone Leg" Yeng, the captain of the men's clubball team.

No question in Tomas's mind what was going on. However it had started, it had turned to rape.

In an instant, Tomas had to make a decision.

If he yelled, he might distract Yeng.

If Yeng saw him coming, he could take Tomas apart like an overcooked chicken. He was twenty centimeters taller, thirty kilos heavier, and could probably lift the back of a pubtrans bus by himself.

Time stretched into infinity . . .

Tomas was no jock, not all that fit, but he did know some basic physics.

He sprinted at Yeng. Three meters away, he jumped, pulled his knees against his chest, and leaned back a hair. He kicked as hard as he could with both feet, aiming at Yeng's back.

He was a little high, which was undoubtedly what saved him from getting beaten into a bloody mess. His right heel smacked into the back of Yeng's head, knocking him off the young woman under him, sprawling facedown onto the soft ground.

Tomas came down, skidded, rolled, banging himself up pretty good and rattled, but not within a parsec of the deeply unconscious state Yeng had just entered.

Leilani came to her feet at the same time Tomas managed that.

It was a glorious view. Shirt open to reveal her breasts— she had pale, pinkish brown nipples—her shorts down, her pubic hair gleaming darkly in the sunshine, trimmed into a long, narrow strip.

Tomas figured he could die now, never to surpass this moment for joy, but that would have been wrong.

"Tomas," she said. "Oh, thank you! He hit me. He was going to—to rape me."

"Yeah, well, not anymore, he isn't."

What she did then surprised him more than anything he had ever seen in his fourteen years. She bent, slid her shorts down and off, and walked toward him. She reached out, hugged him, bit his shoulder, and moaned.

Surprised? No. Astounded. Stunned.

He went with it.

Thirty seconds later, she was on the ground again, and he was on top of her, and being guided into a place about which he had only fantasized.

"Oh, yes!" she said. "Do it!"

Oh, hell yes!

Better than his best fantasies, it was.

Oh!

In that moment, he didn't worry about what might happen if Yeng woke up. Or why on Earth Leilani Zimmer was gifting him with herself. Later, when he learned more about how emotions worked, it made more sense. Her hormones and his were in full battle mode, and he was pumping enough adrenaline to rouse a graveyard full of men long dead.

Pumping other things, too.

The juices flowed, all of them, and the end was so intense he lost himself. He fell into the Void, and a million years of bliss.

It was the most exciting thing that had ever happened to him. And would remain so for, well, forever . . . so far . . .

— — — — — —

"What happened to Yeng?"

He shook himself. "He had a concussion. He didn't remember anything that happened that day once he woke up. He never knew what or who hit him. As far as Yeng was concerned, he had fallen and hit his head while walking alone in the woods going home."

"And the fem?"

"She didn't report the assault. She and I were a one-time deal. We never did it again."

"That must have been disappointing."

"I can't tell you how much, but I was happy for the experience. More than happy. Ecstatic."

"Ah. That explains much."

He looked at her.

In that moment, it *did* explain much.

It was not as if he had forgotten it, that wasn't ever going to happen, but he hadn't made that connection to the adrenaline and testosterone in quite the same way before.

Huh. How could he have missed that?

That the intensity of one was so wrapped around the other? It was so obvious.

Man. *There* was a big fucking blind spot . . .

– – – – – –

"Well, that was easy," Gramps said.

They were in the vehicle Em had gotten for them, a freight van large enough to carry a dozen people, with room left over for cargo. Not the most comfortable thing Cutter had ever ridden in, but sealed and air recycled so as not to be leaking their scent, and hiding them from curious eyes.

"The second vehicle is twenty minutes away," Em said. "Our driver will take this one for a long drive in the country after we switch. We will operate the second one ourselves."

Cutter nodded. "Good job. Formentara?"

Zhe held up the tracker. "Looks like Wink has stopped for the night, and we are assuming that Kay is still with him. Out in the middle of nowhere. Given our location and likely speed, we won't be able to get there before dawn tomorrow at the earliest."

"Why would they be there?" Jo asked Em.

She shrugged. "Who can say? There doesn't appear to be anything there where they are save fields. Stopped to rest? The vehicle malfunctioned? Maybe they've been captured again? We won't know unless we go see."

"What I'm wondering, Colonel," Formentara said, "is why Leeth didn't give us their local com numbers. Surely, she has those."

"I think maybe she doesn't want us involved with any of this. Might be worried we'd try to sneak off and meet up with them if we knew where to meet."

Gunny shook her head. "She didn't trust us? Ah can't imagine that."

"So we head that way, and see what's what," Cutter said. "If you can sleep, once we switch rides would be good. You good to drive, Gramps?"

"Always. I can sleep, too. These damn things can drive themselves—just program in a destination and lean back."

"If it's all the same, I'd rather you keep an eye on the road," Cutter said. "Just in case."

"No problem. I slept last week."

— — — — — —

Kay waded back through the grass, a morning breeze waving the greenery as Wink watched.

He needed to go pee, and even though it was not the most comfortable night he had ever had, he was more rested than he would have been trying to sleep in the cart.

When he got back, Kay had broken out a couple of ration packs. They weren't anything he recognized immediately, but the heat package worked, and the goop inside warmed to something he could keep down even though it had the consistency of white paste . . .

"So, off to see another rich person?"

"Yes. I have spoken to Jak and to Shan. Neither knows I talked to the other, but both named this Vastalimi, who owns a goodly section of a small town eighty klicks north of the town an hour ahead of us. He made a sudden profit trading in hospital supplies used in treatment of the disease. It could be a coincidence, but . . ."

"Probably we should ask him about that," he finished.

— — — — — —

Cutter awoke, aware that Jo was leaning in his direction in the seat across from his. She didn't say anything, but his proximity detector usually stayed on when he was asleep. "What?"

"They are on the move," she said. She looked at Formentara.

"They started out in our direction a little over an hour ago," zhe said, "then veered north. There is a town up that way, just south of some fairly tall mountains, and that's pretty much all there is for several hundred kilometers past. If they stop there, it will be a couple of hours before we catch them."

Cutter nodded. "Okay. Can we get that far without refueling?"

"Yes," Em said. "And we have food and water. Probably best if we stop to stretch and make scat somewhere where you won't be seen."

"Find a spot, Gramps. My kidneys seem to be working just fine. Though these are not the most comfortable seats I've ever used."

"Probably the designer never expected human asses to perch on them," Formentara said.

Em said, "They aren't particularly comfortable for us, either. The People tend to walk or run when they can, and being reminded that mode is a better way is probably part of the design."

TWENTY-SEVEN

"The cart's computer says the population is 1457, and according to the map, our guy lives in the biggest house in the village."

Kay nodded.

"We speak of one *Okloo*masc, and the scat according to the rumor mill is that he likes wine, fems, wine, and fems, not necessarily in that order. His net worth seems to be as much as the last two to whom we spoke. He buys and sells things."

Kay didn't say anything.

"Want to bet against the notion that he knows we are coming?"

"No."

He caught the sharp tone in her reply. "Something?"

"Everyone to whom we have spoken of late has known we were coming."

"Yeah, the criminal comnet seems to work as well as others."

"Perhaps, but that's not enough."

He thought about it for a second. *Yeah.* "How did Rill know?"

"Precisely. The others might have been warned by Rill though that seems unlikely. If Shan did not tell him—and I believe that he would not, after we spoke of it—then who told Rill? Because he knew who we were, and he was expecting us."

Wink nodded. "I just assumed he'd heard about us investigating. Human and a Vastalimi Healer, can't be whole lot of folks like us around."

"Possible. Yet it bothers me."

"Because . . . ?"

"Shan gave us the list of names. If Shan didn't warn them, who else could have known about Rill?"

"Maybe he told somebody."

She nodded.

"So it has got to be Shan, one way or another."

"Maybe."

"What are you thinking here?"

"I am not sure. Perhaps it will become clear after we talk to Okloo."

"Be the first thing that did become clear if it does."

— — — — — —

"Are we there yet?" Gunny said, approximating the whine of a child.

"No. And don't make me stop this vehicle," Gramps said. "Sit there and watch the grass wave. Don't bother your siblings."

Cutter smiled.

"Another hour," Gramps said.

"Ah'm bored, Ah'm tired, Ah'm hungry, Ah have to go pee!" Gunny said. But she grinned, too.

— — — — — —

Kay stopped the cart. "There is the gate."

It was a hundred meters ahead and formidable-looking, especially for a private residence.

"Let's go and—hold up," Wink said. "How many guards do you see?"

"Four."

"Does that seem like a lot?"

"Three-meter-tall electric fence, a fortified kiosk, a heavy gate. Two guards are twice what is needed."

"Turn around. I think we might be in trouble."

Kay nodded. He was right. She put the cart into reverse, wheeled it to the side, made the beginning of a three-point turn.

"Hello," Wink said.

The gate opened. There were two four-person vehicles that appeared behind the guards and headed toward the portal, gaining speed.

"Shit! Go!"

Kay finished the turn and accelerated, but the cart was not exactly built for speed.

"Hurry up."

The two carts cleared the gate.

"The accelerator is fully engaged."

"Then better weave and find cover, because—"

As if on cue, the carts behind them sprouted Vastalimi from the side widows, and they started shooting. A couple of the rounds from carbines blew past, and a few more smacked into the cart, punching holes through the back window, thumping into the body, and sending shards of plastic every which way.

"Dammit!"

Kay slewed the cart to the left, made a skidding turn into a narrow walkway not designed for such vehicles. The ride got bumpier, but there was nobody visible behind them at the moment.

"Guess our guy Okloo knew we were coming, too, and he doesn't want to talk to us. Good thing they can't shoot that well."

An alley loomed ahead. Kay applied the brake, slowed, turned into the alley to the right, banged the rear of the cart into something.

"Hey!"

"Would you like to pilot?"

"I would, but I don't think we have time to switch seats."

Wink had his pistol out, but it was designed for soft targets and wouldn't do much to the carts behind them.

"We need a Plan B," he said.

"Offer one."

"I'm working on it."

He tapped the cart's computer and pulled up a map.

— — — — — —

"Hmm," Formentara said.

"What does that mean?" Jo asked. There was nothing to be seen past the polarized windows to the sides save waist-high, bluish green grass, waving in a gentle breeze, stretching to the horizon. Or at least as far as Jo's opticals could scan, which was pretty much to the horizon . . .

"Well, if you narrow the PPS view and zoom in, you can see that Wink's implant is moving along at a good speed, much faster than it has been. And changing direction frequently."

"He's chasing somebody," Gramps offered.

"Or somebody is chasing him," Gunny said. "Pick it up, old man. Something is going on, and we don't want to miss it."

"Out of the mouths of babes."

— — — — — —

"There's a turn ahead, two streets, take it to the left."

"Why?"

"Because it crosses a narrow bridge five hundred meters past. If we park the cart there and disable it, it stops them from following in their carts."

"They will continue pursuit on foot."

"Yeah, and my pistol becomes useful. Once we get a couple, we can take their weapons and level the playing field some."

"A simple plan. I don't see great odds in our favor."

"It's what I have."

"Very well."

She made the turn. The bridge was visible. The river wasn't that wide, and the bridge was old, a single-lane, stressed-plast arch, gone pale gray with age, probably there for a couple of hundred years. Not a lot of vehicular traffic using it, she'd guess.

"Okay, so we go to the other end, turn the cart sideways to block the road, and find a spot to hide. They get out, I plink a couple of them, then we haul ass."

"That won't get us new weapons."

"Don't be picky; we'll get those later."

– – – – – –

"Fifteen minutes," Gramps said.

"They appear to have stopped moving at the moment," Formentara said. "That could be good or bad."

"Best we hurry and go see."

"Wait—he's moving again."

– – – – – –

"I will draw their attention," Kay said. "Shoot while they are distracted."

They were off the bridge and behind a plastcrete abutment. "You can hit them at this distance?"

"Twenty meters? All day long and twice on Seventh Day."

"Pardon?"

"An old expression. I'll hit them."

The first of the pursuing vehicles skidded to a halt on the bridge, where it was blocked by the abandoned vehicle. Three Vastalimi males piled out and ran for the obstruction.

Kay yelled. Wink didn't recognize all the terms, but he was pretty sure one of them was "Fatherfuckers!"

She stepped out into the clear.

The trio of chasers brought their weapons up—

The second vehicle slewed to a stop behind them—

Wink edged around the corner of the abutment, lined up on the first one.

One dart each, he decided.

He fired, shifted his aim, fired again, and the third one realized he was in trouble and danced to the side, but too late.

Three seconds, three shots, Three hits for three. Gunny would be proud.

The remaining Vastalimi ducked for cover.

"Let's go," Wink said.

— — — — — —

Kay ran slow, to allow Wink to keep up. They were in a residential area, cubes and multiunits, good terrain in which to hide.

"There are five of them left," she said. "We can't outrun them. We need to circle behind them. They won't expect that."

"Really?"

"They are in hunt lust. Fleeing prey runs or goes to ground, sometimes climbs, but it seldom comes around behind to attack."

"Okay."

"To the left, that alley."

They ran.

— — — — — —

"Not far now," Gramps said. "Ten minutes."

"They are moving again," Formentara said. "But slowly, and in an area that looks to be housing. Out of the cart, on foot. Changing direction a lot."

"Chasing somebody or being chased," Gunny said. "Broken-field running."

— — — — — —

"Stay low," Kay said.

Wink nodded, crouched behind a refuse can full of something that smelled rotten.

The pursuing Vastalimi ran past their hiding place and never glanced in their direction.

Kay bolted so fast, Wink felt as if he were mired in the mud as he ran to follow her.

He cleared the edge of the alley in time to see Kay spring and land on the straggler bringing up the rear, taking him to the street. They hit hard, made some impact noise, and her claws were almost a blur they moved so fast. She ripped out his throat—

Wink stopped, took a deep breath, let half of it out, and raised his pistol.

The nearest of the four still on foot was twenty-five meters away, slowing and trying to turn at the sound of his fallen comrade. The farthest was five meters past that. Getting to be a long shot for this weapon.

Wink aimed. Fired. Retargeted and fired again.

Two of them went down.

The third shot missed. *Fuck!*

His fourth shot connected, but there was still one left, and that one had spun all the way around to face them.

He brought his carbine to bear on Wink . . .

Wink realized he wasn't going to be able to get lined up in time—

Shit—

The last of their chasers curled in a sudden spasm, as if hit in the belly, and fell facedown.

What . . . ?

Wink saw Kay, lying prone next to the one she'd clawed

down. She had collected his carbine and fired it, taking out the fifth Vastalimi.

He sometimes forgot she knew how to shoot pretty well. Just like that, they were done.

Eight up. Eight down. Missed one shot, but damn. That's a big win.

He changed magazines in his pistol and walked over to where Kay was coming to her feet.

"Well, that wasn't as hard as I expected," he said. "They weren't very good, were they?"

"Obviously not," she said. "Good would have killed us at the gate."

There weren't any locals sticking their heads out to see what was going on, but Wink expected there would be soon. He hurried up to the first one he had shot, collected the dead Vastalimi's carbine and spare ammo magazines. Kay already had one. "We better move," he said.

Kay nodded.

"Back to the rich man's house, I take it?"

"We haven't gotten what we came for yet," she said. "Nothing has changed."

"You mean other than a bunch of bodies littering the local streets?"

TWENTY-EIGHT

If Jo thought she was going to catch Wink flatfooted, she was wrong. He didn't bat an eyelash.

"Hey, Jo, how you doing?"

She wasn't going to let him get away with it. "So-so. Yourself?"

"Can't complain."

"We happened to be in the neighborhood," Jo said. "Thought maybe you and Kay could use a hand."

"I appreciate that, but I think we got it."

Jo shook her head. "Christus, Wink."

He laughed. "Yeah, yeah, okay, maybe we might could use a little help. When did you get to Vast?"

"Yesterday."

"And it took you this long to come visit us?"

He didn't ask how—he had a tracker implant, and Formentara could locate that easily enough—even if he were dead.

"We wanted to do some sightseeing first. Actually, we

got a late start, and you were way out here in the country, then rolling away from us. We had to chase you."

"The mission on Far Bundaloh done that fast? You been in the Void for what? Three weeks?"

"Seventy-two hours, give or take."

"You took the shortcut?"

"We were in a hurry."

That got him. "Damn. How, uh . . . why . . . ?"

"Kay's brother called us. When you two turned up missing, he became concerned. When the last place you were known to be got blown up? He was more worried. We had pretty much cleared our opposition out, so Rags decided to take a ride."

"You volunteered to risk that trip."

"Of course. We didn't know you'd gotten loose on your own." She paused a moment. "I'm the point—the others are holding a klick back: Rags, Gramps, Gunny, and Formentara. And Singh, remember him? He found us on FB and joined; he's here, too. Plus a newbie, *Mish*fem, goes by Em."

"We got a new Vastalimi? When did that happen?"

"It's a funny story, but how about I save it for after we get this done? Whatever it is."

"That'll work for me."

"So, what's the deal?"

Wink laid it out: "The guy in charge is rich enough to have a bunch of guards, and they are gunners. The compound is pretty stout for a civilian's house, and they don't like uninvited company. We never got through the front gate. We, uh, had to take several of them out."

"Several?"

"Eight."

"Where are the bodies?"

"Mostly piled up in an alley. Couple–three are in a cart by the river."

"Great. You think those will stay hidden long?"

"We think the guy we are after owns the town, and the locals will keep their heads down."

"You *think*."

"Hey, what can I say? It's what we have to work with."

"And Kay is . . . ?"

"She's doing a circuit, looking for a hole. We're observing radio silence because we think they might have sharp hearing."

"Why didn't you call in the local cops?"

He said, "Well, Kay thinks maybe this is a better idea."

"Because . . . ?"

"She thinks there might be a leak. We don't know where."

She nodded. Just good tactics. Fewer people who knew something, the fewer who might spread it around. "This is the guy you believe is good for the disease?"

"Either him, or he knows who is. He made money on it, somehow. His guys killed our ride. Glad you showed up, it was gonna be a long walk home."

"Go on."

"Last few people we went to talk to knew we were coming, and in theory, nobody but us should have known that. Somebody must have told them. This guy was waiting with guns."

"Interesting. We met Kay's sister. One of the reasons we are just getting here—we had to sneak off."

"Yeah, well, we could use some help, and—here comes Kay now."

Jo looked up and saw her friend strolling along as if she owned everything as far as she could see.

Like Wink, Kay expressed no surprise at seeing her.

"Jo Captain. Good to behold you."

Jo shook her head. "Butter wouldn't melt in your mouths."

"Pardon?"

"Never mind. What's the sitrep?"

"There are, in addition to our quarry, an unknown number of guards. The security on the compound is tight. Fence, gate, armed people at the entrance. I take it you did not come alone?"

"Six more of us," Jo said, "including a Vastalimi named *Mish*fem."

"A mercenary? How did you acquire her services?"

"It's a funny story; I'll tell you later. I'm going to go back and fetch the others. Wait here, would you?"

After she left, Kay turned to Wink. "This is an unexpected turn of events."

"Ain't it, though. They came to help us out when they heard from Droc we were in trouble."

"That was but a few days' past," Kay allowed. "They could not have made a transit in such a period."

He nodded. "Not ordinarily."

"Ah."

"Yeah. They risked the *Chomolungma*."

"They have done us a great honor."

"They risked dying to get here in a hurry. Foolish."

"Would you have done any less in their place?"

"Well . . . no. But I'm an adrenaline and testosterone junkie, remember?" He smiled.

"And held in high esteem by your colleagues."

"I'm sure they did it for you more than me," he said. "Hard to give up a good Vastalimi."

She whickered. "Our task is thus made easier."

"There's that."

— — — — —

"Both alive and well," Jo said. "Radio silence because their quarry is probably listening. They killed several guards."

"Good they are alive," Cutter said. "Situation?"

Jo repeated what she had learned.

"Okay, then, we'll mosey on up there and see how best to achieve their goal. Formentara, you okay with manning the hopper here and keeping track of telemetry and coms and all?"

"Why not? Nothing else to do around here. There are fewer augmentation facilities on this world than there were on Far Bundaloh if you can believe that. When are we going to a planet with, you know, running water and power and inside freshers?"

"Maybe next time. Jo?"

"This way. Uh, Rags, maybe you should—"

"No. I'm going. I didn't space all the way here to sit back and do nothing."

"You could help Formentara—"

"Who doesn't need my help in the slightest. Who signs the checks?"

"Mostly me, these days," Jo said. "But I take your point. If you let anybody kill you, I am going to be really pissed off."

– – – – – –

Kay was aware her comrades had drawn nearer. "Here they come," she said. "Take care."

"I wasn't going to shoot any of them," Wink said.

"So you say."

"Was that a joke?"

She smiled.

There were six of them: Jo Captain, Cutter Colonel, Gunny, Demonde Gramps, the Anandan Singh, and one of The People.

Formentara would be with the vehicle.

The unmet fem said, "Ah, *Kluth*fem, I have heard much good about you from these humans. I am *Mish*fem. I can recite my ancestors if you like." She spoke *Govor*, not the most common dialect, which was interesting. *Govor* was the first tongue Kay had herself learned.

"I ken you, Mish. Let us dispense with the relatives. How do you like our team?"

"Best humans I've been around so far, but of course . . ."

". . . that's not saying much," Kay said, finishing the old joke.

Both of them smiled.

"The one called Jo defeated me in bare-hand Challenge. You have taught her well."

Kay said, "No shame, she has beaten me in practice many times. She is the most adept human that way I have ever been around, but of course . . ."

They both whickered.

"Kay," Cutter said. "What do we need to do here?"

"The person who owns that house would seem to have information we want. His people tried to kill us, and I suspect there is a good reason why."

"You and Wink haven't been inside?"

"Not yet."

"Have you come up with a strategy and tactics?"

"Yes. Your arrival has made it much more likely to succeed."

"Let's hear it, then."

"Those hunting us had vehicles. We take those, approach the gate to the compound, we can get close enough to take out the guards there and get inside. We overcome opposition, capture the owner, and ask him some pointed questions."

Gramps laughed. "Want to make *smeerp* stew? First, you catch a *smeerp* . . ."

Both Em and Kay looked at him. "That is obvious," Em said.

He laughed harder.

— — — — —

Em and Kay drove, stuck their arms out, and waved.

The guards opened the gate.

The four guards went down in a hail of projectiles. Served them right for being lax.

There were no guards at the house's entrance, and if there were cameras monitoring the door, they were not apparent.

"Odd," Cutter said. "You'd think they'd have somebody watching the entrance."

"I'm for going in through a window," Jo said, "just in case the door is rigged. No bars on the windows, and if we blow one in, and an alarm goes off, it will be too late."

Cutter nodded.

"All right. Let's do it."

– – – – – –

"Will you take the left?" Kay said.

Jo said, "Yes."

The two fems split, moving fast.

The corridor was wide, but the branching ahead to the left was blind. She couldn't hear anybody down it, but these were Vastalimi, and they could be quiet when they wanted to be.

Jo dropped to her left side and slid the last couple of meters on the smooth floor into the corridor's intersection, both hands on the pistol—

The Vastalimi crouching ten meters away was fast, but not so much so that she had a chance to drop her aim from where she expected a target to appear in time—

Jo saw her eyes go wide as she realized her mistake and jerked the rifle downward—

—too late. Jo squeezed off two quick shots, both center of mass, then tracked upward for the third shot at the fem's head—

—She missed the third because the Vastalimi had curled reflexively forward from the impact of the bioelectric darts that skewered her heart.

—Dead on her feet and falling . . .

Nobody else in sight.

Jo rolled up, gun leading, and ran down the corridor.

There shouldn't be too many guards left by now. Wink had shot one, Gunny had taken three, and Gramps blew one up with a bisector. This one made six, and—

—a pistol went off down the other, a double tap. That was Kay—she could tell by the sound—and there was no return fire, so that would make seven—

Jo subvocalized into her com: "Seven down. Remember to keep some alive—"

A carbine went off, a pair of triplets, and Jo knew from that sound and pattern that it was probably Gramps—

"Repeat—what was that you said?" Gramps said.

"Take one alive," Jo said.

"Sorry. My error."

"You killed the last two?"

"I don't know that they were the last two. Besides, they were Vastalimi, and they were armed."

Gunny said, "A good shot could have taken them down without killing 'em."

"Says the woman who killed three without a nanosecond's hesitation."

"That was different. We still had plenty left back then."

Jo went into the main section of the place. Two dead Vastalimi males sprawled on the floor by Gramps's feet.

Rags came around the corner nearest. "Clear, that way."

Singh commed in: "The domestic staff and some fancy-looking fems are all dead up here. Along with whom I assume is the owner, Okloo. It appears they have been dead for a while. The blood is congealed, and they are stiff."

"Killed before we arrived," Em said. "Is that not interesting?"

"Well, crap. This will make it a little harder to get the information we wanted, them being dead and all," Gunny said.

"It doesn't matter," Kay said. "I know who they were working for."

Wink looked at her. "Really? When did you figure that out?"

"I have suspected it for a time. This is the final piece of the puzzle."

Wink shook his head. "I must be missing something."

"The staff and owner were killed before we arrived, so once again, somebody knew we were coming. They were cleaning up loose ends. I suspect we were supposed to be among those."

Wink considered it for a moment. "So?"

"So, who sent us to see Shan the second time? From where the leaks must be coming?"

" I . . . Oh . . ." He trailed off.

"Yes."

"Well, fuck," he said.

TWENTY-NINE

Leeth arrived next to the building's back entrance and started for the door. Kay called out. "Over here, *Sister.*"

Leeth turned, saw Kay leaning against the wall in the shadow of a tall refuse container.

"Strange place for a meeting," Leeth said.

"Appropriate. A dirty alley seems perfect, don't you think?" She pushed off the wall, stood facing her sister. Her hormones were in flux, her stance tight.

There was a long pause. Finally, Leeth said. "So. You know."

"Yes."

"I am sorry it came to this."

"Are you?"

"More that you figured it out than anything if I must be honest."

"Honest? Why start now?"

There was another pause. "I didn't know Droc was going to call you home."

"Would it have made a difference if you had known?"

Leeth shook her head. "No. It was too far along by then."

Kay shook her head. "My sister, the *Sena*, a murderer. I spit in disgust."

"I wish you had not come back."

"So do I. Aside from a few carefully chosen targets, the rest of them were just ruses?"

"Yes. The plan was for a thousand deaths, maximum, and if fifty of them were major criminals? Nobody would have thought twice about that, they would have been lost in the crowd."

"Including our parents and our siblings."

"That was a hard choice."

"To make certain nobody would suspect you if it came to that. That is beyond frigid, Leeth. You wade in a river of nitrogen."

She nodded. "It was necessary. If I could have stalled you for a couple of weeks? That would have been enough."

Kay shook her head. "You were the most stellar of all the *Sena*. Your entire career. And now this?"

Leeth nodded. "Yes. I was the good fem, doing the right things for the right reasons. But the *Sena* were falling, and I had to come up with a way to stop it."

"You planned it so that somebody would eventually realize that it was deliberate."

"Of course. Our brother would, in time, have been given additional clues, then led down the proper road. It was not contagious, never an epidemic in the making. The majority of The People were never at risk. Droc got there sooner than expected, thanks to your human. I don't think a Vastalimi Healer would ever have made that leap on his own.

"And, of course, your vision was too sharp, much as I tried to keep it clouded. And you wouldn't let it go and leave it to me."

Leeth sighed. "What gave me away in the end?"

"You were too good a Shadow to miss this, and yet, you dragged your feet at every turning, you kept putting me off.

You sent me places where you knew I wouldn't find anything.

"I didn't want to believe it, but when everything else was eliminated, you were still there. The recent trap you set was the final piece in the puzzle. Who else knew Wink and I would be going there? Who sent us to see Shan again? Was he part of it?"

"Not as such. We have Shan under electronic surveillance."

"I never considered that."

"We use his own cameras. He has them everywhere. He is young and vain. He likes to watch himself do things. It makes it easy."

Kay sighed.

"I didn't know your humans would sneak off and find you so soon. How did they?"

"Does it matter?"

"No, not really."

They looked at each other silently for a moment.

"You would have had me killed."

"Caught. Wounded, if necessary, but not killed unless there was no other way.

"The first time you were collected, you would have survived even if you had not escaped on your own. That was the plan. You would have been held, eventually released. The plague would stop, you would leave, and all would be well."

Kay stared at her. "There was a clue there, had I been listening properly. They told me they knew who my sister was. I came to realize what they meant. They didn't know *of* you, you were the one who *set* them on us."

"I would have spared you, if possible, I didn't want you to die."

"Your concern is touching."

"What is it you want to hear? That I would have regretted it if you'd been killed? I would have."

"But you'd have gotten over it quick enough, wouldn't you? As you did the rest of our family you *murdered*."

Leeth said nothing.

Kay let that go. "You set it all up toward an end that would have included a guilty party."

"Of course."

"Anybody I know?"

"*Shard*masc."

"Ah. The Clawproof Uberpatro, Packleader of Packleaders. Cleaning out the den along the way to the biggest prey. It has a certain economy to it."

"It took years to set up and put it into motion. Not many could have managed it."

"I can appreciate that. And how far up are you on the list of plotters?"

"You don't think I did it alone?"

Kay laughed, despite its being so awful. Nothing funny here. It was tragic.

"I am at the top, Sister. Others sharpened their talons for their own reasons, but one uses the tools one has. I was in it for justice."

"*Justice?* You say that despite the hundreds of innocents who have died from this? People you *slaughtered*?"

"I deeply regret it, you must believe that. But their deaths were for the greater good."

Kay stared at her. "The greater good? Are you truly mad?"

"The *Sena* are at a critical point. We are the wall between order and chaos, and we have been crumbling for a long time. When this is done, a diseased pack of longtime criminals—who over their lives killed many more than have died of the illness, but who were too clever for us to spike? They will be gone.

"More importantly, our prestige in solving the crime will infuse our ranks with a spate of new applicants, smart and talented people who will see the Shadows as I saw them long ago. As an adventure. As a higher calling.

"Order will be restored, better than it was.

"Yes, the deaths will stay with me to my own end, and I am sorry for them and their families—our family—you can't know how much; but their lives balanced against the lives of the tens of thousands over the years that a reinvigorated *Sena* will save? There is no contest."

"So the ends justify the means."

"Yes, sometimes it does."

Kay sighed. "But when it comes out that it was a highly regarded officer of the *Sena* who was responsible? What does that do to your recruitment strategy? Do you think that the door will be pounded open by the bright and talented rushing to join an organization that is responsible for mass murder? Or that at least a few Shadows with a conscience won't resign?"

"That won't happen."

"You think not?"

"No one will reveal it."

"Really? My status is low, true, but our Elder Droc's is not, and he will have high-ranking ears to listen. And there are honest Shadows who can verify it. Once you know the guilty party, it is easy enough to backtrack and find the arrows that point to her."

"You won't tell him."

"You *are* mad."

"Lope away, Sister. Leave Vast and go back to playing soldier."

"No."

Leeth pulled her pistol and pointed it at Kay.

Too far away to try a leap.

"That's it? You would murder me?"

"I will regret this most of all, but I can't let you undo it. You left, you haven't seen what I have seen. It is too important to our world. Try to understand."

"Will you offer Challenge instead of shooting me?"

"As good as I am, you did defeat Vial. You aren't the sib

I used to bat around as a cub. I can likely beat you even so, but I can't risk it. I am sorry."

"Gunny," Kay said.

Leeth frowned. "What?"

The shot tore the pistol from her grip, shattering the hard plastic into shards as it flew.

Leeth snarled, dropped into a fighting crouch, her claws snapped out—

Kay raised her hand. "Hold! My comrade—one of those who shoot so well—has you in her sights. Twitch, and die where you stand. She won't miss."

Leeth looked around, didn't see the hidden threat. She relaxed, came up, retracted her claws.

"Again, I underestimated you. Always smarter than I expected you to be," Leeth said. "What now?"

Kay had thought about it, what she would do, and while she didn't like any of her choices, some were less onerous than others. "A bargain," she said.

"I'm listening."

"Give me the names of those involved in the plot with you—"

"No—"

"—hear me through! The names, no omissions. In exchange, two things: You will be allowed to perform *izva-diti utrobu*."

Leeth nodded. "And the second?"

"And the blame for the murders will fall upon Shard, as you planned. I am assuming your evidence, whatever it is, is solid enough to bear inspection?"

"It is." She paused. "You would do that?"

"Yes."

"Why?"

"Because you are right—The People need the *Sena*. If I blacken them with your sin, it serves no purpose. Your way was wrong, but I won't deny that your goal is valid."

"That's it?"

"When I am done here, I will leave our world once more. What remains of our family won't, and what you have done is wicked enough that it will hang over them like a cloud—should it become known. Why should our family suffer any more for your crime?"

"I understand." She paused again. "You really would have made a great Shadow, Kluth. You have found the path that hews closer to right than any other."

"It is still a path too far. Know that your accomplices and coconspirators will be punished. Most of them will likely die, Droc will see to it. Challenges, accidents, sudden illnesses, there is no place upon Vast where they will be able to hide. You cleaned out one kind of criminal nest, we shall clean out another. People who get away with such things will only be encouraged to do worse."

"They understood the risks."

There was a silence that threatened to expand to infinity. Then Leeth said, "There's something else, isn't there? Another reason you haven't said."

Kluth considered it. Yes. There was. And maybe it would be cruel to offer it. Her sister had been ready to shoot her like prey, for the greater good of her cause, but she had told her why. Leeth deserved the truth before she died, didn't she?

Kay said, "Because kinship matters to some of us. We were born moments apart, we lay together as cubs and nursed on our parents' disgorge. You were my favorite sibling. Central in my cubhood. I loved you."

That dart struck home—she could see it. "Even after I would have killed you, you say this?"

"Yes."

"You shame me."

"No, you shamed yourself. Say the names, there is a recorder working. Give a link to the evidence we need.

"Hunt well on the Other Side, Leeth."

Leeth nodded. "Thank you."

Kay turned away.

— — — — — —

When Leeth finished naming names and telling them where to find the faked evidence, she took a deep breath, and her claws snapped out. She looked skyward for a moment, closed her eyes, then crossed her wrists over her abdomen. She jammed her claws into her flesh deeply and uncrossed her hands, flinging them wide, shredding open her belly.

Her entrails spilled out with a gush, blood spewing.

She kept to her feet for what seemed like a long time before she sat down, then fell over onto her side.

On the roof down the alley, sweating in the shiftsuit, but mostly invisible, Gunny said, "Man. That's hard." She relaxed her grip on the carbine.

Next to her, Gramps, his own weapon no longer aimed at Leeth, said, "Yeah. Ripping out your own guts."

Gunny said, "I was talking about Kay."

"So was I."

They looked at each other. Something passed between them, but Gunny couldn't speak to it. She could only nod.

THIRTY

The door to his cube was open, and Wink saw Kay as she arrived.

"Kay."

"Wink. May I enter?"

"Please."

She came into the cube and stood close to where he sat at the small table, honing the edge on his knife with a leather strop. He held the knife up, inspected the edge under the bright light, touched it with his thumb. Done, as sharp as he could get it, given the spine-to-edge thickness. He put the knife into the sheath and clicked off the lamp.

The ship's quarters were small, but sufficient; a place to sleep, sit, attend to small chores in private. "What can I do for you?"

"You recall the conversation we had on our first visit to see Shan, regarding prostitutes?"

He blinked. "Uh, yeah?"

Shan was recovering in a *bolnica* after Kay got through

with him. She had spared his life. Too many had died already, she'd said, and he was relatively innocent. And wiser, now.

She continued: "You asked, had I ever considered sex with other than one of my own species?"

"Um, yeah . . . ?"

"I have considered it twice. One of them is you."

That got his attention. "Really?"

"You find it surprising?"

"Well, my ego wants to grin and dance a little pretending that it knew, but, yes, actually."

"You find the idea repellent?"

"Not in any way. I'm honored. How could I not be? I like you, and our recent adventure only made that more so. A fem of great ability, always an attraction."

"Truth?"

He came to his feet. "Let me close the door," he said.

She grinned.

– – – – – –

Later, Wink said, "Wow. *That* was *incredible*."

"I thought so, as well. I never would have expected it to be so intense." She leaned over and licked the side of his face.

He grinned, and said, "I'm curious. The other non-Vastalimi you mentioned you had considered, it was Jo, wasn't it?"

"Yes."

He smiled more broadly.

"This amuses you?"

"Not amuses, so much. It opens up certain, um, possibilities in my mind."

"Possibilities?"

"We can talk about that later. Show me that trick with your hair again? How can you make it move like that?"

He truly did enjoy skating on the edge, Wink thought. Risking disaster. That might well be the case if what he was speculating upon came to pass. Jo and Kay together with him in a bed?

Oh, my, yes . . .

EPILOGUE

"Here's something," Rags said. He and Jo were alone in the ship's dining area.

"What?" Jo said.

"An old friend from my Army days has reached out. There's a class-one license-limit industrial war brewing in SoNorAm, a region called *Coahuila y Tejas*."

"It's being allowed? On Earth? When's the last time one of those went down? Fifteen years?"

"Apparently somebody got the permits, so there's weight behind it. Both sides are recruiting. My friend has joined one faction, and she's wondering if we might be interested in some freelance guerrilla work."

"What kind of money are they offering?"

Rags grinned as he waved his hand at the hologram. It blinked and enlarged a number. "That's the basic contract for boots on the ground. Premiums for officers, per diem, winning bonus, the usual."

"Whoa! That's serious noodle. She talking ranger stuff?"

"Looks like. Sneak and peek, harry and harass, shoot and scoot."

Jo said, "Well, the board is kind of lean, not like we have anything else big lined up. You trust your friend's judgment?"

"I did. Been a few years since I've seen her, but unless she's changed, she's a good soldier. She was a colonel when she cashed out; looks like she's a general in this action."

He laughed.

"What's funny?"

"Her name is Wood. When I met her, she was just being promoted from captain."

Jo thought about that for a second, then grinned. "Major Wood?"

He nodded.

"Bet she got tired of the dick jokes pretty quick."

"She was a big woman, serious jock, and quick with her hands, too. Lot of guys only made the joke once."

She shook her head. "A real war," she said. "And isn't Gunny from somewhere in that area?"

"Limited, but more risk than chasing bandits or rescuing kidnapees," he allowed.

"Yep. But even if you live in paradise . . ."

". . . you still die anyway," he finished the old saw.

"We have been coasting here of late," she said. "Good to sharpen up our edges."

"I bet Formentara will go for it. Zhe has been bitching about going somewhere with civilization. Plenty of that on the homeworld."

"Such that it is," Jo said.

"Such that it is," he agreed. "What do you think?"

"Been a while since I was on Earth. I wouldn't mind seeing the old homeworld."

"Me, neither. Let's have a talk with the team, shall we?"